The Redcaps' Queen
A Bad-Ass Faerie Tale

Danielle Ackley-McPhail

with illustrations by Ed Coutts

PAPER PHOENIX PRESS

Pennsville, NJ

PUBLISHED BY
Paper Phoenix Press
A division of eSpec Books
PO Box 242
Pennsville, NJ 08070
www.especbooks.com

ISBN: 978-1-942990-70-3
ISBN (ebook): 978-1-942990-71-0

Interior Design: Danielle McPhail,
Sidhe na Daire Multimedia, www.sidhenadaire.com
Cover Layout: Mike McPhail, McP Digital Graphics
Cover and Interior Art: Ed Coutts
Compass Rose: Linda Saboe

Copyeditor: Greg Schauer

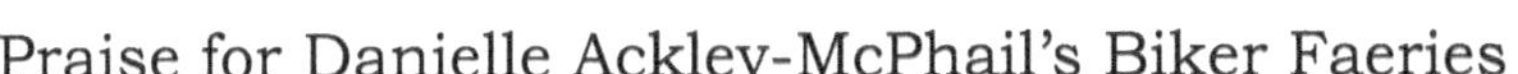

Praise for Danielle Ackley-McPhail's Biker Faeries

"The latest from Ackley-McPhail features an intriguing mix of bikers and elves."
—Publisher's Weekly

"The Halfling Court is a well crafted and thought out book. The characters are immensely likable, and I found myself growing quite fond of them [...] a definite must read."
—5 Tombstones,
Bitten By Books Review

(From reviews of the anthology *Bad-Ass Faeries*.)

"Tugging at the readers heart and hitting all the right notes, "At The Crossroads" is just one example of the treasure trove waiting for readers in Bad-Ass Faeries."
—4 1/2 Mystique Moons, Sarah Gentili,
Mystique Books

"This was a very interesting take on faeries as you don't often hear of faeries being Harley riding, macho guys. I really liked that aspect of the story and the ending wasn't quite what you expected, but in a good way."
—5 Tombstones, Becky Gard,
Bitten by Books Review

"At The Crossroads" by Danielle Ackley-McPhail is one of the true gems in Bad-Ass Faeries. A fine, exciting tale with compelling characters."
—Jim R. Stratton,
Tangent Online

N
W
E
S

Dedication

To my siblings, by birth and marriage:
Barbara Anne (Ackley) Miller
Jamie Adele (Ackley) Remchuk
Charles Nicholas Ackley, Jr.
Richele Denise (Ackley) Sabbara
and Patrick McPhail

A Note of Thanks

I can't tell you how many people helped to make this book what it is…Okay…that's not true. Here they are in no particular order, with the exception of the first, Helen (Halla) Fleischer, who suffered along with me page by page until we found the end of the story. From there we had the help of Jeff Young, James Chambers, Jason A. Starr, Jon Quigley, and Jagi Lamplighter to beat it into shape. And added to that list for this re-release are Jorie Slape and Greg Schauer, both of whom helped clean it up.

Particular thanks go to Debbie Ronca and the Jerzey Derby Brigade for educating me in the unique art of Roller Derby and the delightful personalities they lent to this book, as well as to the fine gentlemen of J&J Miracle Mead for letting me play in their playground and even letting me leave my mark on it. Finally, thanks to Ed Coutts for his infinite patience and vision in bringing my imagery to life.

We all hope you enjoy this mad adventure!

Author's Note

The events of *The Redcaps' Queen* partially overlap those of book one, *The Halfling's Court,* in that they examine some of the same scenes from a different character's perspective.

JERZEY DERBY BRIGADE
WOMEN'S ROLLER DERBY

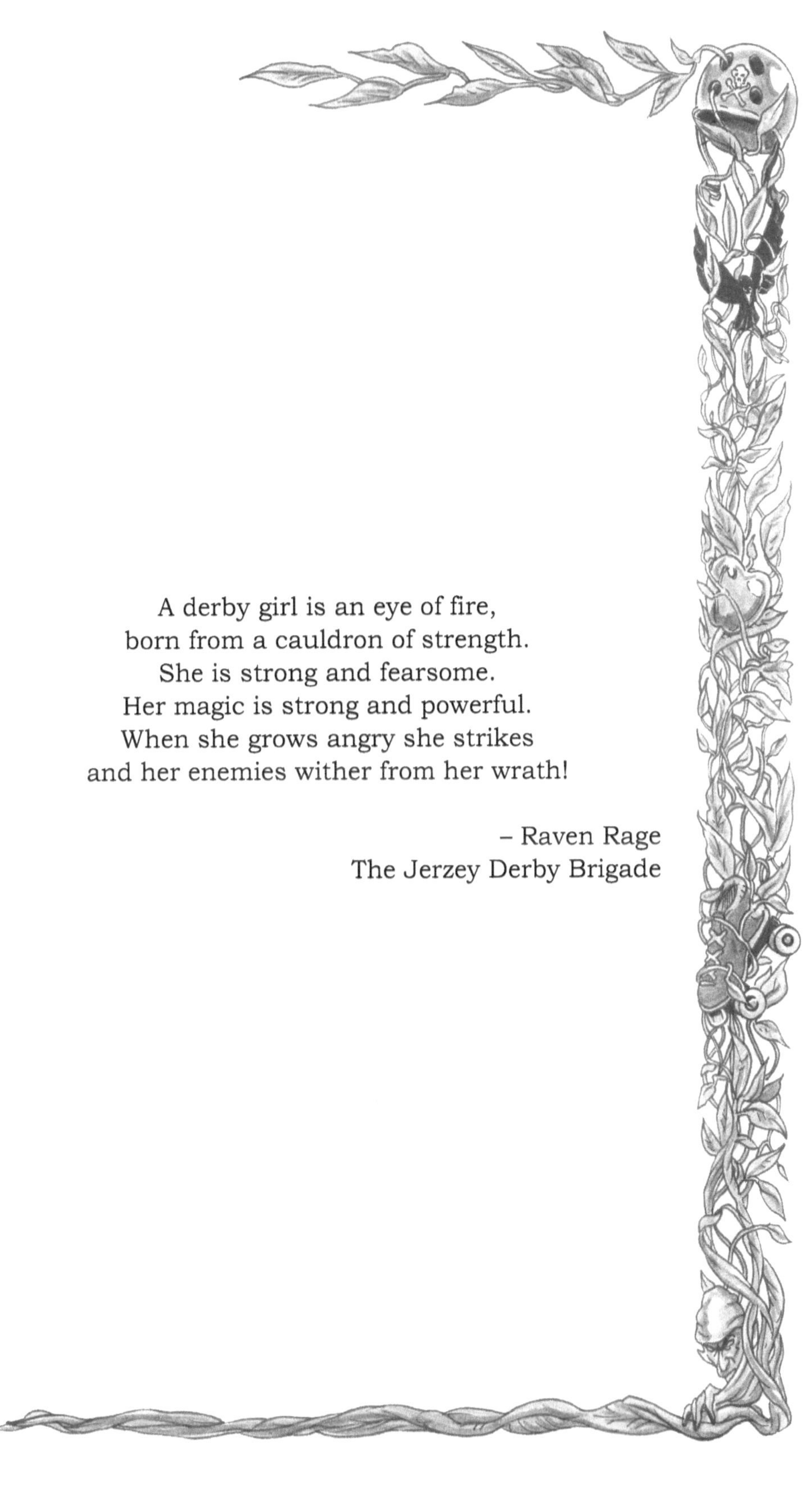

A derby girl is an eye of fire,
born from a cauldron of strength.
She is strong and fearsome.
Her magic is strong and powerful.
When she grows angry she strikes
and her enemies wither from her wrath!

– Raven Rage
The Jerzey Derby Brigade

Suzanne

Chapter One

Suzanne surfaced to the sounds of softly rustling *leaves. The raucous cawing of crows. And sinister murmurs close by her ear. The chill of a breeze tickled her bare back as the sharp pain of bindings on her wrists and legs kindled anger in her breast.*

The impulse to fight surged strongly within her, yet something more than physical bonds held her immobile. Her effort to open her eyes triggered no more than a weak flutter. The blackness shrouding her consciousness briefly lightened to grey before darkening once more. Inwardly, Suzanne growled, drew several deep, centering breaths, and once more bent her will toward moving.

Nothing.

The murmurs increased. She couldn't distinguish what they said, but their growing excitement needed no words. Many hands grasped her. Lifted her up. Bore her away. Suzanne threw her effort into resisting as what felt like sharp-pointed claws pierced her flesh. Her mind fought, but her body remained lax. Her breathing labored the more she strained internally against the force that bound her. The rasp of something like barbed sandpaper swiped across her bare shoulder. Her stomach clenched at the sensation and her muscles screamed to break free of her bonds. Suzanne's pulse picked up and her frustration grew. The more anxious she became the more the fog cleared from her mind.

And then she felt him.

Lance, her lover, was somewhere nearby. The link between them trickled his emotions into her thoughts. Love. Concern. Anger. The last most of all; his temper boiled fierce and hot beneath his skin, even in the bare echo that she felt through their magical bond. Suzanne's soul reached for him but found itself likewise bound. Panic flooded her veins, born of memories long past of childhood beneath her father's control. Kept weak and powerless, her every act dictated. In the here-and-now, Suzanne's breath came in sharp gasps. The darkness deepened until she grew frantic, casting her inner self once more against restraints she could not shake free.

Someone spoke. Distant, yet all too clear. A flat, harsh voice, reminiscent of the crows' caws.

"Service rendered calls for payment due."

Her bearers lowered her to the ground and backed away. Like a rabbit sensing a hawk circling overhead, her inner self stilled, unsure of how to evade.

"No!" Lance roared.

Her eyes snapped open. The world became clear as the esoteric restraints lifted. In the next instant, bitter-cold droplets struck Suzanne's skin. Acid burrowed deep and fast to devour her flesh. No longer weighed down, she bucked and thrashed. The clawed hands returned, pinning her down, and her vision filled with wizened faces grinning beneath brown caps that deepened to crimson as her blood flowed and the redcaps feasted.

Suzanne screamed a piercing, earth-rending scream.

She jerked awake, sweat-soaked, her body trembling and her breath fast and shallow in reaction to the raw, brutal memory that haunted her dreams. Screams still echoed in her mind. Torturous, agonized, piercing. Lance lay undisturbed beside her, arm draped over her waist, breathing in a slow, relaxed rhythm against the back of her neck. His presence calmed her, again a reminder she'd survived. Most mornings were the same lately. Ever since she had been captured by the *Dubh Fae* and his redcap minions—coming within seconds of death—her sleep had been a stalking ground.

She growled in frustration as she edged away from Lance's loose grip. A grey hint of light placed the time somewhere just before dawn. Way too early to be up. She ignored the piercing phantom pains as she slipped from the bed. The chill of the morning air made her shiver as she ran her fingers over naked skin that should have borne scars. She caught her unblemished reflection in the bureau mirror across the room and shivered again. Damp tendrils of platinum-blonde hair clung to her face, neck, and breasts. In the low light, her blue eyes shone dark and startling against her ashen skin. She scowled at her reflection and quickly shimmied into her clothes, reflexively sliding a well-worn bandana in the front pocket of her jeans, an old habit from her childhood.

Behind her, Lance stirred. His arm reached for her in his sleep. The hint of a frown furrowed his brow when he did not find her. Awake or not, his protective nature seeped through. As the leader of the Wild Hunt M.C. he considered himself responsible for every member, but most particularly for her.

Again, frustration burned along her nerves, causing her to tense as she willed him to remain asleep. She loved Lance, had for over twenty years…even before he turned thirteen and discovered the joy of girls, but he never seemed to get the fact that she needed to stand on her own, not because she *had* to, but because it was important to her to be *able* to. She'd even held a human job once. For nearly a year she'd manned the drying furnace at the local auto plant, where intense heat baked the fresh paint into a protective shell. A very unfae occupation; that had been part of its charm. With the resources of the fae world to draw on she hadn't needed to work. What she *had* needed was to prove she could. That she was strong and capable in all things. Not until she proved that to herself and everyone else, could she and Lance move forward and build the kind of life she had always longed for. The life where they were never separate, where family meant love…and children.

That dream seemed even further out of reach now. If only she could conquer this crippling fear. In the military they called it PTSD—post-traumatic stress disorder. Suzanne…she called it fucked up. Just seeing the color red froze her up worse than a seized engine. If she did not overcome that fear on her own, she expected she never would. But Lance kept interfering. He just never seemed to know when to stand down and when it was okay to step in. When he'd learned about her recent issues, he'd actually gone so far as to try and ban anything red from *Delilah's*, the bar that served as a clubhouse for the Wild Hunt. Well-intentioned as his effort was, she stopped him straight away. Besides being impractical, a solution like that threatened to cripple her for good. Remnants of an older fear rose up at that thought. She would let no one make her weak again.

No one.

As she stood there trying to rally for the day, the room around her took on a steadily growing reddish tinge reflected from the rising sun. Suzanne tensed and refused to close her eyes against the sight. She fought to get control of the panic, resisting the urge to crawl back into Lance's arms and pretend herself safe. She wouldn't do it, though; unlike her father, she made a point of never lying, even to herself. The faster her heart beat, the more her skin crawled, as if distant eyes watched her, waiting eagerly for the chance to bleed her. Surrounded by the dawn's haze she relived the attack; the flood of red light swept her back to the blasted crossroads, bound and helpless as the *Dubh Fae's* Dragon Tears ate through her skin and flesh, and the redcaps feasted on her free-flowing blood. Suzanne shuddered. The panic gained ground until she nearly crumpled to the floor. Sheer will alone kept her standing tall, her slender frame too rigid now to tremble. An improvement after last night, where she'd been curled nearly fetal in Lance's arms, but still unacceptable. She reminded herself that those who had harmed her couldn't get past the shields safeguarding the property, including *Delilah's* and the living space above the bar.

It didn't help. The true demons lived in her head.

Deep beneath the trauma from the attack lurked her true fear: that her father was right. That she was weak and could not defend herself. She'd fought against those beliefs her whole life. That was likely the reason so many of her gifts to Lance—and anyone else she cared for—provided protection, right down to the magic tattoo of her likeness that linked their awareness. As if proving that she could take care of others meant she could look out for herself, too. Only...look how well she'd botched that.

Again Lance stirred in the bed behind her; he grumbled and came a little more awake. The flashback lost part of its grip on her as her thoughts latched on to him. His strength and presence tempted her to depend on him, to let him protect her. Furious with herself, she scrubbed her hand hard across tear-dampened cheeks.

Before he roused fully, Suzanne leaned over and tucked the warm blanket back around him, ran her hand gently over the soft waves of his light brown hair, lying long and loose over the pillow. "It's okay, babe," she murmured by his ear, a bit of magic giving weight to her words. Her heart surged and a smile crept across her lips. Impulse took her and she brushed a tender kiss across his brow. "Go back to sleep. I'm going downstairs."

She watched to make sure Lance drifted to sleep again before leaving the room. Grabbing her leather jacket from the closet by the apartment door, she carefully kept her eyes averted from the pile of winter gear on the shelf above it. The knit hats were a mix of all colors, but Lance's favorite—red—dominated. Suzanne shuddered as another flash of memory superimposed the leering, bloody face of a redcap over the pile of hats. Squeezing her eyes closed tight she fought the renewed anxiety the flashback caused. She stumbled back and the sleeve of her jacket caught on something. Opening her eyes, she saw an old air rifle with a blown gasket that Lance hadn't had the time to fix yet. Suzanne reached out, her hand lingering on the stock of the gun. An idea took root as she forced her gaze back to the pile of knit caps. Last night she'd told Lance she would handle this problem of hers…

Now seemed like a good time.

It took a massive effort to fight past her aversion, but she reached up and managed to pick through the jumble of winter hats. Her hand shook violently as she plucked out every red one she could find, shoving them into the sleeve of her jacket where she wouldn't see them until she had to.

Downstairs, in the back room of the bar, Delilah—Lance's aunt—kept an entire closet full of well-maintained paintball gear: from weapons and protection, to marker flags and CO_2 cartridges, not to mention a whole case of paintballs in ridiculous neon colors. That stockpile was the key to Suzanne's plan. Well, that, and the fact the Wild Hunt owned all the acreage within a two-mile radius of the bar.

She headed for Delilah's office off the kitchen to retrieve the ring of supply closet keys hanging just inside the door. She then returned to the back room and pulled all of the gear she wanted from the closet. Everything lay ready and waiting by the time the first footsteps sounded on the stairs. Jon, Lance's uncle and fellow exiled Fae, didn't appear surprised—by her or the pile of gear on the table—though the stack of stocking caps did seem to puzzle him a moment until he clued to the fact they were all red.

"Dušan doesn't have any idea what you're up to, does he?"

Her eyes narrowed. Jon rarely used the name the Four Winds had given Lance when the Hunt was formed; the subtle reminder that anyone wearing colors answered to him brought out her spirit of rebellion. "You going to help, or get in the way?"

Jon's hands went up along with one corner of his mouth. "Me? I know better than that. S'long as you don't plan anything stupid, I got your back." He joined her at the table, picked up a Tippman pneumatic pistol, and made a show of inspecting it, then preparing it for use.

"You know, wanting to protect you isn't the same thing as thinking you aren't capable of protecting yourself," he finally said, without looking up from the air gun he loaded.

Suzanne ground her teeth as she glared at her hands. Her knuckles had gone white. She glanced back at Jon. "It's not what Lance thinks that I'm concerned about."

Across the table, Jon's head snapped up, a protest on his lips as he stared at her intently from beneath a shag of dark brown hair. His natural, deep purple highlights glimmered under the glamour that hid his magical state from most mundane folk.

Before he could speak, Suzanne went on, her words hurried. "Or the Club...I'm the one that has to get my head on straight, before *I* start thinking I can't hack it."

Jon nodded slowly, his rich bronze-brown eyes fairly swirling in sympathetic memory. For a moment both of them remained silent as he held her gaze. Then Jon laid the readied pistol down and settled back in his chair.

"I understand," he said, and she could see he really did—both what she'd said, and what she hadn't—as plain as the haunted look in his eyes. They sat in taut silence, inspecting and readying the gear as they waited for more bodies to arrive.

An odd group marched into the woods, decked out in assorted armor, with a hodge-podge of air weapons shoved into pockets or slung over shoulders. Suzanne had a handful of red canvas flags tucked in the right pocket of her leather jacket and a butterfly knife in the left...just in case. She cradled her air gun in her arms.

Behind and to her left followed Rock, Blow, Bubba, and Dream. They were known collectively as the Four Winds—she couldn't fathom why, for three of them were not of that aspect. Each was a powerful Elemental, respectively: Earth, Air, Fire, and Water. Along with Lance, they had founded the Wild Hunt M.C. They were kin to the Fae, but not of a kind. Most of her race had an affinity for one of the aspects, which drew them to the Elementals. But not Suzanne. If not for Lance, she would have had nothing to do with the four of them. She had something of an aversion. It wasn't personal; she was one of the rare faerie born of all four aspects—generally a mortal trait—a fact she'd grown up both hiding and hating. It had made growing up...difficult. She still hadn't gotten over that. Sometimes it proved an issue, but not today. Today their ambient strength grounded her.

On her right walked Jon and Delilah...her not quite technically in-laws, of a sort. She held them closer than family. She gained from them strength of a different variety, as one whose blood relatives—with the exception of her brother, Gavin—had only sought to undercut her confidence. Even after all her years in the Wild Hunt, Suzanne wasn't used to the support. She breathed deep into her gut and willed the tension out of her body on the exhale. Lance's aunt and uncle were nothing like her kin. She needed to remember that, instead of waiting for the proverbial knife in the back. Trying to shake off her nerves, she turned to Delilah. "Who's watching over Tilly?"

Tilly was Jon and Delilah's daughter and Lance's cousin. She was thirty-four—less than a year younger than Lance—but thanks to an Organ Donor who never should have been allowed on a bike, she wasn't quite right in the head anymore. She could function, but on the level of a four-year-old in a full-grown woman's body. After the accident Suzanne had given Tilly a crystal pendant to protect her from further harm, but the woman still needed someone to keep her out of mischief.

"Gort's keeping her company," Delilah answered, a slight frown on her face, as if she wasn't sure that was the best idea. "She's taken to him. Wouldn't settle in to her cartoons until we said her new friend could watch with her."

Now if that isn't interesting, Suzanne thought. *Imagine…the former advisor to the elven High King babysitting.* She had to chuckle as she pictured him parked on Delilah's couch with his brain leaking out his ear as Tilly ran through the worst that Nickelodeon had to offer. *Poor guy.*

Suzanne hadn't decided if she trusted the newest defector from the Fae Court, but Tilly's endorsement, believe it or not, counted as a mark in his favor. She didn't usually take to people she didn't know that quickly—even before the accident. And, if nothing else, Suzanne owed him for keeping the woman-child occupied and out of the way a while. Today would be much harder to pull off with Tilly underfoot. Bad enough Suzanne had already acquired an audience.

Bubba's wife, Samandrea, and their boys, Zack and Shawn, brought up the rear of their impromptu group. Suzanne could have done without them tagging along, but at least they were proving useful. Between them, they hauled the extra gear. The boys came along strictly as spectators. Not only did Suzanne not want to have to pull her shots, but frankly, she couldn't take more of a blow to her confidence—the boys were too good at this. Sammy chose to sit it out to keep them in line, lest they forget they weren't participating.

Right now their number was uneven, but Suzanne had also texted Gavin. She found herself too edgy to wait for him to show, certain that Lance would come down at any moment and either try to "help" or convince her that this wasn't necessary. Gavin knew where to go; he could catch up.

The deeper they went into the forest, the more Suzanne relaxed as dew-spangled grass slapped her ankles and the distant twittering of the morning birds welcomed her among the trees. She found more comfort here than anywhere else. A different kind of anticipation seeped into her gut; she could beat this...she *would* beat this psychological paralysis brought on by the color red, right here on her own turf.

"Hey! Hold up," a voice called across the back lot, from the direction of *Delilah's*. Suzanne turned around to look, walking backward, while the others glanced over their shoulders. Gavin appeared past the edge of the trees.

He loped across the field toward them, his dark blond hair hanging damp around his shoulders. Suzanne experienced a light jolt as he passed through the protections surrounding the land behind *Delilah's*. Only Club members and their families could cross the shield unaided. Gavin grinned at her as he went through, no doubt feeling the tingle of the magic on his skin. Suzanne laughed back, remembering when Lance had hit puberty and the three of them had gotten giddy on running back and forth through the invisible curtain.

When her brother came close enough, Blow tossed a small ribbed cap at him, which he reflexively caught. The Wind Elemental wore a vicious grin on his narrow face as he quipped: "Last one here gets to play target!"

Gavin just shrugged and pulled the knit hat down over his ears as he turned to Suzanne, his green eyes still a little sleepy. "What's going on, *deifiúr*?"

She tensed at his use of the Gaelic word for sister, something he only did when he felt protective. Usually she hit him for it, but today she let it pass; not like she wouldn't be getting even. "Time for a little therapy," she answered.

His brows drew down in confusion, and his head gave a little tilt to the side. She hefted the air gun she'd armed herself with and pointed at the hat on his head. Understanding finally dawned. Gavin cursed half-heartedly but the love in his gaze made it clear he'd do anything for her, even play target. Long strides brought him to her side where he looked deep in her eyes, deep enough to make her shift her stance. In that instant, but for his coloring, he looked enough like their father that she unconsciously prepared to fight.

"Are you up for this?" he asked, his voice just loud enough for her. He did not mean it unkindly, but the question still battered her resolve. She wanted to say yes, but the word would not come.

As if mocking her, a crow cawed from nearby. Others answered all around, staccato, like a laugh ricocheting from tree to tree. The *Dubh Fae* had had a murder of crows with him the day Suzanne nearly died. The sound, combined with her brother's uncertainty, almost undid her.

It took an effort to keep her breath even, to not lose herself again in the memory. Her skin twitched as if beneath the weight of an unseen gaze. Gavin reached out and grasped her shoulder, steadying her. The faint doubt she had seen in his expression blossomed into full-blown concern. He knew what that day had done to her as no one other than Lance did. She wanted to curse her brother for it. Instead, she shrugged him off and gave a hard nod, daring him to call her a liar. She *had* to be up for this, if not for herself, then for those who depended on her. Ever since the attack she'd withdrawn from the world. Her absence left the orphanage and all the other places where she volunteered even more short staffed than usual. In some ways, that hurt worse than the impact on her personally. Her grip on the rifle tightened as she spun away and stalked toward the area Delilah had long ago set aside for paintball. "Better grab a gun from one of the boys," she called over her shoulder to her brother.

Silent and steady, the group fell in behind. She beat them to the clearing at the center of the combat zone by a good five minutes, earning her a frown from Jon when he caught up. She pretended not to notice while she rechecked her weapon and adjusted her protective gear. She watched the others, purposely forcing herself to stare at the stupid red hats, denying the anxiety that built in her even as it caused her to tremble. Pissed off, she jammed an old, battered motorcycle helmet on her head, but didn't pull the visor down over her face.

"So, how's this going down?" Jon asked, once they were all geared up and ready.

At a loss, Suzanne looked toward Delilah, who stood across the way from her in old leathers, but no helmet. Lance's aunt stepped in without even a blink, giving Suzanne the time she needed to get her thoughts in line. "House rules: no crying foul when ya get hit, no magic, no firing across neutral territory, no head shots, no double-teaming no one. A hit takes you out of the round until you return to neutral ground and one of your team tags you back in." Delilah paused and Suzanne took over.

"We're not out here for me to use you as target practice...I have a problem I have to work through and I have to do it honest or there is no point. I need to get over this bullshit of freezing up every time I see...r-r...*Red.*" she had to force the word out from between gritted teeth. She felt a rush of triumph as she said it, something she'd had trouble doing since the attack. "My job is to find and claim these three flags." Suzanne pulled the markers from her pocket and held them up. "My team...you help me with that and you protect my ass while I retrieve them. You guys..." she turned to those wearing the red caps, "have to try and reclaim your flags before I reach neutral ground...which is right here in the center...or until I nail your butts to a tree. An alert signal will go off when I've claimed a flag. We keep going until I capture all three, or you rescue them.

"And *no* going easy on me..." Suzanne caught each of their eyes. "Got it?"

They all nodded back.

That settled, Suzanne forced herself to look down at the flags, made an effort to actually see them, instead of staring past them. She took a deep breath, willing the crisp aroma of the autumn air to settle her, then drew upon her magic. It took just a touch of energy to lay her spell on them; a simple alert of sound and color to signal when she claimed each flag. Once done she held the markers out to Bubba's boys and one to Sammy as well. "You know what to do. You have ten minutes to plant your flags," she told them. "Then I want your butts back here and out of the war zone."

"All right!" the boys yelled and took off for the trees, each going in a different direction. Sammy went more sedately, if with no less haste. Of its own accord, Suzanne's gaze tracked Shawn, who whooped and brandished his flag in the air as if leading a charge. As the red flickered in and out of sight among the trees, a thin coat of sweat chilled Suzanne's exposed skin. Again her nerves crawled. Growling, she yanked her attention back to those waiting. They stood already grouped in their teams. She forced herself to go on as if she were fine, instead of ready to jump or lash out at every flicker of red. As soon as the boys returned, both teams faded into the forest.

The world closed in when Suzanne pulled her visor down into place, making sure it clicked securely. She focused on her breathing, slow and deep, reminding herself she had plenty of air. She'd chosen an older model rifle, a Sheridan pump-action. Slower, but more reliable, it sat solid and comfortable in her grip. Suzanne charged it, dropping a ball into the chamber, and held it at the ready as she searched for the flutter of a flag.

Something flickered among the trees, barely seen out of the corner of her eye. Suzanne turned to face the direction full on but saw no flag, or anything else responsible for the movement. Scowling, she continued the turn, searching the zone, straining to pick up any sound. The only noise came from the boys, laughing as they fooled around in the clearing. *Cut it out,* she silently ordered herself, fed up with all her chicken-shit jumping at shadows.

The further she went, the more the sounds of laughter faded until only the leaves shushed overhead, occasionally overlaid by the trill of a brazen bird. Behind her another crow cawed, making her jump, and Suzanne had to resist the urge to turn it into a neon-painted corpse. It would take a lot of effort with an air gun, but that was the kind of mood she was in.

With her rifle at the ready, she wove her way through the trees, gaze sharp as she scanned the patch of woods. She spied movement ahead, to either side, about twenty yards off; she'd caught up to her teammates, who bisected the zone looking for the opponents' flags. Joining them in their efforts, she could almost swear she saw other activity as well, caught at the tail of her vision, off to the side...

The boys trying to sneak into the action? Or something else? Suzanne stopped with a jerk, bringing her weapon around, but found nothing there. The skin at the nape of her neck rippled as she turned a tight circle, trying to catch what always seemed just at the edge of sight. Was that a glimmer of brownish red? The gleam of pointed teeth? Flat, red-black eyes burning under the deadfall?

Sweat formed beneath her gear despite the cool temperature of the day. The more the others moved ahead, the more Suzanne noticed the forest scents on the air; predominantly moldering leaves, but beneath that, just the ghost of a smell, a faint coppery tang. She'd smelt it often...or thought she had, anyway...since she'd been rescued. Instinct told her to curl in a protective ball around the acid bath churning her stomach. She fought the urge.

Then she realized what she was doing...creeping and skulking and feeding her phobia when she stood on *protected* land. Of course, it was easy to tell herself she was safe; it was all together harder to believe it when she couldn't shake the feeling of being watched. Still, imagined or not, Suzanne didn't—usually—hide from anything. It pissed her off. She hardly recognized herself. Spunk used to describe her quite aptly; now spooked seemed more applicable.

No, Suzanne thought to herself, fighting the urge to whimper. *Stop doing this to yourself or go home to Father, because you'll have proven him right!* The club wouldn't turn her away for having a problem, but she'd be letting them down nearly as much as herself if she didn't get a handle on this. It could even put them at risk. She'd walk away before letting that happen. But not just yet...she wasn't ready to cry "Uncle." Not even in her head.

Suzanne raised her visor and let loose a primeval battle cry, which her teammates echoed through the wold. Challenge cast, they all dashed off in divergent directions to find the flags. She barely noticed a tingle across her body, as if she'd just crossed the shield, even though the perimeter lay nowhere nearby. Caught up in the hunt, she dismissed the sensation.

A few hours later, Suzanne's team had claimed two flags. She had been back to neutral ground five times: twice to turn in the pennants and three times to get tagged back in to the game. She was tired and beat—by no means the same thing—and she was ready to wring the neck of the person responsible for placing the final flag. They'd clearly gotten...*creative*. She did have some idea who to thank. The last time she'd humped it back to the clearing, shaking ball fragments out of her shirt, Shawn had grinned so big his eyes disappeared, and it wasn't because she'd flashed any skin.

Let him grin, though, and let him gloat at his bit of mischief, whatever it was; Suzanne felt like grinning right back. Her plan was working better than she'd ever hoped it would. After hours of paintball, she barely felt a twinge now, not even when Gavin kept popping up out of nowhere to take pot shots at her. Some hesitation remained, but she didn't freeze up and shut down the way she had just last night. Now if only she could find the final blasted flag they could get back to *Delilah's*!

She didn't know the time—neither mages nor fae wore watches…something about their nature had a detrimental effect on the technology—but a glance at the position of the sun overhead placed it sometime after noon.

As she brought her gaze down from the sky, Suzanne swore the forest blue.

There, only yards away…and about twenty-five feet up the bole of an ancient sycamore…the third flag hung vibrant against the muted greens and browns and creams of the patchwork bark. Shawn, the little shit, had his father's sense of humor and apparently enough of his mother's pixie nature to make things interesting. Locking her jaw, Suzanne headed for the blaze of red canvas, scanning all around for any defenders lurking nearby. Seeing no one, she ran for the sycamore. She lacked the innate connection of the resident dryad, but thanks to her four-fold nature, in mere moments she'd scurried up the tree with the help of Earth and Wind. Only a slight tremor shook her hand as she set her jaw and snatched up the crimson flag. The canvas strip immediately went into her jacket pocket while the sky above her erupted in an indigo light display complete with muted fanfare.

"Game on," she called out, her voice throaty and full, charged with a fresh flood of adrenaline.

She moved by instinct and the force of momentum, barely aware of the answering challenge from below while she began her descent or the *thunk* of spattering paint that twice only just missed her at braced thigh and extended arm. She laughed again and pointed her charged weapon one-handed at Bubba, aiming for his shoulder. Barely flinching as she pulled the trigger, she allowed the recoil to send her spinning from her perch before the ball even impacted. Again taking advantage of her nature, she flowed down like a feather on the breeze and landed in a clear space between the trees, hitting the dirt in a controlled roll that brought her to her feet, already dashing full out for neutral ground.

"Damn, that stings!" Not for the first time, Bubba swore behind her as she disappeared into the forest, already yards away. She laughed, not at his pain, but with the joy of the game, at each little triumph over fear. From farther off she heard the sound of bodies rushing through the underbrush. More concerned with putting distance between her and the opposition than she was with being stealthy, Suzanne kept on running, bounding over fallen branches and dodging among the trees. If they tagged her now, she and her team would lose the game. Any moment she expected the solid *thunk* of a paintball to collide with her back.

Instead, the sounds of pursuit faded and the forest noises slowly increased: scurrying through the leaves, birdsong above, the blasted caw of the crows all around...she felt like the spell beacon still flashed over her head, drawing every eye in the forest to her. Of course, these days she always felt watched anyway, even when alone. Getting over her phobia of the color red hadn't banished that. Suzanne blocked it all out as she slowed to a walk, taking a moment to catch her breath and think. She couldn't run straight back or they'd be on her like anything, but if she went quiet and stealthy, and circled around to come in from another angle, she'd probably have a clear field.

Her steps moved both quick and sure through the undergrowth and deadfall. She set her jaw and straightened her shoulders. One yard...ten, a half-dozen more...She tensed with each step, but it didn't cripple her. Another success. A dangerous smile crossed her lips.

Twenty feet ahead of her stood a clearing. At the center lay a small faerie ring, eight feet wide, maybe less; one of many that dotted the Wild Hunt lands. Altering her steps, she headed for the ring. Each one had a distinct feel. One she could recognize and identify. It would give her an idea of her location in the forest and which way she needed to go.

She stopped abruptly, taking a half a step back. In front of her, a wizened figure out of her most recent nightmares crept from behind the bole of a tree. *Redcap. Powrie. Dunter.* All names for the same vile fae, but she'd always think of them as redcaps. The image of them bathing those caps in her blood so haunted her no other name would serve.

Her stomach contracted painfully and her eyes locked onto the perverse leer on the redcap's face. His right hand curled around an iron pike, the left waggled its fingers at her, like an auld uncle relaxing by the fire. She took in his iron-shod boots and the soft cap on his head, a bit more brown than red today. A distant memory niggled at her mind as she catalogued that fact, but the detail played hard to get. It had something to do with their nature... The knowledge remained elusive, which did not surprise her. She'd never paid much attention to the creatures, having nothing to do with redcaps before two weeks ago.

She wished she could still say as much.

How did he breach the shields? She couldn't help but wonder. Then the bastard licked his lips and looked her up and down, quite familiar, distracting her from the thought.

Suzanne snarled. Here stood the first test of today's success. Combat instinct kicked in and she drew magic to her, the spell on her jacket clearing the way for her fins to unfurl, streaming violet tendrils of energy behind her. A growing metallic tang blanketed the aroma of wet leaves and decay she'd stirred up from the deadfall. It barely registered.

Suzanne faced one foe that she could see. He had not come alone. Somewhere in the forest she sensed more of the beastly fae lurking. Their voracious hunger clung to her like a fog on the air. It pulsed with each pounding beat of her heart until her skin twitched in protest against the sensation. The awareness of being watched increased and the rising wind seemed to carry eager murmurs that had until this moment been relegated to Suzanne's nightmares. She recognized the sound before the feasting. The forest pulsed around her, at once the land behind *Delilah's*, yet reminiscent of the other forest where she'd first been attacked. The disorientation played havoc with her equilibrium.

"No!" she growled, rage conflicting with fear, drawing the outcry both long and loud. "Not this time. Buffet's closed."

The redcap laughed and took a step forward. Was there a desperate edge to the sound, or did Suzanne imagine it? She couldn't say. Feeling a bit perverse herself, she aimed the Sheridan at him and fired. He moved before the ball tagged the trunk of the tree he'd been standing in front of, but then, that had been the point, hadn't it? As he dodged away, Suzanne raced for the clearing, readying her magic and charging the air gun while she closed the distance to her goal.

She heard scrabbling behind her; the sound of many feet converging, accompanied by grumbling and sick, slurping sounds. A gnarled hand grasped the bottom edge of her jacket with the strength of a bulldog. Her violent twist to the side broke his grip. She looked back and thought she saw several grinning faces at her heels, baring razor teeth and blood-red tongues. One followed close. Suzanne put on speed to out-distance him, but as her right foot came down across the mushroom ring, something yanked the other back. Suzanne pivoted and balanced on her free leg. She'd been caught by the one that had first stepped in front of her in the woods. She knew it was him because a few Pepto-pink paint splatters speckled his face. Hatred mingled with the hunger and murder in his expression. Not liking the look in his gleaming red gaze, she blasted him in the head this time with a screaming-orange paintball.

As he yipped and snarled at her, pushed back by the force of the gas-driven ball, she yanked her left foot out of his grip. Pain shot up her leg as she pulled free. Most of her, anyway; she'd lost more than skin in her effort to get loose. The redcap raised his hand and made a show of licking her blood and flesh from his clawed fingers. Though there wasn't much, the red of his hat still seemed to brighten. The memory niggled again. It lingered long enough for her to catch a piece of it. From within the faerie ring she used her magic to close it against them...and herself, as instinct warned her to do. Standing there, breath heaving, she slowly turned a circle as the redcaps converged. She found something unnatural in this, even for matters involving the Fae. Six of them surrounded her, all familiar, though she wished she could say otherwise. It was a rare thing for these solitary fae to band together.

She narrowed her gaze as she realized *her* blood dyed their caps. As long as they were wet with it, a bond existed between them. It let them spy upon her, it let them find her, and—she realized now—it let them pass the Wild Hunt's defenses, which had been keyed to let her through. That tingle! Damn, she had actually felt them cross the shield.

Something else still eluded her, but she found herself too distracted to pinpoint what. At the moment the creatures paced around her haven, stomping and grumbling and lashing out until their clawed hands set off sparks against the transparent barrier of her shield.

Agitated did not seem a strong enough word for the actions of these murderous fae.

With a calm she did not feel and an urge to poke them further, Suzanne sat down to contemplate her situation—and the redcaps—more closely. Her left foot rested on the ground and she bent her knee, raising her pant leg and baring her bloody ankle. The redcaps' movements grew frenzied. She had to laugh as they flung themselves at her, only to be sent flying back with a flash and a sizzle, repelled by her magic. Each time they rushed the shield, a shiver traveled through her at the impact, a disruption in the energy. The protection held, but for how much longer?

Then something occurred to her. She could leave. She didn't have to stay here. Didn't have to confront them. Didn't *need* to, did she? From within this gateway she could go anywhere in the Fae or mortal worlds with but a thought. Yet the question remained: if she fled, would she ever be free of the hold they had on her? Her fingers tightened on the stock of her weapon as she considered that. The stink of her own sweat filled the magically enclosed circle. Forcing herself to breathe deep, she realized something else. The terror tasted stale. Old. Done.

Yes, her pulse pounded, and yes, her muscles knotted, but the redcaps had not trapped or even overwhelmed her, they merely had her outmanned. Sense had sent her scrambling, not fear. Adrenaline kept her tense and trembling, ready for action, not flight.

She found peace in the revelation.

Suzanne raised her left hand, tilted her head coyly to the side, and let her fingers waggle at their leader. Not even bothering to get up, she started the spell to open the gateway. Before she could complete it, a flicker of movement among the trees caught her eye, followed by a faint sound of roughhousing drawing nearer. She spied two familiar figures goofing off among the trees.

"Fuck!" she yelled aloud. She reacted out of pure instinct, not thought, scrambling to her feet with a twinge of pain in her ankle. The gate spell remained partially formed around her, giving the air a rippled effect. Her sudden action drew all eyes to her, those in the distance and those up close. The movement she'd noticed stopped dead, as did the frenzy taking place directly around her. If the redcaps became aware of Bubba's boys, they'd be on them in an instant. They had no choice.

Suzanne knew what she must do as the last bit of forgotten redcap lore surfaced from the depths of her memory. If the caps upon their heads dried out, the creatures died. They might lust after her blood as a matter of pride—they were not known for leaving survivors—but any would do when it came down to preserving their lives. The unsuspecting boys represented the easier target. After all, even with the bond between them broken, the recaps could always target her again later, at their leisure, once their caps were properly moist and crimson.

Suzanne calmly slid her hand into her pocket and palmed the butterfly knife she'd stowed there. She brought it out and flicked it open in one smooth move, raising both arms over her head. She clenched her right hand into a fist then flicked her fingers wide, meaningless to the redcaps, but an order the boys knew well, to split up and scatter. Her effort came too late. Several of the redcaps turned away from her and began to stalk the boys. She couldn't allow that. Her other hand swept down, drawing the open blade in a shallow slice down the back of her right hand. As the blood welled, those redcaps that had broken off came rushing back again.

She had their attention now. For them, the world outside of her no longer existed. Tongues flicked and lips smacked as red-tinged eyes avidly followed the trail of blood snaking down her sleeve. Certain of their complete focus on her, Suzanne willingly called upon Earth and Air and Fire and Water for the first time in her life, not quite knowing what she asked, but instinct telling her she must.

Nothing happened.

Well, nothing more than the wind lashing the forest into a thrashing maelstrom. The redcaps ignored it.

Suzanne's eyes closed and her head flung back, a flash of despair arching her spine. The brief moment of weakness broke her focus. Just enough. Down came the shield and Suzanne nearly dropped with it as the force of the winds hit her on the heels of the broken spell. The air around her shook and shattered as all six redcaps rushed the circle.

No. Not again. Never again, not for the feasting, not for the fear...with her or anyone else. Her eyes snapped open and her chin lowered until she met the redcaps' gazes with an unholy glare.

"Bring it," she growled, as she carefully, gently cut her spirit off from the connection to Lance, safeguarding him from what would come.

Her arms came down, ready and beckoning at her sides, and her knees bent, legs spreading a bit wider in a fighter's stance. At her back, her fins—flooding with magic—unfurled with a whip's crack, trailing tendrils of energy primarily colored in lavender and blue. She stood there in challenge while they rushed her. The winds continued to tug at her, one dry, one cool, one hot, and one wet. Other than to brace herself, Suzanne barely had a chance to wonder at them before the redcaps descended, clutching and tearing. The leader—looking more painter's cap than redcap—fairly scaled her, catching the seam at her shoulder with his dagger-like nails, slicing right through her leather jacket to flesh. He laughed evilly as he rubbed his head—and his cap—against the flow like a macabre cat. As the others tore with less success at her leathers, Suzanne could think of only one more option, one way to ensure the boys' safety, and her release from this hateful link. She brought the shields back up again, encapsulating herself, the redcaps, and the errant whirlwind. Her mind turned inward as she held two things alive in her thoughts: first a spell to bind the redcaps to her, no matter how they sought to flee, and the second a destination. Once all six gripped her, she loosed her magic and ordered the gate to whisk them away.

Suzanne barely noticed that the winds followed.

The seven of them landed on the hard, superheated floor of the paint-drying furnace Suzanne used to run. The wicked fae shrieked as their flesh seared away. Five of the redcaps would never rise again; they burned to cinders around Suzanne as their caps dried out in an instant. Her nose pinched against the acrid stench. The ashes whipping around the chamber, borne upon the unnatural wind, stung her eyes, but the extreme temperature did not harm her. The rogue winds wove around where she crouched, insulating her from the intense heat of the furnace.

The sixth redcap, the leader, clung to her leg, apparently within the scope of whatever protected her. Half of his cap remained fresh-soaked and his gaze promised retribution. Suzanne couldn't breathe, but she lashed out at him. With a sharp jab, she slammed her right fist into his face; with the left hand, she swiped the crimson hat off his head, blood dripping from her fingers as she crumpled it in her fist and shoved it into the pocket of her jeans.

The redcap fell away from her with a shriek. Hatred and malice burned bright in his eyes like embers as he reached for her too late. His skin crackled and flaked away in an instant, like paper flash-incinerated. The memory of his expression lingered even as his ashes fell away.

Suzanne gasped, fully expecting she foresaw the means of her own death.

Instead, the winds swirled tighter around her. Again she felt the separate currents, sensed what she'd missed before as Earth gently cradled her flesh, Air filled her lungs, Fire drew away the painful heat, and Water cooled her scorched throat. That safeguarding done, the Four Winds wrapped around her in a protective funnel and lifted her away, back through the newly opened gate.

She came to on the forest floor, in the middle of the neutral ground, blinking up into ten anxious faces. Her helmet and rifle lay beside her. A grin came to her face as she fumbled with her jacket pocket, pulling out a crumpled canvas flag. "I win," she crowed as she held it aloft, and only four of those staring down at her knew how thoroughly.

Callan and Tilly

Chapter Two

Underhill came apart a little more with each passing day. It fractured and splintered apace with Dair na Scath's mind. Even now the Ard Ri—High King—of Underhill ranted and raved, sending a rain of leaves falling from the chronicle trees that lined the Great Hall. A bitter wind whirled around him, shredding those leaves already littering the ground. The stench of decay overwhelmed Callan's senses as he stoically stood attendance on his liege.

Very few others did. Fewer with each day, as their world crumbled. Courtiers were fickle beings no matter the realm they hailed from.

As leader of the Fae armies, Callan had little choice. Not that he wouldn't have been by the *Ard Ri*'s side regardless. How better to know your enemy than to keep his council? Though Dair did not know it, they had been enemies from the moment the first oath had been broken between them at the High King's whim... just over forty mortal years ago. Callan had patience. No need to move in haste. For now, he listened and did as his majesty bid.

"He betrayed us! How dare he betray us?! We will crush him, body and soul!" The High King spit the words, rife with venom. "He lied about our Anai, hid from us news of her child, and stole our ceremonial dagger. Why are we so beset by treachery? We have surely been too kind."

That would not have been the answer Callan returned, had he been asked and free to answer truthfully.

Dair turned to look down on Callan, a long-suffering expression adding bitterness to his mien. "None but you have kept faith with us." And with these words of false praise Dair reinforced his champion's personal vow to see the usurper standing before him bludgeoned to a bloody pool beneath the pommel of Callan's own sword. Such goals strengthened his resolve to bide his time, particularly now, when the High King's expression made it clear his warrior's seeming faithfulness appeared in his eyes more a product of weakness than honor.

"What is your will, *A Shoilse*?" Callan asked, his tone neutral as he went to one knee, as required when addressing the High King in his Hall.

"Our will? You ask our will?" Dair paused, as if the answer should be self-evident, before raging once more. "Destroy them! Destroy them all! Feed their living entrails to our hounds. Drag their torn and bleeding bodies face down across the Salt Desert!" He darted across the intervening space and leaned in close. Too close. Callan stared at the tendons standing out against Dair's thinning skin and resisted the urge to gut the High King as he loomed. "Make. Them. Suffer." Foam flecked Dair's thin, dry lips as the words hissed across them.

"It shall be done," the warrior responded, and waited for more precise instructions.

"We have sent the Black One after the thief who stole our Anai away."

At the mention of his once-betrothed, Callan tensed, his jaw locked against his own impulse to rage. Dair, of course, did not notice or acknowledge Callan's personal right to vengeance. He did not even admit the pledge he'd once made to a mere warrior, which he'd violated long before his daughter's death.

"By night's end, Cameron Cosain," Dair ground out the name, "will be as dead as our Anai,"—he of course used the royal we—"and the Abomination with him."

Callan understood the High King spoke of Lance Cosain, the halfling with more right to the *Ruada-an* Throne than Dair himself, and perhaps even enough power to claim it, though mercy upon anyone foolish enough to think that truth, let alone voice it.

"You we will send after the other," Dair continued, his gaze narrowing as a smug smile blossomed across his face. "We have ensured you a path into the heart of the enemy camp which they cannot guard against. Go...now...and secure our future. Deal with Gort as you will, but bring to us the woman with him, unharmed. She is precious to our cause. But before you return, deliver this message. The Abomination is to meet us at the field of Destiny on the floating island of Avalon. In exchange for himself and our dagger, we will return the girl."

Dair spoke of the woman, Tilly, another halfling possessing more royal blood in her veins than Dair had spilt over the time of his rule. She was damaged...or flawed, it did not matter which. Better, in Callan's opinion, to slay her, rather than to introduce more madness into the Fae Court.

Of course, Dair held Callan's opinion in even less regard than he did Callan himself.

The warrior rose, waiting in patience as Dair opened the gate. Part of him wondered if he had waited too long to claim his vengeance.

Perplexed and more than a little unnerved by this thing called television, Gort rose from the couch and moved around the mound of pillows on the floor to stand before the contraption, searching for a means to turn it off. He understood his current situation had been a calculated move on Lance's part. Annoyed, the halfling had left the apartment this morning with the little control box in his possession. The biker clearly did not care for Gort. But why? Because Dair na Scath once called him advisor, or because Gort made the man uncomfortable by knowing more about his family than Lance seemed to? There being little he could do to combat either prejudice, Gort huffed, his hand coming up to rub his temple where a slow, dull ache had settled, and drawing down over the rest of his face as if he might wipe away his frustration. He winced as he encountered the tender wound on his cheek where Dair na Scath, out of displeasure, had lashed Gort with a whip-like root from one of his shadow oaks. It ached and would not heal, unusual as the Fae were all fast healing. Yet another annoyance in his already beleaguered life...

Well, perhaps he could do something about the current exasperation, anyway.

Considering the television, he slowly reached out and pressed one of the protrusions. The image changed, but not for the better. Lights flashed while people moved violently across the screen. A shrieking, raucous noise projected into the room, catching Gort point blank. Crying out, his hands pressed over his sensitive ears, the druid backed away. He stopped abruptly as he came up against a soft body.

"Hey! What did you do?" Tilly cried out over the noise. Her small fist pounded his back. Gort grunted with the blow and pivoted out of striking range. The woman's mind might be trapped in childhood, but her strength remained that of an adult, and not a weak one. Her displeasure enveloped him in a swirling, emotive cloud of sorrow, anger, and disappointment. The strength of those currents pulled and tugged Gort off balance, threatening to overwhelm his composure, like a riptide would his body. Hastily he shielded himself against the emotional onslaught.

For a brief instant her physical appearance distracted him, so like her aunt, whom Gort had known and cared for long ago, before Dair na Scath had riven the *Rudha-an* family line. Yet so unlike Tilsaia, who would never have clad herself in a bright pink tee shirt and soft cotton pajama bottoms. Clothing choices aside, the resemblance was enough that Gort fully suspected this young woman had been named for the other.

"I don't like you any more today." This Tilly glowered nearly as impressively as her cousin Lance...and her aunt, for that matter. Gort dragged his attention back to the matter at hand.

"That saddens me," he said, meaning it, yet startled at how deeply. "I thought to propose a game to you."

Tilly looked doubtful and hopeful all at once. "Nobody ever wants to play games...'cept Lance. An' Suzanne...an'..."

"What game would you like to play?" Gort interjected, foreseeing that the list of willing participants perhaps was not as limited as Tilly would have him believe. He had to raise his voice uncomfortably above the noise still pouring from the television. "Might you turn that off so we can decide?"

Now eager, Tilly complied. She then hurried back to him and rattled off a stream of names that had no meaning to him. Somewhat concerned, he worried perhaps games meant something different in this place. He cursed his limited familiarity with the mortal world, wincing as he glanced toward the television, dreading he might actually need to figure out how to turn it back on. But then he considered that his charge did not have full command of her intellect. One would presume that any game intended for her would be simplistic.

"Perhaps your favorite?"

Tilly's face brightened in an instant, any lingering signs of doubt or displeasure fleeing.

"Poker!" she said quickly. "Nobody ever wants to play poker."

Gort frowned at the smug set to her features, wondering how quickly he might regret his offer. "This is a new game to me," he told her. "I am glad to play but you must explain how."

She drew her teeth across her lower lip and her brow creased. He could see her mind struggle with his request, but after a moment she gave a soft sigh and nodded.

"I can do that. But first we have to set up." Reverting to her sparkling smile she skipped out of the room. An inordinate amount of banging and thudding came from the chamber she'd entered. So much so that once more Gort grew worried. He took a step toward the doorway, thinking to intervene, only to have Tilly bounce back into the room. Her arms were full of stuffed dogs—and a single stuffed dragon—and she wore a transparent green visor askew on her head. One hand clutched a number of plastic chips in red, blue, and white while the other held a small rectangular box.

"We has to do it right," she declared as she made her way to the table, the odd dog or two falling off the pile in her wake. Focused on her task, Tilly seemed unaware.

She divested herself of the pile, or rather all but two of the animals, which tangled in a cord hung around her neck. With a huff, Tilly took the pendant off and set it on the table to disentangle her toys. A glimmer of mage energy clung to it, catching his eye, but Tilly's bustling drew his attention away.

Gort chuckled as she arranged the plush canines in their own seats with stacks of colorful chips arrayed before them. The visor landed at a jaunty angle on the bulldog's head. From the small box she drew what Gort now recognized as playing cards, something even the Fae Court were familiar with. The expertise with which she shuffled them gave him pause, a stark reminder that she had not always been so childlike. He cleared his throat to get her attention.

"And where would milady like for me to sit?"

Tilly giggled and pointed to an empty chair between the dragon and a shocking pink poodle. Dutifully moving toward his seat, Gort suddenly lurched as a sharp current of mage energy burned across his skin. He gasped. Another jolt shook his body, sending him to his knees. He reached out to grip the back of a chair and missed. Tilly squealed, but Gort barely heard her for the buzzing in his head. Reality warped as a surge of mage energy washed through him from his toes to his head, ending in a knife-edge of pain tearing across his cheek. His body stiffened. Something ripped free from his flesh. Gort landed hard on the floor staring at a sliver of blood-coated wood before him. He recognized it as oak and dread pierced his heart as he realized why his wound had not healed and how thoroughly Dair na Scath had used him.

What danger had Gort brought down on those he'd sought to protect?

"Tilly! Run! Downstairs, now!" he yelled, the words slurred and broken. She listened, but she ran toward him, panicked concern leaving her face pale and drawn. "No...no! The other way," he tried to tell her, but the warning came too late. She'd just reached him when reality tore up the middle, starting at the splinter on the floor.

Gort struggled to his feet, drawing himself up by the table leg, waving away Tilly's attempt to "help." He managed to come upright just as Callan, the High King's chosen warrior, stepped through the newly opened gate. Pushing Tilly behind him, Gort swayed with the effort. It startled him to hear her growl over his shoulder. A full-blown snarl that made his skin chill with a cold sweat. Emotion not his own sent his focus spinning as adrenalin surged and his muscles tensed contrary to his own reaction. His limbs locked as two sets of impulses attempted to drive them to action. He forced Tilly's feelings of rage and confusion aside to regain control of his body. Raising a shield against the woman's empathic sendings, he turned toward the threat.

Lacking anything that remotely resembled a weapon, Gort grabbed the brown and white bulldog from the seat beside him and flung it in the intruder's face. Futile really, even as a diversion, but there wasn't much more that Gort could do as he swayed, still clutching the chair to remain upright. The moment he let fly with the plush animal he knew it was a mistake; Callan drew his elven blade and cleaved the dog in two, scattering white fluff all over. For a moment, stunned silence on everyone's part, then a roar of deep, intense rage swept through the room.

"Brutus was my favorite!" Tilly screamed as she launched herself at the dark elf. The waves of intense emotion she projected overwhelmed Gort's shields and completely staggered both of the fae. A single tear trailed down Callan's cheek. It clashed with the malice tightening his features. Surprisingly he did not strike, though his muscles stood out taut against his garments, poised and ready to engage. His gaze held a flood of emotions Gort suspected the elf had never before let himself feel, let alone express even in this subtle manner.

By sheer will Gort regained his balance and composure, his own eyes freely streaming heartache's tears, his expression set in grim, determined lines. He had been charged with safeguarding this woman. He could not fail in that. Forcing his limbs to move, he placed himself between Tilly and Callan's wrath. The elven warrior shook off the paralysis caused by Tilly's empathic overload. His arm came up. Gort could not evade the backhanded blow, his own limbs moving sluggishly, reluctant to respond. The impact sent him crashing into the infernal television. Glass shattered. Jags of pain sent bright, angry flashes across Gort's vision. He struggled to rise from the wreckage, shards of glass slicing his flesh as he stumbled toward Callan, only to slip as his foot came down on Tilly's nest of pillows. He looked up from the floor in horror to see her engage the foe in his stead.

The warrior snarled but restrained his natural response to the woman's forceful attack. Rather than strike out, he grabbed for her. Like a wildcat, she twisted away, then circled back to exact further retribution for her beloved Brutus. Each time she moved near the table, her pendant flashed and the mage energy linked to it tried to wrap her in a protective field she slid away from each time she attacked. Her hand lashed out as Callan reached for her. He hissed at the bloody gouges she left across his cheek before dancing out of his grip once more. Feminine laughter rang in bell-like peals.

Gort gasped and shoved the pillows out of his way. He clambered upright, lurching to his feet, to assist and hinder, respectively. Callan's eyes narrowed and a calculated smile came to his lips. The warrior ceased reaching for Tilly and instead snatched up the poodle. Gort cried out a warning, but it came too late. With a tortured wail, Tilly cast herself forward.

"Babette!"

The instant Callan's arm locked around her, he dropped the stuffed dog, drew himself straight and dignified, despite the woman thrashing in his arms, and sneered toward Gort.

"Inform the Abomination he is to meet the *Ard Ri* alone at the Field of Destiny. He is to bring the dagger you stole from the High King. In exchange for it and himself, the woman will be freed."

Message delivered, Callan stepped back through the ripple of the still-open gate, taking Tilly with him. The portal crashed closed behind them with a wave of released mage energy that sent Gort back to his knees. He groaned and scrambled for the door, grabbing Tilly's pendant as he passed the table, half crawling–half lunging, until he exited the apartment and gained the stairs. His vision greyed out as he struggled to stand completely upright. Misjudging the first step, he tumbled down the length of the stairs. He fought to remain conscious as he landed at the bottom, just barely holding on as startled bikers streamed through the door leading to the bar.

Jazzed and triumphant, Suzanne sauntered across the back lot just ahead of her pack of cohorts. They must have made a sight; all of them sweaty and half spent, most of them in their tattiest gear, tagged with bright splotches of neon paint. Except for Rock and Blow. They must have given up the chase early and gone open season on each other because orange and pink paint nearly covered Rock head to toe, and Blow looked pretty much the same, except in yellow and green. Both still shed paint droplets and fragments of ball casing with each step.

Their ongoing sibling rivalry faded from Suzanne's thoughts, though. The smile that hadn't left her lips since she'd regained consciousness in the center of neutral ground grew even bigger. As she approached the back door to *Delilah's*, Lance walked out of the kitchen onto the stoop. She lengthened her stride, leaving the others behind while she skipped up the back steps and settled into Lance's arms, barely feeling the injuries to her ankle and shoulder.

That first kiss of the day? It nearly sent her running back to bed again, dragging Lance behind her. Intense enough that she barely heard Zack and Shawn acting grossed out in the compound. Suzanne got into it a bit more than she should have out there on the stoop as she reopened the link between them and soaked in his pleasure. Her blood raced even more than usual and she had the oddest urge to nip at Lance's lip. She resisted, though she did let her hands wander. When she slid one under Lance's favorite muscle shirt he stilled and made to draw back. Of course...he wore red.

Suzanne smiled against his lips. "I told you I'd take care of it."

She could feel his pride at the edge of her consciousness only slightly tinged with doubt and concern. That didn't bother her as long as he kept it to himself, which he did. Right up until he noticed the bulge in her pocket and tugged the redcap's hat into the open. On first glance it appeared to be no more than a scrap of cloth. Unfortunately, it left a reddened stain on her jeans and a corresponding smudge on Lance's hand.

"Suzanne?" She didn't need the link to feel his concern increase and his testosterone guns go into overdrive, or to know that meant trouble.

Suzanne willed him to back down. Willed it hard without pushing it on him through the link they shared. It was a near thing. With determination edged with desperation, she clung to the confidence she'd claimed for herself that morning and broadened her smile.

"It's nothing. I took care of it," she said with a shrug of her wounded shoulder. Satisfaction sent warmth throughout her body, which she knew he couldn't help but feel as well, if less intensely, through both empathy and his tattoo. She then took her trophy from his hand before he could recognize it for what it was and slid it back into her pocket.

His pinning gaze left her to scan those just coming up behind. She gritted her teeth as he searched their expressions for anything that might contradict her claims and watched as he struggled with his alpha tendencies. The next few seconds, she feared, she'd either kill him or he'd crush her. Suzanne held her breath, not wanting either to happen.

Relief hit her so hard when his stance relaxed that she barely heard as he bantered with her. Her tension evaporated as he snugged her tight against his hips. She had a vague impression of more wisecracks coming from those on the ground, but Suzanne couldn't care less. He'd trusted her! He let it go. The resulting rush empowered her. The iron grip of her inner demons loosened slightly and deep down she wondered if she and Lance might finally be ready to swear vows. Perhaps even talk of a...family. She had denied herself that desire so long she had to force the thought out.

Some of that must have leaked through to Lance. He grinned at her and drew her around beside him, beneath his arm. "Best we go around the front today, unless Delilah wants to find a new cook before dinner; Rock and Blow look like they might still be dripping and Mongo's on a tear."

The small group laughed. Except for Delilah. Her eyes grew a little stormy and her lips pressed flat on hearing something had annoyed her temperamental cook. The exchange came across so natural and family-like that Suzanne could practically see the glow of contentment settle over them all...or perhaps that was Lance unwittingly sharing his empathic gift among them. Suzanne didn't care which. She loved the sensation. Bathed in good-will, she slid her hand to his hip and gave him a squeeze as they started down the back steps. It had been a long time since she'd let herself indulge in being happy. A part of her couldn't help but poke at the sensation, expecting it to pop.

She hated when her inner cynic was right.

One minute Lance had his arm draped loosely around her shoulder. The next his back arched and his body tensed. A cry forced its way past his clenched jaw. Before Suzanne could grab for him, he slumped backward and slid down the concrete steps.

"Lance!"

At the first thud of his skull hitting the stair edge, Suzanne stopped breathing. She scrambled to catch up with him without falling herself. Her ankle burned, but she ignored it. She wanted to howl and lash out at the others when they converged on him and blocked her path. The link reassured her that he lived, but her panic and aggression increased with his growing turmoil. Before she could reach him, Lance shoved the others away and struggled to his feet.

"No!" he roared as he gripped the handrail with stark white knuckles.

Suzanne flinched as his wing fins unfurled with a whip-like crack. He looked ready for a take-down fight, yet the soul-tearing anguish in his cry stopped her dead. Her muscles locked up so tight she trembled and for the third time that week tears burned unbidden down her cheeks.

Dream and Bubba each erected hasty shields with a corresponding snap just as the tendrils of magic streaming out from Lance's shoulder fins lashed over those clustered too close to him. The air danced with multi-hued sparks as mage energies collided with the shields. Both Winds grunted with the effort to keep the protections in place; not just against the energy Lance projected, but also the waves of power gravitating toward him from every direction. As the currents converged where he stood and his body jerked with the overload, Lance glared in his uncle's direction and ground out, "Get to Cam's."

Suzanne felt Lance's shock as the words acted as a guide for the rogue magic swirling around him. A gateway opened where he stood, swallowing him whole and presumably jerking him away through the aether to his father's home.

In the sudden magical and emotional void, Suzanne crumpled to the ground, her limbs trembling. Her vision went monochromatic one moment and Technicolor the next, before settling into a formless haze. For a long, helpless moment, gravity pinned her to the ground. Breathing took effort and staying conscious was a battle. Panic clawed up from every cell in her body. It was as if an equal volume of sand had replaced all the air surrounding her. The echo of her father's voice murmured in her thoughts, as heard throughout her childhood each time he turned his back to her dismissively and walked away: "worthless... powerless... useless..."

She fought against that, fiercer than all the rest.

Slowly, natural color returned to the world. A whisper of breath crept past Suzanne's lips to torment her lungs. They burned as she greedily sucked the air, somehow finding the energy to scramble to her knees. All the magical folk around her seemed similarly affected to varying degrees. Only Delilah stood, her expression fierce, looking around like a momma cat ready to fight death's shadow with nothing but teeth and claws.

Reaching for the handrail, Suzanne dragged herself to her feet.

"What the fucking hell was that?" she demanded. Her voice sounded as rough and strained as talking felt. She locked her knees to stop them from trembling, willing her body to recover so she could go after her man. An equally strong urge ordered her to rise and care for those stricken around her.

Either way, her body remained uncooperative.

"Ah...sheesh..." Blow groaned from where he still sprawled on the ground. He looked much worse than Suzanne felt. All the Winds did. With guilt, she remembered all they'd already done for her that day. For all of a minute, then concern for Lance won out.

"Come on, get your asses up," she said, her voice marginally firmer than a moment ago. "He needs back-up...bad. I can feel it."

"Yeah, not likely, and no shit," Samandrea snapped with only a portion of her usual heat. She laid at the edge of the grass, awkwardly spread atop her sons, her beautiful, horribly scarred pixie wings fully extended and visible. Her natural black markings, a pattern vaguely reminiscent of bird's-eye maple, seemed to swirl sluggishly against the marred crimson membranes cupped protectively over Zack and Shawn. The boys seemed fine. Ready to jump to their feet, even, but something had drained Sammy as badly as the others. That did not prevent her from spending herself further to protect her children. Suzanne's heart ached at the sight.

At the sound of his wife's voice, Bubba stirred, grumbling and growling like a mountain about to blow its top. In one massive heave, he lurched to his feet, hands fisted and a pale blue flame flaring from the rough spot in the center of his forehead. The others scrambled upright, Jon going to Delilah, who began to tremble in reaction, while the Winds shook off the effects of having all the mage energy sucked out of the area.

"Someone explain," Delilah said. "*Now...*"

No one got the chance. Not that they could anyway.

Even as the ambient magic seeped back into the void left by whatever the hell Lance had done, Mongo came tearing out the back door, somehow coming across as both fierce and frantic, all without a single expression on his face.

"You best get inside right now, we have a situation."

"Yeah, like we're not dealing with one out here too," Suzanne said, pivoting around to glare at him. "Break out the mead." The magical properties of the drink would aid their recovery from the energy drain they'd all experienced. "Everyone out here needs to recharge and hit the road before..."

Mongo cut her off. "Some fae BUG gated in and grabbed Tilly right out of the upstairs rooms."

Suzanne nearly found herself back on the ground as Delilah and Jon shoved past her on their way inside. In that moment, Lance's aunt rivaled any *bean sidhe*, loosing a sound somewhere between a wail and a battle cry. Fear for both her man and her friend, Tilly, helped Suzanne to shake off the lethargy better than any restorative. Guilt and worry burned Suzanne's gut at yet another failure of her efforts. The pendant she had given the woman should have safeguarded her! Gripping the handrail, she turned back to the rest of her group. "Inside." She then pivoted and leapt up the back steps, pausing as she passed Mongo. "The mead. Now. The best we have. Get us ready to fight. We need to move."

A sudden crash sounded inside, along with the sharp *thunk* of knuckles hitting flesh and more of Delilah's screams, rage-filled and piercing.

"Ah, crap!" Suzanne hurtled across the kitchen and through the doors to the bar in about three strides. Her eyes bugged a bit at the sight of about six bikers hauling Delilah back from a man-shaped, bloody mass on the ground. The woman spit and kicked and thrashed as only a protective mother could, deprived of putting a further hurt on the one responsible for harm coming to her child. Just past the roiling mass of bodies, Suzanne spied Jon pinned to the wall by his own bunch of handlers. The bar itself looked as if a tornado had ripped through. Nothing appeared broken, beyond some bottles and one of the dartboards, but talk about one hell of a mess... Fortunately, there were no outsiders there this afternoon.

As her gaze took it all in, Suzanne crossed to the bloody pulp on the floor. She grimaced as she spied the crystal she'd given to Tilly laying by the person's head. Damn! She'd told the woman to never take it off. Kneeling, Suzanne scooped up the pendant and shoved it into her pocket before tugging the man out of his protective huddle. She drew a sharp breath. Not that she hadn't had an idea of who lay before her, but the sight of his condition made her wince. Gort—the recent defector from the Fae Court and former advisor to the High King, and now failed protector of Delilah's pride and joy—lay there, barely conscious, his breath coming harsh through his battered lips. Suzanne didn't know what amazed her more: that two people did this much damage in less than five minutes, or that Gort still breathed at all. She glared over her shoulder at the still-raging parents.

"Not going to learn much kicking his head into next week, are you?" she said, as she drew the fae to his feet and guided him into a nearby chair. The damage, for the most part, clearly came from fist-pounding and a few well-placed kicks, though there were some nasty cuts along his back she was at a loss to explain. Yet nothing life-threatening, especially for one of the fae... In fact, unless he came to further harm, he would heal swiftly. Suzanne frowned, though, to see an inch-long gouge in Gort's cheek that confused her for other reasons. The flesh looked torn from the inside out and the wound still bled. Unusual for a mage-born creature. She ran a finger over the raw edge. The fae flinched away and his breath hissed a bit sharper past his lips. Suzanne sensed remnants of magic embedded in the wound.

"Most of that ain't their handiwork," Kelly said from behind the bar, where she'd wisely drawn the riot gate down over the liquor shelf as a precaution against flying...anything.

"He came fallin' down the back stairs already bloody and purpling up."

"Hmm," Suzanne responded as she turned back to examine the gouge more closely.

"It's…Dair's doing," Gort struggled to speak. "Sent his—" The fae gasped and his breath whistled unnaturally in Suzanne's ears. She pressed a hand to his shoulder and turned to Lyman, a tall, quiet man with piercing eyes and light brown hair. Also, the nearest club member not holding someone down. "Get the first aid kit. Patch him up…"

As he moved to do as she ordered, Jon and Delilah renewed their yelling, along with their efforts to get back to the ass-kicking. Suzanne ignored them, raising her voice to be heard. "Stabilize him until Lance…" Her breath caught as she realized she'd forgotten about Lance in light of the current crisis. Pushing to her feet, her instructions half spoken, she turned toward the kitchen to find Mongo leaning against the door jamb. Zack and Shawn peered past him from the safety of the other room. Sammy paced beyond them, between her children and the back door, her temper still roiling.

"The rest drank up and headed right over to Cam's," Mongo said.

Relief and hurt warred in Suzanne. Good that someone rode out to help Lance, wicked bad that she again found herself left behind…proven useless, unimportant, or so it seemed. It didn't matter that she had to deal with the crisis here. Common sense didn't enter into it. Her man was in trouble and someone else rode to his rescue. Closing her eyes she sank her awareness into the link between her and Lance. The connection couldn't tell her what had happened when she wasn't paying attention but his emotional state now told her it had all come out okay. Without her.

She shoved the irrational pain down to get back to the matter at hand. Yet, even as she refused to dwell on it, a part of her heart kept poking fingers in the ancient wound. After the morning she'd had she lacked the energy to fight her self-doubt. Clenching her teeth against the emotional sting, Suzanne turned back toward Gort just in time for the next shock of the day. Garm, Mongo's scarred and wary Irish wolfhound, had moved silently past her. The guard dog took up a defensive position in front of the very fae most of them currently wanted to pound into the ground. *First Tilly, now Garm. What is it about this guy that makes those that don't even know him take his side?*

Suzanne narrowed her gaze as she met Garm's, searching for the wisdom that had the dog aligning with the supposed enemy. She didn't understand, but she had more faith in Garm's sense than she did in half the riders in the club. That said a lot since there wasn't one patch holder in the club she wouldn't trust at her back in a fight or anything else. For the time being, she accepted the dog's judgment of who was worthwhile to stand by and who wasn't.

Garm must have been satisfied she wasn't going to go after Gort herself because the hound relaxed the slightest bit, leaning his mass carefully against the wounded fae's chair without jostling him. While Lyman cleaned his wounds and Garm stood guard over him, Gort explained what had happened. On hearing what he said, Suzanne fought down panic at the potential for disaster, for Tilly and her family, as well as for herself.

Suzanne turned to the rest of the club with a grim look. "Kelly, call everyone in you can reach, tell them to come ready for a rescue run." She then turned toward Jon and Delilah, motioning for their guards to let them go. "Both of you pull it together. This isn't helping."

"We trusted him to watch over her," Delilah growled, glaring at her husband as if that were his fault. "He was supposed to *protect* her!"

"Yeah, I know. That didn't work out," Suzanne answered keeping her voice calm and low. "I'm sorry, so sorry. We'll make it right, I promise, but right now I need you to calm down. I need you to wait until Lance gets here. He's on his way."

Delilah nodded hard, but didn't lose the iron-jawed grimace or the lethal looks darted in Gort's direction. Beside her, Jon breathed so heavily through his nose that Suzanne expected puffs of cartoon steam to come billowing out. He nodded as well, and his arm came up around his wife's shoulders now that she stood still and reasonably contained. As he tried to guide her toward one of the booths along the wall, though, Delilah shrugged him off and started pacing, her gaze going from the front door to the clock above the bar. She gave the impression of a barely restrained tigress.

Suzanne knew exactly how she felt and dearly wanted to ride off to the rescue herself. The urge to kick ass and reclaim one of their own rode her like a hog.

Instead she stood there feeling helpless again; not because she was weak, but because a few fae—most of them lesser—weren't enough to go against the High King and all his Court; even less so, a group of humans with little to no magic to call upon. It amazed Suzanne that the men had managed to keep Jon and Delilah here this long.

Expecting trouble, Suzanne caught the eye of the bikers in the room. A tilt of her head set them lining up in a human blockade between Delilah and the door. A glance toward the kitchen confirmed Mongo had moved full into the bar, letting the connecting door close behind him. He'd planted his feet right in front of it, his arms crossed over his chest.

With everything seen to, the weight of all that had happened came down on Suzanne like an avalanche. She trembled and swayed, feeling like her blood had all run down to her toes. Before her knees gave out, Lyman appeared beside her, taking her arm and guiding her toward the bar. Good choice on his part. She would have torn into him if he'd planted her in a chair or worse picked her up. Even so, she snatched her arm from his grip, willing her steps steady and strong as she moved away from him and hopped up to sit her ass on the bar. With her eyes she challenged anyone in the room to call her weak.

No one spoke. No one even seemed to notice her, except for Lyman, who shook his head as he returned to the med kit and packed things up, tossing the garbage but leaving the kit out, like he expected they may need it again soon.

Suzanne frowned at that thought.

The gentle *thud* of thick glass on wood broke the uneasy silence. Suzanne turned her head and looked down to find a half-empty bottle of mead next to her, the cork popped and a glass standing ready. She arched a little further and pinned Kelly with a sour glance. The bartender grinned back with a shrug.

"Mongo said you asked for it," she said unrepentantly and completely unfazed.

Yes, she had, hadn't she? No wonder her ass was dragging. For a moment she'd forgotten the mage drain from less than half an hour ago. The bottle weighed heavily in her hand, as if carved from granite. Ignoring the glass, Suzanne lifted the bottle's neck to her lips and drank a quarter of the contents straight off. The mead flowed down her throat warm and smooth, soothing an ache she hadn't realized had settled there. Her spine straightened and she drew a deep, centering breath in reaction, her muscles tingling as the tension melted away. She couldn't call the drink an instant fix but it did clear the mental static and let her body get down to the business of reabsorbing the magic missing from her reserves. Another swig left her good. With one hand, Suzanne wedged the cork back in the bottle. With the other, she reached over and snagged Kelly's pen, using it to scrawl her name on the label before tucking the mead beneath the counter where they kept non-customer stock.

"Enough! I'm done waitin'. Get outa my way!" Delilah looked like the spokeswoman for the wild women of the world. The whites showed all around her eyes, standing out like bright beacons against her anger-reddened face. Her fiery red hair fell partly down to frame her face and aggression stiffened every muscle in her body. Suzanne bit her lip and scooched to the edge of the bar ready to hop down. It looked to her like the woman just might blow a blood vessel. Literally. Jon hovered near, but didn't move to stop his wife, his face all hard planes and sharp lines. In some ways his calm quiet frightened Suzanne more than Delilah's raging ever could. The way his eyes darkened until they swallowed the light. The way his jaw flexed and his fists didn't. Suzanne shivered.

"I said get out of my way, now, or you'll never cross that threshold again on your own feet!" Delilah screamed still pacing, her steps so forceful Suzanne had to wonder when one of those boot-heels would snap.

The club members keeping Delilah corralled didn't budge. Some frowned as she watched them closely for signs one of them might break. Some crossed their arms, others looked mighty uncomfortable defying the woman who'd mothered each of them at some point or another, but they all held their posts. Delilah went back to pacing. Each pass seemed to act like a watch knob, winding her tighter and tighter.

Boots, bar, and men all received a reprieve heralded by the roar of familiar cycles pulling into the lot. Moments later Lance stalked through the door, scoping the scene before him. The moment she saw him, Delilah threw herself at the wall of bikers keeping her from the door, and now Lance. Suzanne's throat tightened as her man pushed through and went to the distraught woman.

"She's gone!" Delilah screamed. None of the new arrivals had to ask who. There existed an innate rage peculiar only to mothers. "She's gone! They took her and you will get her back!" Delilah punctuated the words by pounding her hard little fist into Lance's shoulder. Suzanne felt the echo of an unexpected pain travel up their shared link. She frowned as he jerked back and brought his hands up to still the assault.

"Yes." That was all he said, quiet and lethal.

It was like someone punched a hole in Delilah's gas tank. She stilled, trembled, then her legs gave out as a single sob broke loose. Lance drew her close before she fell but she wasn't in his grip for more than a few seconds before Jon came beside him and pulled her away.

"Dair na Scath?" Lance asked.

Jon nodded, murder in his gaze as he shared what had been explained to them. "Gort claims the High King sent his champion through a temporary gate anchored to his face."

"What?!"

Suzanne's heart screamed the same thing. Her breath sounded harsh in her ears, coming in shallow huffs, and the tips of her fingers began to tingle. *No,* she thought, *please no...Maybe it wasn't him. Maybe someone else assumed the post....* Jon went on while her mind jabbered. She forced herself to focus, to calm and listen.

"The wound contained a splinter of oak, enough to enable Dair to bypass the protections. The bells didn't even ring. We wouldn't have known at all if Gort hadn't fallen down the stairs."

Lance cursed. "Where is he?" He stalked forward to the center of the bar, stance wide and his muscles tight as he turned in a circle, meeting the gaze of each biker crammed into the place.

Suzanne hopped down from the bar and started to go to him. She stopped as Lance spied Gort slumped in the corner with Garm at his feet. He stalked over and hauled Gort up by the collar of his shirt, shook him hard until the fae's eyes returned to focus, then let go.

"Back room, now."

They disappeared and Suzanne found herself shut out again. Perhaps forever, once Lance and the Hunt found out....

She shuddered and shoved the thought away.

Eventually the door to the back room opened and Lance stalked back into the bar. Suzanne noted the grim set to his features. Part of her wanted to rush to his side; the other wanted to disappear into the background, haunted by memories of her father's temper when things did not suit him. This was not the first time she'd recognized a faint similarity between the two men.

Lance stopped beside Jon, and spoke to him briefly. Suzanne couldn't hear what he said, but she relaxed as Lance ignored her and everyone else as he then stomped into the kitchen. The back door slammed a moment later. She almost followed him but noticed Gort leaning against the doorjamb to the back room. The druid gave the barest shake of his head, his expression somber.

Suzanne frowned, but eased back onto her stool, eyes locked on the kitchen.

Less than ten minutes passed and she heard the back door slam again, then the kitchen door swung open hard enough to keep swinging as Lance strong-armed through. He moved to stand beside the bar—bikers swiftly clearing his path—and turning, stood with his fisted hand raised overhead, the signal to stop, in this case, talking.

"The High Court has decided to get into our faces," he said once everyone looked his way and shut their mouths. As Lance spoke, Jon came out of the back room holding a cloth-wrapped Court dagger that mirrored the one that bound the rulers of the Fae lands to their throne. He handed it to Lance, who barely nodded before going on, "They've taken one of our own, violated our turf, and messed with us on the road. We don't take that crap from the Red Dawgs," he said, naming The Wild Hunt's rival gang, "we sure as hell aren't taking it from Dair na Scath and his Court." He nodded at Gort. "I'm told they issued a challenge. We just accepted. The Winds and I are going to Avalon to get Tilly back. I need some of you on the rescue run in case there's trouble."

Suzanne didn't hear much after that. Dread clutched at her chest. Her lover was about to go head to head with her father on a legendary floating island. What could go wrong?

Lance started calling out names, dividing the masses into two groups: one to stay behind to protect the families, the other to ride the Wild Hunt against the fae. Except for their toughest brawlers, Lance ordered most of the humans to stay behind. Likewise, most of the fae and halflings got tagged for the rescue run, except for Jon—who needed to anchor Delilah—and one or two others to provide a magical arsenal for those defenders staying behind.

All that made sense to Suzanne. She agreed with most of his choices, though she would have sent Lyman on the run with the field med kit and kept Mongo here. She stopped analyzing the division of forces as Lance looked her way. His lips thinned and tightened. Before he even said a thing she bristled. Then her name joined the roster of those staying put. She opened her mouth to protest; Lance crossed his arms and cut her off with a glance before she could argue. "Stay here and do your part, or turn in your colors," he said to the room at large, his gaze traveling from face to face, but stopping with hers. When everyone else nodded agreement Lance turned and headed for the door. Jaw set, Suzanne evaded Gavin's effort to stop her as she went after Lance. She intercepted him at the end of the bar and blocked his path. Her jaw hardened and her eyes went cold as her fingers twitched. "I can handle this," she growled.

Lance nodded. "Good, glad to hear it, but I still need you to *handle* it here. You are my strongest mage…" despite herself Suzanne felt warmth kindle in her belly, rising until it softened her expression. She leaned in like a flower turning toward the sun at praise so rarely heard for most of her life. "…and my biggest distraction. I need you to stay here to protect the families not because I don't think you're up to the battle, but because I can't afford to not have my head in the fight."

And the warmth went out of her like a fire smothered by ash.

She'd been all set to back down and he handed her that crap. Her fingers inched closer to her colors. Lance looked like he wanted to grab her arm away. Suzanne thrust out her jaw and dared him to try with her eyes, ready for a throw-down. Itching for a reason. The side of her lip edged up. She expected his temper to flare; he didn't oblige. His gaze remained serious and focused, as if nothing—not even this crisis—existed, just her. He kept his hands where they were.

"I'm trusting you, angel…I'm trusting you with your life, with theirs; I'm just not ready for you to be in harm's way, not against these kind of odds. I need to know you're safe. You only just kicked this and I'm already rattled. Right now, *I* can't handle it."

As much as she didn't want to, Suzanne sensed he dealt honestly with her. He projected urgency and understanding, tinged with a desperation he tried to bury deep. He pled with her in silence as she knew he couldn't afford to aloud.

Still unhappy, but not unreasonable, Suzanne banked the heat in her gaze and nodded sharply as she turned and stomped away. Part of her felt that if the fool insisted on haring off into a fight without her, he deserved whatever came to him; the other part edged into a panic at the thought of him facing down the forces of the High King…maybe even…. No. Anxiety threatened to turn her chest as stiff as stone at the possibility of Lance injured, or worse…never coming back again. Her mind shrunk from the thought and her steps quickened until she took the stairs three at a time. If she couldn't be beside him in this confrontation, she would protect him the absolute best she could.

Then give him hell later at her leisure.

She hurried past their apartment and went straight for Delilah's, where she kept stuff she didn't want Lance nosing around, in this case his birthday presents. Snatching them from his aunt's closet, Suzanne pivoted and half ran back down the stairs, not slowing until she reached the front door, despite her burden. Reaching out a hand she snagged one of the biker bells from the Guardian Wall for Lance's bike—there for the express purpose of giving protection here in the bar or to those going out on a run—and hurried out the door. Her boots clicked against the pavement as she stalked up to where Lance stood beside his father's Panhead and thrust the massive box into his arms, then dropped the bell on top. She worked real hard not to snarl at Gort, or even look at him as he straddled the bitch pad, patiently waiting.

"Happy Birthday," she said to Lance through clenched teeth, a scowl twisting her expression. The intent, closed-down look on Lance's face transformed as he briefly pocketed the bell so he could open the box, revealing the custom-made leathers she'd spelled with every protection she knew, not to mention a few other features. Her jaw flexed and her breath caught in her throat as Lance stripped down right there and put on the new gear. He fairly glowed with love and pleasure, not to mention the adrenaline rush of pending battle she felt zing across their link.

Suzanne's heart threatened to soften. Before the weakness took hold completely (or so she told herself), she shoved the rest of his present—a new helmet, also heavily spelled with protections—against his chest and pivoted away, unable to stand there and watch as he went off to engage the enemy.

The words she could never bring herself to give him slipped out in a whisper as she walked away. "I love you." She hadn't meant for Lance to hear her...really. But he must have, for his jubilance bled through there link to her and he whooped out loud before revving away.

Tension ran through the bar like electric wires strung from person to person. Suzanne scanned the room. Everyone there wore Club colors. When she'd been out front the non-combatants must have headed to the bunkhouse in the back. Wise move. That building had more protections on it than any other on the property. She should know. She'd set many of them.

Those that remained in the bar moved about like dogs scenting an interloper in their territory. The newer members of the Hunt grumbled and paced and shot glances around as if waiting for intruders to come through the walls. The veterans prepared in their own way. Some readied a wide array of bladed and bludgeoning weapons—no guns; they weren't allowed in *Delilah's*. (Too dangerous with Tilly around. She liked guns.) Others stretched out across the extra-long benches lining the wall to catch some rest, or channeled their nerves through a game of darts or pool. Even they looked around with pointed gazes from time to time. The Fae and other mage-gifted did none of this. They conserved their energy, doing no more than steadily sip on mead to charge their magic.

Suzanne nursed her own glass as she kept watch over the mortals. This was the first time many of them had come up against Fae that were not members of the club. Few of them knew what to expect, or how to prepare for a fight likely to involve the arcane. She searched the group for signs of anyone at risk of losing it before the conflict even began. They all held it together for now.

If only she could say likewise. She already fought a personal battle today. The longer she waited, the more her muscles contracted and the demons in her heart climbed her spine to whisper poison in her ear. One moment a sense of love glowed within her, the next she fumed. No matter what his reasons were, Lance had once again left her behind. First he claimed he needed her here to help protect the families. Then he admitted he just didn't want her with him. Couldn't afford *the distraction* of worrying about her. With a snarl, she brought her glass down on the bar. It always came down to the same thing. Coddling. Cotton wrapping. No trust, no faith. Proving once more that he saw her as weak and incapable. If things were like this between them now, how bad would his attitude get when they were bound one to the other? Worse, how controlling would he be with any children they might have? Her grip tightened on her mead. The subtle sound of creaking startled her, followed by the sharp, sudden pop of a fissure. Looking down, she spied a fresh crack running the length of her glass. She resisted the urge to toss the half-filled tumbler across the room just to hear the sound of it shattering. Downing the mead anyway, she dropped the empty in the garbage. All that got her was a dull thunk and a snap as the glass split after landing on a spent bottle. Not nearly as satisfying. She looked around for something else to throw after all, her lips pressed tight together and her fingers twitching with the need to bust something...or someone.

Between the situation with Lance earlier, the atmosphere in the bar, and the agitation seeping across their joint link, Suzanne's temper balanced on a hair trigger.

"This isn't like you. You need to calm down, baby-girl," Mongo said from beside her as he set a warm, fragrant brownie in front of her. "That, or find some kinda way to work it off."

Only he could get away with calling her baby-girl. Even she didn't know why...Maybe because he usually never spoke the endearment with anyone close enough to hear...or maybe the brownie had something to do with it, because when Mongo brought her one of those, she didn't care who said what.

For a brief moment she leaned against his shoulder, then straightened just as quickly. "I'll try," she promised, fully meaning it, though not too hopeful of her success. Her nerves crackled like silent lightning dancing through the clouds.

"I'm serious, Suzanne. You keep things bottled up like this and the bottle's gonna crack until it all busts out." Mongo narrowed his eyes and looked her over, like he debated his next words. "I ever tell you about my cousin?"

"What? I thought you were raised by wolves..."

Mongo smirked back at her and kept talking. "Deb's a real decent broad. Tough and spunky and competitive as anything. She's coming down in a few days for a visit. She's a derby girl with a team up in New Jersey." He flashed a picture from his wallet but in the dim light of the bar Suzanne couldn't make out more than slashes of war paint beneath the woman's eyes, a flirty pose, and what looked like a massive cupcake in her hands. Mongo just kept talking as he put the picture away. "I should have her talk to you; tell you what it's about. Nothing like roller derby to work off aggression. You need something, before the top of your head blows clean off."

Suzanne shook her head, annoyed even Mongo wouldn't leave her alone. "Come on, Mongo...lay off, will you?"

He scowled and reached for the brownie.

"I'll calm down...promise!" Suzanne smiled with a sweetness she didn't feel as she snatched the treat closer to her and dropped her shoulder forward to block his reach. "Ohm.... Ohm...." she started chanting.

"Yeah...yeah...a rebop...a rebop." Mongo grinned ruefully. "Yank the other one."

She shrugged and her smile flattened out. "I can't help it. I know what kind of danger he's walking into."

The cook nodded his head, a slow and steady bounce, before he stilled and pinned her with a hard look. "You should tell him." He wasn't talking about the coming conflict or her connections to the wrong side—a secret he knew but would never tell.

Suzanne frowned sullenly.

Mongo's eyebrows shot up in warning. He looked like he might make a more concerted effort to take away her brownie. Grabbing it, Suzanne took a healthy bite. Her mouth instantly flooded with deep, rich chocolate just hinting at bitter, tempered by smooth caramel and a sharp, salty sprinkling on top. Her eyes drifted closed and her breath came out in a hum as her consciousness visited its happy place.

It was a short visit. Mongo gave her shoulder a hard thump.

"I did," she said hurriedly. "...kinda."

"Ain't no kinda about that sort of thing."

Mulishly, she scowled at him. "He heard me."

Silence, then Mongo frowned, his eyes darkened and his easy manner retreated back behind his gruff façade. "That boy don't deserve what you're serving him, young lady."

Suzanne set her brownie down as the bitterness teasing her tongue increased, overwhelming the pleasure of the chocolate. Not the brownie's fault, but the enjoyment had gone out of the moment. Doubt uncurled from her heart and scratched to be released.

She felt Mongo's disappointment as he brushed the back of his hand across her hair and turned to head for the kitchen.

"Mongo..." she called after him. A subtle pause in his next step. "I do hear you."

Somber eyes met hers as he glanced back over his shoulder and nodded.

In the end, regardless of everyone being hyperaware, there wasn't much in the way of forewarning. First all the bells on the Guardian Wall jangled wildly, then seconds later thunder cracked overhead, despite the clear, blue sky outside. Every mage and Fae in the place experienced five rapid-fire jolts; hard, like someone smacked whatever surface they touched. The sensation echoed like a twitch in the straight-up mortals.

Suzanne lowered the butt of her pool cue to the ground and straightened.

"Okay, people, time to get serious," she said, laying her cue across the table. Grabbing her favored sword—an elven blade somewhat resembling the Japanese tachi—and slinging it over her shoulder, she strode quickly for the door, drawing magic as she went. Suzanne's shoulder fins unfurled. Crackling tendrils of magic, in shades of blue and lavender, trailed from their delicate arches. Drawing a hair band from her jeans pocket—the one not containing her trophy—she bunched up her long, silver-blonde tresses in a rough knot at the back of her head, keeping them out of her way and the enemy's grip, then headed out the door.

At her back, the Wild Hunt streamed from the building and formed up battle lines. Suzanne grinned wolfishly. Her blood coursed through her, hot and fast, as she positioned herself at the forefront of the defending forces. At the edge of the property, where the gravel met the road, the air rippled and twitched. Dark and dire colors tinted the threshold of the forming gate. As the mortal realm fissured, the cool, moist air of springtime wafted through the portal to clash with the crispness of autumn. Instinctively, Suzanne inhaled, eager for the scent of home, only to discover the intruding breeze carried an undercurrent of sickly sweet decay. She coughed and kept the rest of her breaths shallow.

Any other impressions faded from her awareness as she spied Lance and the Four Winds already in the middle of the lot. Dream and Rock looked a little fried, but they all stood braced and ready for battle. Each brandished a weapon in keeping with their elemental nature, Bubba for a brief moment fully enrobed in flame before dialing it back. Everyone on the Wild Hunt side of the conflict glared as an unexpected forerunner tumbled through the gate. Face bloodied and his left shoulder fin sheared away, what could only be the *Dubh Fae* scrambled across the gravel lot as if running toward sanctuary.

Suzanne snarled.

As if! she thought, certain a blow to the head must tally among the bastard's injuries. *Let him come within slicing distance of my blade and* I'll end all his worries. Raw images of her capture haunted her, surfacing from the shadowed depths of memory: the crossroads, the agony of Dragon's Tears consuming her flesh, the redcaps' feasting. But she'd survived all that, and the redcaps, *their* deaths had come at *her* hand.

With that realization, confidence flowed through her veins. Snapping in the direction of her personal foe, Suzanne unsheathed her sword and surged forward, ready to engage. Then her silver-blue gaze met that of an icier hue beyond the fallen fae. Her soul whimpered and her body seized in automatic reaction, locked in place against her will as Callan swaggered through the gate at the head of the High King's army.

Hissing, Suzanne fought the compulsion, resisted the conditioned response, clinging to the assurance that weakness did not define her. The dark elf smirked, looked her up and down, then lifted his nose in antipathy. He turned from her as if she merited no attention, as he had for all of her formative years.

"No!" she screamed, her face contorted with rage.

He did not even flicker an eye in response as he bent his focus on Lance, pounding him with mage bolt after mage bolt, all the while working closer and closer to the *Dubh Fae*. The battle lines converged on Lance and Callan, then flowed around them to engage the biker horde. Suzanne found herself beset on all sides by the lesser fae that made up the bulk of the High King's army: spriggans, kobolds, even a road gremlin or twenty, to name a few. Her elven blade slashed in graceful arcs and drew Fae blood over and over until the air sparkled with the droplets, barely feeling the light hits she took in return. She pushed her opponents back, traveling across the field of battle in a series of parries and lunges, determined to reach her lover's side and to stop Callan from obtaining whatever he sought. She held that focus so tightly she barely noticed the split in her lip, until she caught her tongue darting out to swipe the blood clear. For a bare moment, the sharp, mineral-rich taste tingled on the tip before a flash of heat and hunger welled up from her belly. She recoiled, losing her focus. In that instant of distraction, Callan struck, siphoning away her energy until her fins drooped and the tendrils faded; he stole her magic and turned it against Lance.

"Mine!" she snarled, fighting the involuntary connection.

If not for her brother's vigilance and that of the other members of the Hunt she would have fallen in that moment. All awareness of the greater battle faded away in light of this personal one. Gavin, Irish, and two or three others defended her body as she fought for her soul. Desperation edged her efforts as blow after blow rained down on Lance, draining her further. She watched as his gaze narrowed and he switched tactics, holding his own against the High King's warrior. The sight left her in awe. He galvanized her to dig in her arcane feet deeper in resistance. Physically slashing her blade through the space between them, Suzanne visualized the steel severing the link Callan had forged, bending her will toward that reality.

The bond weakened and a grin spread across her lips.

Across the battlefield the dark elf's attention shifted. She felt his glare upon her, the weight of his displeasure too familiar by far. With Callan diverted, Lance attacked, encapsulating the dark elf within an ingenious shield, severing his links to the mortal realm.

Mage energy jolted Suzanne all the way to her knees as what remained of her power returned to her. She braced and would have surged forward to Lance's side if not for the bog wraith that moved against her. The battle drew her back in, demanded her concentration. Suzanne lost herself in the defense of the only home she knew, and the only family that mattered.

Jarring and abrupt, the battle ended. Suzanne blinked, then shuddered, her weapon poised as she looked for a foe to engage. She blinked again as none presented themselves, then lowered her sword arm, pointing the blade toward the ground, but not enough for it to touch. Slowly she turned, sweeping her gaze over the lot. A detached segment of her thoughts noted they were fortunate the mage shields on the property prevented those outside from noticing things like pitched battles and their aftermath.

Bodies lay strewn over the gravel lot. Some groaned. Some did not. Most of their own rose in varying degrees of unsteadiness, under their own power or by a hand-up from a bro. Those that didn't would never rise again. Mercifully there were few of those.

Suzanne stood there, muscles taut and blood burning, as instinct continued to urge her to fight those that had fled. None lingered but the corpses, and those already flickered with eldritch flames that would ensure not even ash remained. Her breath sawed harshly in her chest as she struggled to accept the conflict had ended. The muscles in her jaw locked tighter than a bound up tension rod with the effort. A half-dozen barely noticed wounds dribbled thin ribbons of blood across her skin, making it both tickle and itch. With an air of distraction she dabbed at the cuts, then wiped her blade and sheathed it, before sliding the cloth back into her pocket. All the while, instinct sent impulses to her brain that insisted on the need for further violence. She had to continually remind herself that wasn't so.

As she came down from the battle high, she turned a slow circle searching for Lance. For the first time since she'd gifted him the tattoo, she couldn't sense him. Why couldn't she sense him? Panic clawed her gut as only one explanation presented itself. Even with her this wired, nothing should have blocked the link between them. She'd anchored it deep. Fresh adrenaline infused her veins as she spun around. Her hand came to rest on the hilt of her sword as her gaze raked the battlefield.

When she spied the dead husk of her former assailant, the *Dubh Fae*, Suzanne shouted and surged forward, her gaze searching for the one responsible for bringing down her personal foe. No longer would she, in the private corners of her mind, fear him coming after her again. And yet she had been robbed of the satisfaction of dealing with the threat on her own terms.

And then she saw Lance sprawled unmoving on the gravel beyond the *Dubh Fae*. The Four Winds lay crumpled around him. All of them wore stunned expressions. A glint of horror sparked through their expressions.

They looked as if someone had died.

At this seeming confirmation of her fears, pain bit Suzanne deep, hard, and fast until she felt she might shatter beneath the pressure. She'd unconsciously moved in Lance's direction when she'd spied him. Now she stopped dead, fists clenching and jaw flexing as two impulses warred within her: one urging her to cry, the other to scream, the extremes of either reaction completely out of character. The strength of those impulses caused Suzanne to hesitate where she stood. Before she could break free of the conflict, Lance and those surrounding him hauled themselves to their feet and shook off whatever gripped them. A glazed expression lingered in their eyes. The urge to cry won out as relief and joy surged through her. She trembled and fought to regain her calm, unnerved by the extremes of her emotions, not to mention her lack of physical control. Before Lance or the Winds could look her way, Suzanne turned and grabbed the arm of the nearest injured biker and helped him inside, needing a chance to compose herself. The familiar, if rare task soothed her. She was always at her best helping others. With each one she led to Lyman's triage area she found a bit more of her balance.

Gavin caught her eye as he passed on his way to the kitchen.

"You okay?" he asked, his gaze intent on her. Just her brother's presence alone helped to settle her further. She grimaced in response, then nodded, her expression tightening once more as fear added itself to her emotional mix. "You saw him?"

"Yeah, saw you hold your own, too," he answered with quiet pride.

She smiled her thanks and Gavin gripped her shoulder before returning to his objective. When he was gone, Suzanne assessed herself. Warmth in her cheeks remained the only outward sign of her lingering agitation. If she were to glance at her reflection a faint red flush would mock her. She refrained from looking as she busied herself helping with the wounded.

With each moment that passed she had to resist the persistent compulsion to hurry back out to the lot. Whether to make sure Lance was okay or to kick his ass for scaring her, she couldn't say. A long five minutes passed before he and the Winds straggled in, all of them looking somber and just a bit rattled. Seeing the pain few would recognize in Lance's gaze, Suzanne's protective instincts surged forward. Her gaze ran over him in a visual inventory of the minor hurts he'd taken in battle. She frowned as she noticed the tip of her tongue run along her lower lip and her breathing pick up in a manner that had nothing to do with after-battle sex urges.

Her reactions continued to confuse her, making her again hesitate before stepping toward him, but just a moment. When she did move forward something dark shifted in Lance's gaze and his expression tightened. She faltered as he took a half-step back away from her and pivoted, handing off a rather ornate Court dagger to Bubba. Anxiety hit Suzanne like a wave as she reached down their mage link to reassure herself he was okay, only to discover he'd cut her off.

"I'm going to get Tilly," he announced, his tone hard and unyielding. "You will *all* stay here."

She barely heard as Lance spoke, for the roaring in her ears. Hurt and anger heated her blood. He'd actively, willfully, blocked her. Bad enough, that, but her backbone rose, shoving her heartache aside to clear room for fury as her lover channeled echoes of her father. *How dare he?!* Before she could get into his face, Lance disappeared. Literally.

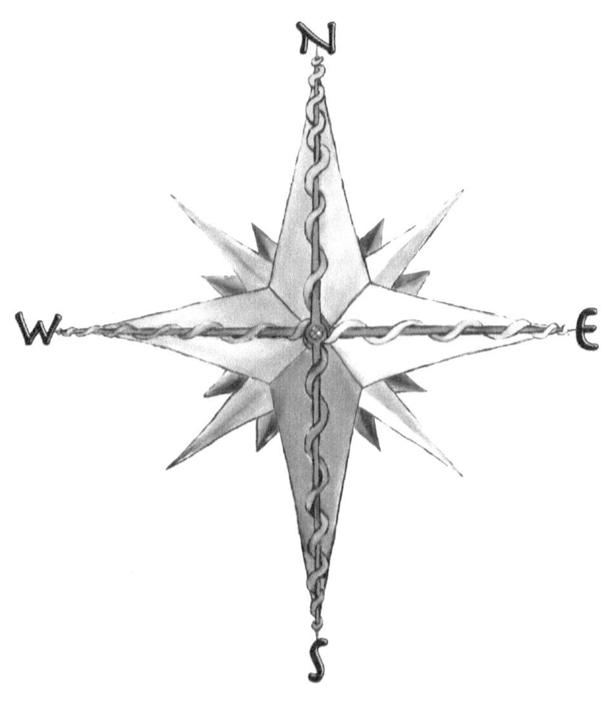
N
W
E
S

Saia

Chapter Three

Her vows forbid Saia to leave the clouds for the world below, but that didn't mean she couldn't keep tabs on her earth-bound kin. Leaning over the pool in the heart of Avalon's orchards, she felt the constraints of her choices more in that moment than all the time she'd served as one of the nine guardians of the Island of Mists. Briefly the waters reflected back her own appearance: warm, caramel-colored eyes set amidst delicate features, all framed by long, golden brown hair falling in waves around her face. The image quickly faded until the waters showed her glimpses of a pitched battle between Lance's Wild Hunt and Dair's warriors, the death of the *Dubh Fae*, and after in the bar, *Delilah's*. She watched the familiar aftermath of battle: glazed eyes and pain-taut muscles, bloodied limbs, bone-deep bruises...and still bodies. Saia's fingers tingled at the sight and the urge to go down among them, giving aid and healing, nearly swaying her to defy her duty.

Nearly. But more than vows kept her in her chosen place.

Saia turned her back on those thoughts and stared intently at the reflection of the mortal world. Only the clean-up remained. Short and fast and bloody as the encounter had been, Lance Cosain and the Wild Hunt had taken the day, but hardly the war. Did the biker know that the High King was not the sole threat to him and his people? Dair had obsession; his champion, the elven warrior, Callan...*he* had ambition. And worse: pride, now challenged. Saia worried her lip and wished for some way to warn them.

The sound of a snapped twig served as faint warning, then water splashed full in Saia's face as one of the legendary apples of Avalon broke the surface of the Oracle Pool, and with it, not inconsequentially, the image. She looked up into the cold, angry eyes of the Morrigan with an expression carefully schooled to neutral. Saia went still. She had just witnessed the death of the *Dubh Fae*, named Kerwin—this goddess's cast-off son—but so inscrutable were the Morrigan's thoughts that Saia could not tell by her expression if his death mattered to the war goddess, or if she even knew he'd been slain.

The moment passed, not with enlightenment, but the narrowing of the Morrigan's eyes and the curl of her immortal lip. "If it isn't too much bother," the Crow Queen murmured, "we are summoned..."

Saia nodded, but the Morrigan had already turned away, her white, sleeveless robes a sharp contrast to the ebony raven tattooed upon her bare arm. As she stalked away, she spoke over her shoulder in cutting tones, "You might consider changing."

The Fae princess dared a silent hiss at the goddess's back, self-consciously running her hands down the black leather bodice-vest and thigh-hugging jeans she chose to wear on her own time. Silly, perhaps, but it made her feel closer to those she held in her heart but could not hold in her arms. Turning her back on the cranky bitch, Saia smoothed now-shimmering hands along her curves a second time, transforming her gear until clothing identical to the Morrigan's clad her body, with the sole addition of a delicate chatelaine, bearing two keys, which girded her hips.

Longingly, she glanced beneath the shadow of the trees at her second, sentimental mimicry: At a quick glance it appeared to be a fanciful interpretation of a tricked out lowrider...looking vaguely like a Harley, with a burnished steel, dragon-head prow, and an engine that took the term "burning rubber" to heart. With a rueful grin she sent a mental caress to the bad-ass "bike." — in truth, an eager dragon kit nearly as fixated on "the world" as she was. In return she received a playful burble with a hint of heat, followed by a mental image of the Morrigan with a scorched butt.

The last startled a chuckle from the depths of Saia's gut.

"Better not let *her* catch a glimpse of that," she said, shaking her head.

As she turned away, the air beneath the trees warped like the superheated air of a volcano's breath. In response, her eyeballs felt as if they would twitch, if only they knew how. Disoriented, but familiar with the effect, Saia stayed her steps and closed her eyes until the sensation passed. She took three deep breaths before she chanced opening them again, just in time to see her friend, the self-named (and made) Chopper, slink away among the apple trees in his dragon form.

In that brief moment of pausing, the waters of the Oracle Pool calmed until they once more appeared as smooth as glass. Saia gasped as swirling beneath the surface caught her eye. Never, in all her time on Avalon, had an image formed independent of a mind's focus. She had been told of such things, but never witnessed it herself. She'd also been told that such unbidden visions were foretellings, seldom pleasing and always true.

Part of her longed to turn away, but the vision compelled her.

She jerked and shuddered as the foretelling began, straining to be released from the onus of watching. Dread coiled in her belly as the faces of her loved ones once more formed out of the mists. The vision unfolded, forcing her to witness as one by one they fell, slaughtered at the hand of one they trusted. She could not look away from the brutal bloodletting, no matter how hard she tried. Her eyes instead narrowed on the murderer as she tried not to see the victims. She knew that face. Knew it from her time before Avalon, and more recently from the battle. She would not have believed that one capable of such horrors.

Finally, in rebellion, Saia cried out, and though her gaze remained locked upon the pool, she broke the surface of the water, shattering the vision. It made no difference. The horror of what she had seen would not leave her.

Forgetting her duty, she collapsed at the edge of the pool, sobs wrenching her body with their force until night descended on the Island of Avalon.

Doubt and frustration battled within Suzanne as she waited, along with everyone else at *Delilah's*, for Lance to return. Not wanting to deal with the others, she sat huddled in the corner of one of the wall booths, feet on the bench and her chin tucked against her knees. Inside her personal battle still raged.

Why? Why did he do it?

She could think of only two reasons. One, he felt he had to protect her from what he'd come up against. After all, whatever had happened left him shaken and on the ground. Two, she had held him at bay so long he was done with her. Had, in fact, never cared for her as deeply as he'd claimed. The first boiled her blood and sent red flashes across her vision like a cape waved before a bull. The second—that insidious doubt that always hovered in the crevices of her heart—left her soul shredded.

Unease tripped down her spine as her hindbrain insisted she pay attention.

This was not like her. Though these emotions visited her frequently, the intensity rattled her. She was not prone to extremes, let alone conflicting ones. Such was the antithesis of her upbringing. In self-defense, Suzanne bled away the strength of her emotions, exerting a control learned long ago at Callan's instruction. Her pulse slowed as she drew deep and methodical breaths, only to ramp up again in an instant as a gate snapped open in the middle of *Delilah's*. Bikers scrambled out of the way as the air warped, crackling and shimmying in warning. The skins of time and space and perception split, the edges raw and angry, the effort at once both crude and powerful.

Suzanne scrambled from her booth and drew magic to her the moment she sensed the portal opening. She spread her stance and readied for yet another battle, though faint tremors throughout her body warned how close exhaustion loomed. Around her, others similarly readied themselves.

A frown tugged Suzanne's lips as she stared across the bar and into the High Court of Faerie. She barely noticed the decrepit state of the once grand Hall. Her gaze locked on the figure standing before the portal, her lungs barely remembering to breathe. Lance...leathers torn, his flesh still bearing signs of battle, muscles defined and glistening. In his right hand he gripped the lesser Court dagger he'd borrowed from Jon. Suzanne barely noticed as she took in Lance framed by glowing white tendrils of mage energy trailing from proud, erect, shoulder fins. She knew he'd changed, had even seen his "wings" one time before, through the fog of trauma and extreme pain, but this was the first she'd seen them since. The wonder of his transformation robbed her of words.

It took her a moment to notice the triumph radiating from his gaze. He spread his wings with an exultant cry. Huddled beneath the arcing magic, tucked close enough against Lance's side that the tendrils would not snap along her skin, Tilly peered out. An answering shout went up across the bar. As Lance and Tilly strolled across the threshold of the portal, Delilah and Jon converged in a jumble of tears and laughter, hands darting out and back again, not quite touching, as if afraid to test the truth of their sight.

"Mama...I'm back!" Tilly said quiet and peacefully, her face infused with joy as she laughed and opened her arms to her parents. Delilah swayed and nearly laid herself out on the ground for the second time that day. Jon's arm went around her and they stood holding one another, faces slack with shock. Tilly smiled a sympathetic smile and reached out, slowly stepping forward until she stood right before them, arms spread wide. They grabbed their daughter to them. All three of them spoke at once, laughing and crying and 'oh my God'ing, oblivious to those around them.

Suzanne watched for several minutes, both pleased and bitter at their good fortune. No reunion between her and her kin would ever resemble the elation playing out before her. She could not look away. The more she watched the more her frown deepened and took on a perplexed twist. Tilly seemed different. The girl had changed. Gone was the simple, placid expression. Gone was the cloud that had for the last five years obscured her bright gaze. When Suzanne actually listened to what Tilly said, it all made sense. Adult sense. Something had restored her, leaving her alert and aware and in full grasp of her intellect.

The moment held her attention so tightly that Suzanne jumped and flinched as powerful arms closed around her shoulders, pulling her back against a muscular chest.

"Whoa...steady there, babe," Lance murmured against her neck. "It's just me."

Relieved, she reached her spirit out and tried to reconnect through their link, only to find it still closed to her. She stiffened and went to move away, but her body betrayed her. In the aftermath of battle she could not resist the comfort of his embrace. As Lance pressed his lips to her neck in a gentle, loving caress and nuzzled his head against hers, Suzanne gripped his arms and snugged herself tight against him. Behind her, he shuddered and sighed, softly enough that none but she could tell.

"I'm sorry," he whispered.

At that Suzanne's temper spiked a bit. He didn't specify for what and his tone came out casual, like he knew he'd better apologize, though maybe he wasn't quite clear what for. Or maybe—if she looked at it objectively—like he was too exhausted to do much more than breathe. The need to ask what all happened when she'd been left behind ate at her, but now really wasn't the time.

Leaning her head back against his shoulder she pressed her lips beneath his ear and breathed a gentle breath against the fine hairs along the lobe until he shuddered. "Come on," she said, rubbing her rear lightly against him. "Tomorrow's soon enough to sort everything out. Tonight you can try and get back on my good side."

Lance chuckled. "Babe, every side you've got is the good side."

She swatted his arm and drew away, heading for the back room and the stairwell leading upstairs. Suzanne felt Lance's gaze follow her, hot and heavy. She couldn't resist giving her hips a little sway as she started up the stairs, swishing her hair so the strands had to have brushed his cheek his footsteps sounded that close. His breath rumbled behind her and his hand came down on her thigh, practically burning her through her jeans. With that one touch he both stilled the sway and urged her to climb faster, but he didn't speak. Suzanne skipped light and fast up the remaining steps. Lance, with a chuckle, took them two at a time behind her.

"You don't need wings to fly, angel, I'll take you to heaven."

His words triggered a sultry shiver down her spine and into her belly. Lance growled at the resulting shimmy. As they both came off the top step, he kept going right on her heels until Suzanne's body rested flush against the wall and his pressed firm against hers.

"Brat," he murmured in her ear as he slowly ground himself against the curve of her ass. She pushed back and swiveled her hips in a way she knew made him nuts. In retaliation, he buried his lips against her neck, sucking and nipping until Suzanne's breath shuddered.

"Better not let Mama catch you doing that out here...the spray nozzle from the kitchen sink does reach out into the hall, you know."

It took a moment for the words to sink in. For it to make sense what they meant and where they came from. Lance groaned and took several stiff steps back, while Suzanne clung to the wall, turning glazed eyes toward the stairwell, where the comment came from. Not the least apologetic, Tilly leaned against the far wall. She grinned at them and gave a little nod toward the apartment belonging to Delilah and Jon, to which the two of them had blocked her route.

"I'm a bit wiped...all the excitement and all...figured I'd turn in early."

Suzanne smiled as Lance stepped out of the way, pulling Tilly close to plant a kiss on her forehead.

"Ew!" Tilly cried. "Ew! Cut it out! Not when I know what you've been doing with those!" She played it up, hands flapping and face screwed into a comical grimace, but hugged him hard. Suzanne had to laugh. Restored or not, Tilly was and always would be an imp of the adorable variety.

As the woman went past, Suzanne pulled the nearly forgotten pendant out of her pocket and handed it back to her. Not saying a word, but grimacing slightly, Tilly hugged her as well before escaping to her own room in her parents' apartment.

In awe of the transformation, Suzanne turned to Lance. "How? How is it she's restored?" she asked once Tilly had closed the door.

He shook his head slowly from side to side as if he couldn't quite believe the change himself. For a moment, Suzanne wondered if he was going to tell her. If he *could* tell her...

He took a deep breath and let his head fall back. For a moment he closed his eyes, before looking back at Suzanne. His gaze held wonder still lightly tinged with anger. "On Avalon," he began, his jaw clenching briefly before he went on, "on Avalon, Dair na Scath had her spelled under his control. When we tried to get her free I drew all the magic I could and willed her free from whatever clouded her."

Suzanne gasped and reached out to grip his arm, barely realizing she did so.

Lance nodded and gave her a sheepish half-smile. "I didn't know how well it worked until I went Underhill to take her back."

She didn't know which awed her more, having Tilly back or the power it must have taken Lance to restore her friend. Uncomfortable with either one, Suzanne turned her thoughts away from such things. Instead she moved forward and draped herself over his chest, her fingers reaching behind him to wrap around his ponytail in a slow, suggestive tug.

"So, hero, you want to...turn in early?"

"I think I could stand to get horizontal," Lance answered, a smug, almost-smile flitting across his lips, though Suzanne couldn't help but notice tightness lingered around his eyes. "You gonna tuck me in?"

Before she could respond his lips came down on hers, worrying and nipping until she groaned. Something drove him harder than usual, but the link between them remained closed and she couldn't quite tell what. It startled her how much more intense things seemed without that glimpse of insight. Apparently she'd gotten dependent on the link when it came to reading emotions, Lance's anyway. Uncertainty added depth to their encounter. Right now his expression appeared both haunted and hungry.

Well...she'd just have to do something about both of those.

Reaching one hand behind her, she leaned back until she gripped the doorknob. With a tug she drew Lance toward their apartment. A soft *snick* and the door swung open. Suzanne groaned as he walked her backward into the foyer. The door then closed with a shove from his booted foot. She chuckled at the resulting slam, the sound dying on her lips as Lance again pinned her against the wall.

It took more than a while for them to actually get horizontal.

Never in all her years on Avalon, had Saia been so tempted to forsake her vows.

For days the vision haunted her. Each night in her sleep, her family died as she watched their slaughter reflected in the Oracle Pool. She knew their killer from her long-ago life, though she hardly recognized Callan's pale, insipid daughter in the bold, brutal figure the vision revealed. Saia had thought Fleur different from her father, kind and decent, if altogether too much under his influence. In those days Saia had noticed the girl had fought against his control in subtle ways. From what Saia saw in the vision the child had lost the battle.

Did she act on Callan's orders or had she formed a vicious nature of her own?

In either case, Saia would do everything in her power to prevent this dire act. She had learned from her fellow guardians that while ever true, such visions could be thwarted. Not much left in the world beyond Avalon mattered to her; what remained she counted precious. She saw but one way to foil the Fates. One bold move she could make against the events unfolding below. A single chance and no guarantee it would be sufficient to shift the balance.

It would not be the first time Saia made such a gamble.

Grabbing a reed basket, she snatched apples from the trees as she hurried past until the fruit nearly topped the brim. Her robes rustled the grasses and caught on brambles taking root at the base of each trunk. Those guardians chastised her but did not hinder her passage or her harvest. As a guardian herself, she had claim to Avalon's unending bounty, even though the cause this particular batch would serve was primarily her own.

The tree branches murmured in her wake and more vigorous rustling ahead warned her that she did not tread the orchards alone. Saia ignored the ruckus and lengthened her stride. Through the sun-dappled leaves she saw the pool that marked the center of the grove. Tucking the basket beneath one arm, the other she used to reach for her chatelaine, hauling the delicate chain up until its dangling keys rested in her palm. One came to her with her duties as guardian. The other stood as guarantee of a favor owed. She'd never thought to call in that favor...

For the sake of those she loved, she would use every resource she could claim.

Standing in the center of the grove before a natural arch in the trees where two gnarled limbs intertwined, Saia held that special key, letting all else drop from her hand to dangle across her white-robed thigh. One finger stroked across the back of the honeybee engraved on the thick bow. The heat of her touch raised a bead of honey near his bum, startling a chuckle from her. Only the Js—or one of them, anyway—would come up with something like that and actually *use* it.

Grimacing, she began the next part of the summons. "Wine, women and, song, hurry along," she said her cheeks burning. "My throat is dry and trouble is nigh."

Nothing.

A breeze rustled the trees. An apple plopped into the pool behind her. Somewhere nearby Chopper lurked, the carbon scent of his breath faintly flavoring the air. But beneath the arched boughs she saw nothing except the gnarled limbs of yet more apple trees. Had she done it incorrectly? This was the first she'd attempted the summoning.

Then she remembered. She'd left out the final part. Muttering under her breath she lifted the key up above her mouth and ground out the words, "Bottom's up." As the displaced drop of honey landed on her tongue the air shimmered, then darkened until a set of thick, oaken doors stood open before her, framing the perfect replica of a Viking Mead Hall. High ceilings, broad, smoke-blackened beams, heavy plank tables, and hogsheads of mead stacked everywhere. Oddly enough, anything movable— short of the people—was in some way lashed to the floor. Weaving throughout the chamber were women, provocatively dressed in corsets and hiked skirts, draped blouses and killer boots. Each of them bore a tray containing carved wooden tankards, which they ably distributed around the room, all the while dodging groping hands and sprawled legs, not to mention the occasional knife, dart, or axe lobbed at the targets leaning against the far wall. Surprisingly, though chaos reigned, it did so in a well-choreographed manner.

Not much had changed since the last time J&J Miracle Mead Hall came to anchor in the middle of Avalon, though by some reckonings a lifetime had passed. Hardly surprising, given the hall's trans-dimensional nature. Saia stood in the doorway and peered around the low-lit chamber, searching for her quarry, but the chaos defeated her.

With a huff, she shifted her heavy basket to a two-handed grip and hurried through the door. As she passed into the Hall, something warm, dry, and supple brushed her ankle. A warning went off in the back of her thoughts, altogether too faint, virtually drowned out by her worries. The unexpected sensation startled her, causing her to jerk her foot away. And the chaos folded her in with welcoming arms. The sudden move nearly sent her colliding with a mead maiden's full and impressively balanced tray. The woman frowned and with an adept hitch step avoided the disastrous crash. Apologizing profusely Saia hurried over to the counter and out of everyone's way.

On the far side of the counter stood a delicate woman with skin a light cinnamon hue and hair the dark, black velvet shade of a bumble bee's stripe, tumbled into a messy bun. She wore a man's white silk shirt under a brocade vest in shades of green and blue and purple. Pinned at her throat, she wore a Wing emblem bearing a Major's rank markings. Up close, one could see the thin slash of a scar that ran diagonally across the woman's face, just missing her right eye, remnants of a wound that predated her Valkyrie Corps days.

"Melisande," Saia nodded in greeting to the Hall Mistress.

"You do realize all you need do is grip the key and think of the Hall, yes? Once she is stationary she appears."

Saia frowned. "You don't say? I'll have to remember that."

"It was Coyote that told you this other silly nonsense, was it not?" Melisande did not wait for an answer. "I will have words with him."

Not wanting to dwell on the matter, Saia heaved her basket onto the bar.

"I need a favor."

Melisande considered her carefully before speaking, looking from the apples to Saia and back again. "So serious, even for you. I am thinking you should not speak of this to me, m'lady. You are not one who asks a favor lightly. I've no doubt this is one the Messrs. will need approve. Jonathan, I think..." she added half to herself as she raised a hand and beckoned to one of the women bearing trays. She spoke discretely to the woman and sent her off.

Before the mead maiden could return, a solid man came ambling up, his eyes bright and sparkling above his full and impressive beard. Atop his head, a well-brushed bowler tilted at a jaunty angle. As his eyes rested on Saia, the faint smile on his lips erupted into a full-blown grin.

Of course, it might have been equally inspired by the sight of the basket of apples beside her. Saia's lips smiled gently in return while her gaze remained solemn. She allowed herself to be enveloped briefly by those brawny arms.

"What brings us to you, my dear?" Jason asked as he leaned against the counter next to her in a pose she suspected he intended to show off his kilt.

Melisande shoved him upright with a frown and wiped the polished wood where he'd rested. "Behave yourself," she told him, "I've sent for Jonathan. We must have reason to balance your daring, you Don Wannabe."

Jason shot her a good-natured grin. " 'Sande, you say the sweetest things."

The Hall Mistress scowled and pressed her lips thin. The pale scar bisecting her face took on a pink hue. "*Melisande.* Or Major, if you don't feel you can manage the first," she said, her features stretched long and stiff, as if shortened names offended her dignity.

Saia took a step back from the tension sparking the air and came up against a lean, firm chest. She turned her head and saw a well-dressed man in a brown bowler at her back.

"Now, children," Jonathan said, both his voice and tone pleasant and mellow. "Play nice in front of our guest." His hands came up to rest on Saia's shoulders. "She doesn't visit often...I'd hate to think this is why."

He then bent down and murmured in her ear, "Actually, she quite likes him…just not his habit of rushing to the assistance of other nubile young ladies."

Saia laughed at that. Imagine, herself being called young…when even by Fae standards she'd reached a respectable middle age. His comment did cause her to reconsider the encounter unfolding before her, though. She twisted at the waist to look more directly at her friend, Jonathan, the more dignified J of the pairing that was J&J Miracle Mead.

He quirked an eyebrow at her and let a rakish smile draw his lips. An eager glimmer sparkled in his gaze as he looked past her at the basket of fruit. "Shall we discuss favors…and apples?"

"Not here," she answered, her own expression devoid of any flirtation. She had no time for playfulness. Both Jonathan and Jason straightened and briefly assumed a somber, business-like demeanor.

"Of course. If you'll adjourn to our office, madam?" Jonathan responded, sweeping his arm in the direction of a spiral staircase leading to a loft over the bar.

Saia reached for her basket of apples only to have Jason lift it from her grasp. The weight hardly constituted a burden, to her, but she allowed him his gallantry. The good-natured giant scowled as Jonathan then offered her his arm, mischief's sparkle dancing in his eyes. She couldn't help but laugh as she slipped a hand in the crook of both men's arms.

It was really rather silly in the end as they walked all of ten feet before the narrow stair leading to the office loft required they proceed single file.

"So," Jonathan said as the door closed behind them, leaving the room in a sudden pocket of silence. "Speak to me of…favors." He quirked his eyebrow suggestively as a faint smile flirted across his lips. His gaze, however, remained sober as he perched a hip against the edge of a battered worktable.

Saia could not blame him. Truly it was rare for her to grace the Mead Hall. And never before had she'd done the summoning. Moving to sit on an age-worn divan she pursed her lips and ran her gaze around the inner sanctum; another first, her visit here. What a hodge-podge of wonders: libatious, historic, and tinkering in nature. If anyone was equipped to help her it surely must be these two purveyors of miracles. One corner appeared a cross between a kitchen and a mad chemist's workshop, with vials and beakers and the odd cooking implement scattered about, not to mention racks of herbs and raw honeycomb precisely labeled. In the far other corner a workbench of a completely different sort held baskets of gears, brass tubing, and an impressive array of tools from the most delicate watch maker's set all the way up to a sledge hammer of carnival proportions. Nearer to the tinker's side stood a door oddly marked FLIGHT DECK. In the spaces between sprawled leather-bound journals and priceless art, fine furnishings from nearly every culture and age of design, including the most hideous plaid sofa anyone had surely ever seen, which looked exceedingly comfortable, if somewhat out of place along the back wall.

Jason set her basket beside her and Jonathan gently cleared his throat.

"Forgive me. Your lair quite captivates."

Nodding, Jonathan lightly crossed his arms and Jason moved to a locked cabinet on the far side of the cluttered table. Taking a key similar to her own from the brim of his black bowler he opened the door, revealing an array of hand-labeled bottles. Saia watched as he sifted through them until with a satisfied grunt he drew one out. He returned with three glasses and set them and the bottle on the butt-end of a cut-off cask beside the divan. The label, which she could now see clearly, read Avalon's Kiss. Briefly she smiled, delighted at the tribute, though it likewise served a reminder of her dilemma.

Saia sighed and considered the only two men she knew capable of helping her. She feared what she was about to ask far exceeded the favor the Js already owed her, but by how much? And could she meet the price?

Squaring her shoulders she faced them. "I need a new doorway established."

The Js sobered completely and straightened. With a con-sidering *hmph*, Jason reached for the bottle of mead and broke the wax seal. Pouring three stout glasses, he then passed them around.

"You don't do anything by half, do you, my dear?" Jonathan asked her.

"I can't afford to," she answered as a past the Js could not hope to imagine scrolled across her memory in brief, sobering glimpses. Past mistakes had already separated her from her family. All she had left to comfort her was the knowledge they were well and happy somewhere. She would do anything to preserve that.

The perceptive manner in which Jonathan met her gaze made her feel uncomfortably exposed. He left his perch at the table and moved to sit on the far end of the divan, the basket of apples between them.

"Not that we protest the visit or the gifts you bear," he said, concern darkening his gaze. "But what is so important that it drives you here to us, when little else does?"

"Family."

Two sets of eyebrows arched up under their respective bowler brims and the corresponding jaws went slightly slack.

"What? You thought I dropped from one of Avalon's trees?" The words stung her lips they came out that sharp, her heart aching for all she'd sacrificed. She could not blame the men for their assumption but it made her angry and not a little reckless.

Two things kept her calm and reasoning: the time of the vision was not now, and the facts of it were not immutable.

"I have seen their murders. I must warn my loved ones and only you can help me," she told them, her expression set in grim determination. "I can never leave Avalon's shores. The Mead Hall is my miracle. Only here may our realms cross. Only here may I speak aloud with my own voice."

Jason nodded as his cheeks puffed out on a blown breath. "Everywhere at once and nowhere at all," he quoted aptly.

"Precisely," Saia said, and nothing more.

Odd ticks coming from the tinkering workbench constituted the sole source of sound for several long, taut moments. As she sat there, waiting for the verdict, the aroma of her forgotten drink wafted up to tweak her nose. Willing herself not to push the Js on this, she raised her glass and sipped this new blend of Miracle Mead. Smooth, light, yet flavored with the mellow crispness of Avalon's own apples. She sipped again and let the sampling rest on her pallet, teasing out the faint notes of ginger, threaded through with hints of vanilla. Despite her worries, a smile lifted her lips and she relaxed into the padded back of the divan. "Oh...oh, well done, gentlemen."

Both beamed at the praise.

"The fine work of Darkan, our newest Mead Man," Jason told her proudly. "He's a master of the melomels and cysers...the apple-based meads," he added at her puzzled look. "He'll be pleased you've enjoyed his first effort for us."

As she took a further drink the Js joined her, sampling the finished blend for what Saia expected was the first time if the looks of satisfaction and delight that they exchanged were any gauge. Some of the heaviness lifted from the room's atmosphere and Jonathan leaned forward. "Miracles are our business, my dear. Tell us where you wish us to berth the Hall and, if at all possible, we'll make it so."

"Delilah's Roadhouse," she answered.

"But where?" Jonathan prompted her when she said no more.

Heat filled Saia's cheeks as a wince twitched her lips. "I don't know," she admitted. "It's all the same to me from up here. We don't exactly exchange postcards."

Jason chuckled. "No, I don't suppose you do...where would you get the stamps?"

As if *that* was the issue.

"You say family is involved...? With this place, I mean." Jonathan asked, his gaze intent as his mind mulled the problem.

Saia nodded and Jonathan's features took on a faintly grim cast.

He let out a breath and met her eye. "Okay, you have a deal...but this cancels the debt between us, and there is payment required beyond. Given this fine restorative we've just sampled—of which said apples are a key component—it will cost you more than one bushel. We'll want an additional three, and what you ask will require a touch of your blood."

"Done," she answered promptly, holding out her hand.

Jonathan took it in his and swiftly dipped to brush the back of it with his lips, gentle, but firm. He glanced up at her with sincere eyes and a roguish grin. "And sealed with a kiss, though I'd gladly make a better effort at that."

With a solemn look, she drew her hand away, though again a blush heated her cheeks. Her vows stood in the way of what he only half playfully asked.

Tipping the edge of his bowler toward her in concession, he then turned to Jason. "A key, if you will, fine sir," he said, with a twirling wave of his hand, playing up the silliness as if he hadn't been quite serious the instant before.

Jason moved to an apothecary cabinet on the mad-chemist side of the room, rooting around until he drew out yet another key similar to the one that hung from Saia's chatelaine. Bringing it across to the divan he handed it and a small utility knife that hung from his belt to Jonathan. He then dipped his hat toward Saia, with a slightly uncomfortable look on his face, his attention still on the blade. "I best go warn Melisande to start battening down the bar."

Jonathan acknowledged Jason's departing words with a distracted nod as he again took Saia's hand. She braced herself as he laid the knife's tip on the pad of her little finger.

He dipped his head to catch her eye. "This will take a while to lock in...if it does at all. We've never had cause to try this method before."

She nodded sharply, her attention fixed on the knife point ready to pierce her skin.

Sudden, pounding steps on the staircase caused Saia to jump, resulting in the blade more than slightly pricking her finger. She hissed and shook her hand reflexively. Blood from the shallow gash spattered her white robes, as well as the divan and Jonathan both, leaving tiny crimson circles on his tan work shirt. She pressed her hands to her mouth and her eyes widened. "Sorry," she mouthed, as Jason pushed open the door.

"You have to stop him," he said through heaving breaths, sounding more than a little frantic.

Both she and Jonathan turned to him, their brows surely drawing down in identical confusion.

"Your blasted dragonet! He's eaten the whole roasted boar in one gulp and has started eyeing the mutton. There'll be nothing left for lunch!"

"Oh, no!" She hadn't realized Chopper had followed her through the door. He simply adored well-seasoned meat, which he did not have ready access to on Avalon.

"What the heck is a dragon doing on Avalon, anyway?" Jason asked, his beard bristling as his lower lip jutted out.

"Hiding from St. George," Saia said, faint and distracted. Beside her, Jonathan burst out laughing. She barely took note of him as her brow creased and she turned her attention to the open door. At the escalating uproar drifting through it, she half rose from where she sat, ready to rush down to the hall. Only Jonathan's grip on her hand kept her from doing so. He tugged her back down.

"Don't worry," he said, still chuckling, "we'll order out." Turning to Jason he said, "Have the crew open the door in Thailand." And with that bizarre reassurance, he laid down the knife and brought the key to her finger, squeezing one drop of her blood over the engraved bumblebee on the bow. This time he brought her hand to his lips, pressing them to the slight wound. Saia forgot to draw it away.

Suzanne drifted in a sated haze, relaxed for the first time in what seemed forever. Lance had, indeed, done everything imaginable to get on her good side...every one of them. Eventually they'd made it to the bed. Hours had passed until the faint moonbeams filtering through the gauze curtains provided the only light.

Reaching back over her shoulder, she tugged on a strand of Lance's hair as they lay entwined together in their tussled bed, the sheets and blankets around their feet, what hadn't fallen to the floor. "You never told me what happened today."

He pressed his lips to her shoulder. "Oh, stuff..."

With a languid chuckle she smacked his arm, which draped her waist. Lance remained silent a long time. The subtle flexing of his muscles against her skin spoke of the turmoil she still could not sense. Needing to know, she patiently waited.

He sighed and nestled in close. In the darkness he began to speak, his tone low and flat, like it got when he locked down on his empathy hard.

"Dair put a hit on my father. I got there and he was bleeding out. It was the *Dubh Fae*. Whatever I did that got me there, it left me next to useless. I tell you, I was reeling. I thought he was going to finish both of us off, but when he saw Gort's dagger he just grabbed it and ran."

Suzanne gasped and half sat up, twisting back to look at him. "Cam…?"

Lance drew her back down beside him. "He's okay…now. I don't know that I can explain, but somehow I healed him, and *he* healed me. Then I get back here and…well, you know about that mess."

Suzanne hugged his arm, but said nothing.

"I've never been so frustrated, so angry, and there was nothing I could do."

"We went and stormed bloody, friggin' Avalon, with our hands tied. It was a set-up. Dair na Scath shows up with Tilly just sitting quiet behind him, and *Callan* by his side."

At the mention of the High King's champion, and with such venom, Suzanne tensed, fear robbing her of breath. *Does Lance know? What will he do?*

"Not to mention a few thousand of his closest lackeys," Lance went on, not even noticing. "There I am with only the Winds behind me and a counterfeit dagger because the *Dubh Fae* stole the real one. I tried to bluff." He growled and his arm tightened. "No one told me there is no lying on Avalon. Then I tried to talk Tilly away from him. When that didn't work, Sammy tried to snatch her, but Mr. High-and-Mighty King bolts with Tilly, telling us we better show up with the right dagger."

Suzanne wiggled around until she could see his face, if only faintly in the moonlight. "The one you and…Callan fought over?" she had to force out the name.

Lance nodded and his expression shut down. She wouldn't have thought it possible, but his voice went even flatter.

"The *Dubh Fae* died for that dagger. I didn't intend for it to happen; The Winds and I linked to fight off Callan. The *Dubh Fae* got caught in the meld somehow." Lance's voice grew more strained. "Callan kept pounding us with mage bolts. The energy was too much, it would have fried us. When I dumped it I didn't pay attention to where it went and I fried the *Dubh Fae* instead."

Suzanne gasped, but hugged him tight, sensing the torment he felt even without the benefit of the link.

"Then, after all that, I went into the hall of the High King...and you know what I found?" Something shifted in Lance's expression, triggering a bitter twist to his lips and a deepening scowl. He hesitated, but it did not feel as if he waited for a response. He blinked hard and his lips flattened. "I found a broken king in a dead court. I held up his greatest nightmare and shoved it in his face. Then I took what was mine and made it clear it would stay mine." He spoke that last low and lethal, his emotional control slipping.

Suzanne braced herself against the unexpected onslaught. For a moment it distracted her, but then she realized something about Lance's account rang incomplete. Again, he kept something hidden. From the closed-off look on his face, whatever it was would remain unsaid. She pressed her lips and turned away. A part of her wanted to believe all was well. The rest wanted to call him on whatever he kept from her. Not wanting to disrupt the closeness they'd regained, she forced her suspicions aside.

They lay there a while breathing. Caressing. Coming down from the tension caused by what Lance shared. Suzanne let herself drift into a gentle doze, her eyes fluttering, ready to close. She jerked fully awake as Lance spoke next to her ear.

"My turn...what had you beyond pissed at me?"

She winced and hunched in tight until her skin barely touched his. Determined, Lance pursued the matter, leaning in until their bare flesh again pressed together. "Come on, tell me so I can make it right."

Even without the influence of Lance's empathy, her emotions snarled up inside: fear, doubt, annoyance. Why could they not have this one, peaceful moment?

But you started it, reason whispered in her thoughts.

Suzanne gritted her teeth and pushed the perception away. All her earlier anger boiled up from the crevices of her heart. More pissed that he'd brought it up than she was at the original offense; she pounded her fist down hard on the arm locked around her waist. "Can't you ever let things lie?"

Lance grunted, then placed a kiss on her shoulder just shy of where the redcap had slashed her. "Nope," he answered, completely unrepentant.

"How about we start with the fact you only told me half of what is going on,"—she felt him twitch in response, and knew she'd been right—"not to mention you've pulled me out of the first decent doze I've had since I can't remember when. I could deal with that, but you shut me out of the run, and *then* you cut me off from our link...I thought you were DEAD!"

"I'm sorry, babe..."

She snarled. As if sorry was enough.

"You don't trust me...you don't believe in me."

He sighed and leaned away from her. "If I didn't trust you, I wouldn't have left you holding things down on this end."

Not feeling particularly close at the moment, Suzanne didn't bother to respond. Cold without him against her back, she hunched into the pillow and reached down to draw up the blankets.

"Come on...I made the best call I could in every situation."

To be fair, she knew that, on a rational level. Unfortunately, her demons dwelt on a more unstable plane, and they'd decided to come out and play. Realizing this and hating the weakness it represented, Suzanne focused on her breathing, on finding that balance deep at her center. She made a stand and shoved the demons back.

It took a little longer than usual to restore some sense of calm. That disturbed her.

Still chilled, and not particularly happy with the strain creeping between them after such closeness as they'd shared, she squirmed back until Lance's body again cupped hers. He let out a long breath and some of the tension radiating from him eased.

"You never told me what you did in the woods. How did you make things better?" He spoke the words casually, but the weight of his attention threatened to force the air from her chest.

Her demons broke lose again, shattering the little inner compartment she'd locked them in. Damn! She'd thought Lance had let that go as well, taking her at her word that she'd solved the problem. Her muscles started to bunch and any hope of contentment drained away.

"We played paintball," she muttered into her pillow letting her voice trail off into a sleepy grumble. Lance pressed closer against her until she had no doubt he knew her body was too tense for her to be as sleepy as she'd sounded. He ran a hand over her shoulder and stopped to knead a newly forming knot. "Maybe they did, but you got up to something more." The more he spoke, the more he pushed, the tighter her nerves bunched.

"Sheesh, you make it sound like I went out there looking for trouble!" She moved out of his embrace once more, visualizing his scowl.

"No, but you found some."

Suzanne flinched as his hand traced the scabbed-over gash on her shoulder. With a tug he laid her flat on her back and into the moonlight trailing from the window. He stared her in the eye. "Tell me you didn't," he challenged her. "Tell me one of ours did this...or this..." His foot brushed across her torn ankle, drawing a hiss from Suzanne's lips. "Or maybe you tripped...is that it?" His empathy sent waves of frustration crackling through the air.

"No more than you did," she answered in arched tones, pushing against the red splotch of newly healed skin on his shoulder. There had been no mention of that in Lance's telling, though Suzanne assumed it was the *Dubh Fae*'s work—may his spirit rot at the gates to the Summer Land.

Lance glowered down at her, but did not elaborate.

Teeth clenched, she rolled back to her side. If he wasn't willing to be truly open with her, the least he could do was back off.

Zero chance of that happening.

"Come on, Sue, talk to me," he said low and intent, his breath hot on her neck, although at least six inches of cooling sheets stretched between them. "What's going on? How come I had no clue? The tat didn't even twinge..."

He kept at her and kept at her, going on like a cat worrying a mouse. Or a friggin' two-year-old, endlessly asking why. Suzanne had enough. Sliding from the bed she turned to face him, body poised and her hands fisted. The autumn air chilled her skin. She ignored it. "This is not the first time we've had this conversation, Lance. I'm a big girl. I can take care of my own problems. I *need* to take care of my own problems. You didn't know because I didn't want you to. You would have been on my ass the whole time making sure I didn't stub my toe or something." His expression shifted uncomfortably at her words and she knew she spoke truth. "I had to deal with this myself or I would have never gotten better. Why can't you understand that?"

Lance rose on the other side of the bed. A muscle in his jaw twitched, and she watched him rein back and get himself under control. Again, protecting her, even from himself. Suzanne snarled and pushed harder, suddenly wanting him to lose it, wanting him to stop treating her like she would break...wanting him as pissed off and miserable as he'd made her.

"You didn't know because I closed down the link so I could do what I had to do without you holding me back." Not precisely accurate, but close enough. She hadn't wanted him to feel her die, if it had come to that, and look what that had gotten her. Next time she wouldn't let herself care.

Her lover's eyes went flat and hard, nothing but a faint glimmer in the darkened room. For a brief instant he again resembled her father. She must have flinched. She heard him draw a sharp, deep breath in response and slowly let it out, and then her Lance stood before her again; as pissed as she'd intended, but recognizable.

"Excuse me?" The words ground like granite past his lips, but he didn't raise his voice. Delilah had taught him to be polite to a woman even when furious. Faint tremors through his arms and torso betrayed how much effort it took for him not to strike back, though. Suzanne realized she'd gone too far as the vein at his temple pulsed. Even still, he did not snarl or yell.

"So...what you're saying is that you did the very thing you gave me hell for...*first?* What you're saying is that it's okay for you to be like your father, but God help me if I even try and protect you?" He no longer shook, but his muscles bulged. She had never seen him so furious, though the faint echo of a pain-hazed memory told her that day he'd rescued her at the crossroads he had looked quite like this.

"I guess here's where I apologize for caring so much," he said the volume of his voice slowly climbing. "Though I don't know why I should bother seeing how you don't care at all." The last roared from his lips until she needed no link or empathy to feel his pain. His anger. His betrayal.

How had things gone so horribly wrong?

Suzanne opened her mouth to refute his claim, but she could not do so in good conscience and he knew it; Lance snarled and got down into her face. "You want me to stop 'coddling' you? You want to feel what I had the *gall* to shield you from? Fine!" With a brutal twist of will and a mental yank Lance reopened the link between them, throwing it wide, no barriers. Suzanne crumpled to her knees with the force of the *Dubh Fae*'s death throes. The agony tripped up and down her spine, firing rogue impulses across her nerves: agony, terror, despair. The raw intensity of that last betrayed its source as Lance.

"I've been wrestling with that for hours. Fun, isn't it?" His lips pressed tight until all color drained from them, leaving a thin, white line. For a split second she saw remorse darken his gaze. As she watched he raised an emotional barrier between them, but not fast enough for her to miss the desolation glinting in his eye. Slow enough for it to echo in her heart.

She tried to apologize, to confess how much she loved him, but the words would not come. She had waited too long, pushed him too far in what she recognized now as the most unfair of tests. The emotional maelstrom emanating from him overwhelmed her, leaving her gasping as tears burned tracks down her face. She slumped to the floor until only her braced arm kept her from lying fully prone. "Lance..."

"Don't bother," he snapped, as he headed for the door. "A stray dog gets treated better than this shit." And her dreams of building a loving family shredded, destroyed by her own willfulness. With the raw force of his will he completely severed the link between them, rather than just shutting it down as he had before. Suzanne collapsed, sobbing, forsaken, and more alone in her head than she had been in decades. She looked up at him begging for forgiveness with her gaze.

Lance stood at the doorway, eyes bleak, but hard, his hand clenched tight enough to shake. "We're done." His eyes slowly closed and his body briefly went rigid before he pivoted, grabbed his jeans from where they draped over the corner of the dresser, and stalked out the bedroom door.

The apartment door slammed closed on his final words.

Suzanne
EdCoutts/2013

Chapter Four

DEEP IN THE ROTTING HEART OF FAERIE, THE ELVEN KNIGHT Callan stood alone in the ravaged Hall of the *Ard Ri*. Once the proud line of Rowan had held sway from this tree-lined Court. Now their grip on power had all but shaken loose. Dust and debris littered the once-grand floor and brown edged the leaves of the fading *Rudha-an* throne. Dair na Scath had fled. Or perhaps he'd merely wandered off, useless and broken, his mind crumbled by the weight of his obsession and subsequent defeat. The Abomination...spawn of Dair's own daughter...had stolen away both the last woman of the *Rudha-an* line and the charmed dagger that would have bound her to the High King, strengthening his claim to power.

Callan stared at the dilapidated dais. Upon a time, he had been promised everything: the kingdom, the hand of Princess Anaiphal, the throne. Now... The kingdom fractured more with each passing day. His betrothed had thrice been stolen from him, first by the Dair himself, then by a mortal, and finally by death. Only the throne remained within Callan's reach, but still beyond his grasp. No matter. He had no desire for that pitiful seat of power. Let it rot. He would claim Underhill for his own and forge a new throne. Only one thing stood in the way of that goal. Not until the last blood of Rowan drained away to feed the soil would the Fae realm be open to his conquest. Two remained: Lance Cosain—son to the woman who was to have been

Callan's bride—and his flawed cousin, called, of all things, Tilly.

They would not bar his way for long. Not with what he'd learned in the midst of the battle.

Callan pivoted and moved across the chamber toward a literal wall of trees grown trunk to trunk, with no space between. He tasted the bittersweet tang of decay on the air and sheets of torn bark crackled under his feet, while a harsh breeze tugged at his braids. He barely noticed, his attention locked before him. He came to a halt in front of the living chronicle of the *Rudha-an* line, staring at the desecrated bole of the one recording the current age. The runes spell-etched into the revealed flesh confirmed what the High King's chosen had discovered: the location of Callan's faithless daughter...his greatest disappointment...yet, ironically, also the unexpected key to his ascension to power. After all of these years to discover the petulant, rebellious child aligned with the enemy. And oh the muck she'd gotten entrenched in. As if consorting with mortals was not bad enough, he'd sensed a dark, familiar taint on her, one that left her vulnerable. At last, a fissure in her blasted defenses. Not one to miss an opportunity, he considered how to best use it to his advantage. Already she teetered, a few careful nudges would send her tumbling, and the Line of *Rudha-an* with her.

Callan smiled. It was not pleasant.

One pale, elegant finger reached out to trace the runes, the damaged wood rough beneath his skin. Little Fleur had changed her name... *Suzanne*...she now called herself Suzanne. Callan frowned, his lip curling in disgust even as his eye took on a calculating gleam. His child whored herself to the *Ard Ri's* bastard grandson. Callan could work with that. Reading on, his mind laid a plan.

The High King may have crumpled like a dry leaf beneath a boot heel, but Callan's power remained. No other knew of the true state of Dair na Scath. As the leader of the High King's forces who would dare question Callan's command? He knew no one so ambitious or foolish to do so directly, but by subterfuge and scheming...all too likely, particularly now. For the time being, he could not leave Underhill, lest in his absence that changed. He would have to delegate. Returning to his chamber, comprised of great, arching ironwood trees that betrayed no signs of the realm's decay, Callan summoned the nearest redcaps.

They grumbled and glared and thumped their pikes, but they came, creeping in one solitary powrie at a time, circling and baring their teeth, lunging at one another until Callan placed his hand atop the nearest redcap's head and quicker than the fae could react, called on his element of fire. The resulting shriek ended abruptly as the cap dried out and Callan's object lesson burnt down to ash.

"Your disrespect offends me," he announced to those remaining. "You should work on that." And one by one he held their gaze. "I have a task for you. Execute it to my satisfaction and you will have an unimaginable reward."

They assumed respectful positions, as near to which they were able, heads lowered and ears cocked. Waiting. And waiting. No sound breached the silence but that of the will-o'-wisps murmuring in the tree boughs above. The scent of ember and ash lingered in the air, a suitable reminder for best behavior.

Just as various muscles in those wizen faces began to twitch, Callan spoke. "Your brothers have fallen,"—he paused as a curious mix of glee and rage crept over their faces—"and a cap has been taken."

At that the powries very nearly gave in to their impulse to frenzy. They did not bear competition well and clearly did not welcome yet another redcap among their number. Callan lifted a single brow and gave his head a slight tilt. His half-raised hands took on a subtle red glow. They settled instantaneously.

"You are to watch the taker. Tell me what you see. And if the opportunity presents itself, you are to bring her to me."

Every redcap stilled at the word "her." That was a cat of a completely different color. Their faces lifted and their eyes gleamed.

It had been a very long time since the redcaps had a queen among them.

Other than staff, *Delilah's* was empty. Mongo manned the bar until Kelly came on shift, and though she wasn't actually an employee, Suzanne covered for Joan, the waitress on that afternoon, so she could take a break. Neither one of them had much to do; a little straightening up, sweeping the floor—staring at each other with long faces like kids told they can't go out to play. Mongo's longing gaze kept drifting toward the kitchen. The dead hours between the end of lunch and the beginning of the evening crowd sucked.

Suzanne found herself picking at the scab on her shoulder. Not on purpose, it just kind of happened. She didn't notice the sting or the blood until the front door swung open, sending a cool breeze across her shoulder. Absentmindedly, she reached into her pocket to pull out her ever-present bandana. As she brought it up to wipe the blood away she turned her gaze to see who the newcomer was.

A woman Suzanne had never seen before walked in. A tough chick, from the look of her; not very tall, built, but compact, with short, sassy hair just this side of cherry red. The grin on her face made her eyes sparkle. She wore jeans and a trendy leather jacket, with a messenger bag slung over her shoulder. Something rang familiar...

"Mongo-bongo!" the stranger called out from across the room as she lifted her arms in the air in a long-distance hug.

Mongo responded with a growl that rumbled through his chest like a cascade of thunder, his expression set in a miniature storm cloud, not quite hiding the pleased look in his eye. "Knock that off, Cupcake," he said as he came stalking around the bar.

"Okay, *Eugene*," she said, a devilish smirk on her face as she crossed to the bar in a few powerful strides.

Suzanne's expression rapidly shifted to stunned, her brow puckering as her mouth hung open. Normally, woman or not, anyone mocking Mongo's name could expect to have her head handed to her. Of course, it shocked Suzanne that anyone else even *knew* Mongo's given name. She only knew it by accident. He didn't exactly use it more than necessary. Like...ever.

"Ah, sheesh! Will you shut up already?" Mongo turned bright red but his expression softened. Smiling, he held his arms open. The stranger chuckled, deep and throaty, and propelled herself into them. Then it clicked. This must be Debbie. "What are you doing here so early?"

"We have practices all week," the woman answered as she took a couple steps back to get a better angle on his face. "So we can get a feel for the rink before the actual bout. Don't have to be there until seven, though."

Mongo nodded as if that made some kind of sense. If it did, Suzanne couldn't tell. Then he seemed to remember she was there. He turned to her wearing the broadest smile she'd ever seen grace his lips.

"Suzanne," he said, looking beyond pleased, "meet my cousin, better known as Molotov Cupcake of the Jerzey Derby Brigade."

"100 proof!" The woman grinned, elbowing him before she held out her hand to Suzanne. "Debbie. But if you want, you can call me Cupcake. Nice to meet you, Suzanne." It came out 'nice ta meecha.' Suzanne just nodded and put away her bandana before she shook Debbie's hand. She didn't know which she found more amusing, that this tiny firecracker of a woman was related to the laid back man-mountain, or that the cook had a cousin called Cupcake.

Pleasantries observed, Cupcake turned back to Mongo.

"Mind if I hang a flyer for Saturday's bout?" she asked.

"Go for it," Mongo answered, nodding his head toward the cork board situated by the door. "That's what the board's there for." As she sauntered away, flipping open the flap of her bag, Mongo turned to Suzanne. "Deb's here with her team for a roller derby bout over in Dalton. Talk about tough broads...roller skates, attitude, and a hell of a lot of aggression..."

"Sounds like fun," Suzanne said, her voice as flat as her expression. Biker chick that she was, and more than ready to defend herself, she wasn't exactly the sort to look for a fight. Cupcake didn't seem to pick that up, though.

"It is!" she chimed in on her way back to the bar, clearly having overhead Suzanne's comment. Her grin turned just a little fanatical as her face lit up with excitement, "A total blast. You should try it. It's one of my favorite ways to blow off steam."

Mongo must have picked up on Suzanne's annoyance. "Yo, where are the tickets?"

Cupcake turned to stare at him, her expression slightly confused.

"For the bout?" he prompted her. "You do want us to sell them, right?"

"Sweet!" She put her hand on his shoulder and gave a little bounce on her powerful legs to plant a kiss on Mongo's cheek. She landed back on her feet as if she'd never left solid ground. Without missing a step, she reached back into her bag to pull out a rubber-band-wrapped stack of tickets. Suzanne found herself impressed. It must have shown because Mongo nodded in agreement. "You should see her on skates."

"I don't know about skates, but I can definitely picture her on a cycle."

"Nah, nothing against them, but I prefer eight wheels to anything else." Cupcake said. "Hardly anyone ever ends up dead from a fall off skates." Then she grinned. "Bloody, broken, bruised...but hardly ever dead."

Suzanne's gut fluttered in an odd way at the word bloody.

"Well," Cupcake said as she handed over the tickets, "it's been a *long* time...we're gonna go bake something, right?" She looked at Mongo with soulful eyes and a confident smile. "It's been *forever*..."

Mongo looked pained. His gaze traveled the empty room, lingering on the bar he was supposed to be manning before flicking toward the kitchen. "Deb, I'm on shift..." he started, trailing off as his cousin put on the pout. Mongo sighed.

"Oh, go ahead, already," Suzanne cut in on his inner dilemma. "It's not like we're swamped."

Both Cupcake and Mongo grinned the same grin as they darted for the kitchen door. Mongo paused beside Suzanne on the way to plant a rare kiss on the top of her head. She looked up when he hesitated. He stood looking down at her, his brow furrowed. "What did you do?"

Suzanne followed his gaze to her shoulder and gasped. Her cut looked angry and seeped more blood than it should have from a picked scab. Just looking at it made her a little sick. She fought against showing how much as she waved Mongo away and reached into her pocket to pull out her bandana. Holding Mongo's gaze, she pressed the cloth over the wound. "Nothing...I just picked at it. Go on, I'm fine."

Mongo wore a doubtful expression. "You've been getting dinged up an awful lot lately." Suzanne refused to make a big deal about it, but a cold shiver swept over her as she realized he spoke the truth.

"It's nothing, Mongo. Please, forget about it." His brow creased deeper, but he did head for the kitchen, his steps slowing each time he glanced over his shoulder at her.

"Go! Bake me something yummy to make up for abandoning me out here alone." Suzanne faked a pout. When he disappeared through the swinging door, the pout slid into a frown. Suzanne lifted the rag to glance at her wound more closely. The edges looked red and annoyed, the damage fresh, instead of days old. The skin around it seemed paler than usual and the bleeding appeared to be picking up instead of slowing. Her stomach fluttered again and Suzanne caught herself both swallowing back bile and wetting her lips. Unsettled, she went to the medical kit—still out on the table where Lyman had left it. She laid down the bandana and took out some triple antibiotic and a bandage to treat her shoulder. As she set them on the table her gut clenched as she got a closer look at the bloodied cloth.

It wasn't her bandana at all. She cursed and braced a trembling hand on the chair back in front of her. With the other she reached out. The familiar scrap of cloth left a gory smudge on the table's surface when she picked it up.

How long had she been under its sway? How many cuts had she mindlessly dabbed, feeding the vile thing? Suddenly it became hard to breathe.

Her skin rippled in aversion at the damp feel of the red cap. Her first impulse was to cast it away; trash it and forget about it. Just thinking about doing so triggered panic in her heart. Straightening her spine, she forced herself to do it anyway, thrusting the cap deep into the can beneath the garbage, where no one would see. As she walked away it was like someone impaled her on a pike, shoving it a bit deeper with each step until Suzanne hunched over clutching her gut. Beads of sweat streamed down her face and her heart pounded until she found herself in the midst of a full-blown panic attack.

Not for the first time.

Her breath came in gasps. The urge to vomit nearly overwhelmed her. Stumbling back she rooted around until she came up with the cap, surprisingly unsoiled. All but sobbing, she grabbed a plastic sandwich bag from behind the bar and dropped the cap inside, not wanting to answer questions about blood stains on her jeans. She then shoved the baggy into her pocket before someone came in and caught her.

God, good thing Lance isn't here. One look at the mess of her shoulder, and that scrap, and he'd have been all in her face wanting to know what happened.

Or would he? After the other night she really wasn't so sure.

Not letting herself dwell on that, she tended to her shoulder, and then retreated behind the bar. To distract herself, she tried to focus on her plans for the rest of the day. Lyman's sister had the flu and Suzanne had cooked up some soup to take her for dinner. She just had time to stop on her way to the crisis center where she'd man the phones for a couple of hours. She knew firsthand how vital it was to have someone to reach out to. Each time she helped another, even if it was just by listening, a bit of her soul healed. Helping others not only filled her with purpose, it also strengthened her confidence, an element sadly lacking in her earlier years.

There was no hope for it, though. While she sat there, alone, waiting for Kelly and Joan, questions kept forming. Uncomfortable questions that left her tense through the shoulders, with a belly full of acid. Her demons acquired new faces.

Aside from her issues with Lance, one fear clawed at her thoughts more than all the others: *What is happening to me?*

If only she knew the answer.

Barely hearing the rumble of the late-night crowd partying around him, or even the crashing blare of heavy rock currently shaking the speakers, Lance stared down into his glass, not really seeing the amber glow of the untouched whiskey. The sides of his mouth cut hard lines into his face, the match to his scowl. Inside, his heart died a little more; though his expression did not betray that.

"If that glass knows what's good for it, it'll get out of town."

Lance closed his eyes at the sound of the clear, sweet voice. His brow smoothed and the corners of his mouth drew up into an almost smile. He straightened and pushed away from the bar, turning to glance at his cousin Tilly. His breath caught hard in his throat for just a second as he stared into her un-clouded eyes.

"Hey, Dumplin'," he said, reaching out an arm to pull her against his side. He made an effort not to crush her to him. The urge hit him strong. After years of heartache and frustration, they had her back—hale and whole. No matter how wonderful, that took some adjusting to.

Tilly gave him a squeeze then tugged herself free.

"Rein it back, Lancelot."

He grimaced as she used her old nickname for him. There were some things he hadn't missed.

Grinning back, she bumped his arm with her fist, but her eyes stayed dead serious. "No, really, you need to pull back on those he-man impulses of yours. That's the problem, you know...between the two of you. Suck it up and patch things up, the right way this time."

His grimace became a glare. They were *not* discussing Suzanne. From the corner of his eye, he saw Tilly smile a sad smile and raise her hands in surrender. She then climbed onto the stool beside his. Lance turned his attention back to his drink, grabbing the glass and finally bringing it to his mouth. He'd just gulped half of it when Tilly spoke.

"Hey, Kel, how about a chocolate milk?"

Lance nearly spit the mouthful across the bar, but managed to spill it back into his glass. With a cough he turned to stare at his cousin.

"What?" she asked innocently. "It wasn't all bad."

He just shook his head, not sure what to make of this new Tilly, a peculiar melding of the damaged, child-like woman she'd been for the past five years and the self-sufficient biker chick she'd been before that. Clearly that was his hang-up, though, because she cheerfully turned to accept the whiskey glass full of chocolate-flavored moo juice. Watching her enjoy the first sip, he had to smile.

"You want some?" she asked, mischief glimmering in her eyes. She didn't hold out the glass, but he reached for it anyway, taking a healthy swig.

"Hey!"

"You offered," he said.

"Yeah, but you weren't supposed to take me up on it," she whined just a little, pouting at her now half-empty glass, still in his hand. Lance couldn't help it. He laughed, loud and full, relaxing at least a little for the first time in weeks, and definitely since his split with Suzanne. Before he could tease Tilly any further, Kelly set another full glass of dairy down on the bar, snagging his whiskey away with the other hand.

He mimicked Tilly's pout, his eyes following the vanishing drink. Putting on an exaggerated sigh, he lifted the milk to his lips once more and took a long drink, ending with lip-smack that nearly sent Tilly tumbling to the floor, she laughed so hard. Unfortunately, his empathy told him nervousness amped her amusement. The merriment ended abruptly, rather than trailing off.

They sat for a while, Lance trying to stay relaxed as Tilly quietly drank her chocolate milk. He couldn't keep it up, though. She watched him the whole time; in the reflection of the mirror backing the bar, in sidelong glances—even turning toward him in a nervous bob he pretended not to notice. When she started to chew on her lip, he gave up.

"Say it," he grumbled, unable to ignore the growing edge of anxiety, which even shielded, his empathy could not help but pick up from her.

"I'm worried about you."

"Yeah, I know."

"I'm more worried about Suzanne."

Lance quirked his eyebrow at that one as he took another swig of milk.

"I'm serious, Lance. Something's going on there. She's tense and snappish. And she's got a new scab every time I see her. She needs help, but she's the last person who will ask for it...and your alpha tendencies are making that worse. She was almost there, ready to believe you were something other than she expected. Then you made it worse by walking, reinforcing every insecurity she ever had." Tilly set her jaw and her expression grew stern. "You make this right! She needs to know that you're there if she can't handle her problems...Up until now you had her feeling she was there if *you* couldn't handle her problems. That's not taking care of her. It's taking her over."

The glass suddenly felt fragile in his grip. Lance scowled so hard the muscles in his face ached. It wasn't Tilly's place to take him to task over this. She had no clue what he'd been through, what shit he'd been dealt. How hard he already tried to do what she was telling him to do. And all of it for nothing. He couldn't bring himself to rail at Tilly, though, not as grateful as he was to have her back.... So, unless he wanted her pissed at him too, he really needed to extract himself from the conversation. He carefully set the milk down and sat back away from the bar. Tilly continued to glare at him from her stool, looking ready for a throw-down now that she'd worked herself up to saying what was on her mind.

No way was Lance going to give her one.

"I've heard what you have to say."

"And?"

Lance slid off his stool and scooped up his jacket. Planting a kiss on her cheek, he turned and headed for the door. "Thanks for caring enough to say it."

The whole bar fell silent as he came face to face with Suzanne walking in the door. She paled and it was like a kick to his gut. Lance just concentrated on breathing steady and politely stepped to the side so that she could pass. Now that Tilly had pointed it out, he couldn't help but notice a couple of angry cuts on her hands. He frowned as she hurried past.

Echoes of Tilly's lecture popped into his head and wouldn't shut off, tormenting him as he stalked out the door.

Seeing Lance shook her. Shook her bad. Suzanne hadn't realized it but this was the first she'd come face to face with him since the breakup. It might just be that she would have to move on, make a new place to belong. Seeing him had been beyond hard. She had to get past that, though.

"You get a cat or something?" Tilly asked, her gaze shadowed and a faint frown creasing her face. Her mind elsewhere, Suzanne did a double take at the fine trace of milk mustache on her friend's lip, not really hearing the question.

"Well?"

"What?"

Tilly scowled and nodded at Suzanne's hands. "I'm seeing an awful lot of scratches lately. Thought maybe you got a rebound cat."

That jolted Suzanne like nothing she ever experienced before. Sweet, kind Tilly had landed a sucker punch to her gut.

"Who pissed in your glass?" Suzanne snapped, turning to walk away.

Tilly laid a hand on her arm. "Wait...please? I'm sorry, that was mean. It just gets so frustrating, feeling like no one is listening..." The halfling dropped her eyes, but not fast enough to hide her pain. "Like they all think I'm still cracked in the head."

"Oh! Honey, no..." An edge of guilt rippled up from Suzanne's belly, as she reexamined her recent dealings with her friend, finding herself not completely free of fault. "It's just going to take some time for everyone to adjust."

A grimace passed over Tilly's face.

"So," she said with an arched look at Suzanne's hand. "What gives?"

Sighing, Suzanne looked down as well. She'd certainly never been the clumsy sort—her Fae nature precluded the possibility—but she had noticed herself how prone to mishap she had become. She feared it was the cap, winning points in their private battle for dominance, but she could hardly admit that, could she?

"It's nothing to worry about, Tilly. I've been really distracted with everything that's going on." It was not a lie. Just not all of the truth.

Another grimace, paired with a narrowed gaze, as if Tilly knew she hedged.

"Yeah, well much more distraction and we'll be building another pyre." Another reason the Hunt owned so much of the surrounding land, and kept it shielded. They took care of their own.

Suzanne's frown deepened. "I'm fine."

"*Ooo!* Both of you! More stubborn than a pair of leprechauns! Get over yourselves and try thinking of someone else for a change! I can *feel* neither of you is okay, so stop handing me bullshit like I'm not capable of grasping the truth. You don't want to talk, fine, but be straight about it!"

The crowd in the bar went silent again as Tilly's voice escalated until that last part rang out like Lance barking orders. Suzanne twitched under the combined stares of the crowd. Tilly just shook her head before stalking out the front door, channeling more echoes of her cousin. Making a serious effort not to glare at those around her, Suzanne mirrored them both, stalking in the opposite direction, eager to end one of the worst days ever. She made it as far as the upstairs landing.

Sliding to sit on the top step, Suzanne couldn't bring herself to walk through that apartment door to a host of memories of what she'd lost. Willfully, and by her own hand lost. Yet she did not have the fortitude to run the gauntlet of the main room once again, and nowhere to go if she did. Weary, she leaned her head against the wall where the faded cabbage roses bore a water stain from some past encounter with the hose from Delilah's kitchen sink. Below her, the stairs creaked. She didn't bother to look up.

"*Deifiúr*, tell me what I can do."

Suzanne tilted her head and opened one eye to look at her brother. Her heart clenched at the sight of him; worry added creases where none belonged. His very presence shored her up. Managing a weak smile, she held her hand out to him. "Come in and talk to me." *Distract me from the heartache,* she added in her thoughts. *Drown out the memories a while so I can rest.* To Gavin she merely said, "I've missed you."

They talked for a long time about everything and nothing, until Suzanne found the strength to shoo him away, to brave her bed and the memories there. The sheets still held Lance's scent, and he'd left strands of hair on the pillow. Likewise, the echo of his hurt left a bitter tang to the air. The good outweighed the bad when it was all she had left.

Suzanne crawled into Lance's spot and wrapped herself in the memory of his arms.

Tears soaked his pillow as she relaxed her vigilance in the dark.

Suzanne came to, walking through moon-dappled darkness, with the rustle of dying leaves overhead and a chill wind slashing across her bare skin. Blinking against debris that swirled around her, she looked around in confusion, recognizing nothing, and brought her arms up around herself in a futile grasp at warmth. With no conscious decision to do so, she continued walking forward, drawn further into the trees until all sign of light vanished.

Deep in her belly she realized where she went, she just didn't want to acknowledge it, until suddenly she had no choice. Her steps stopped abruptly and every naked inch of her began to tremble. Before her—limned in moonlight—lay a familiar clearing. Both her shoulder and her ankle throbbed and a different sort of chill traveled along her neck and down her spine. Turning in a slow circle, Suzanne struggled not to panic. Somewhere overhead a mockingbird protested, apparently disturbed by her shuffling among the crackling leaves that littered the wold. She had no memory of leaving her bed, let alone the apartment, yet she stood surrounded by shadow and trees, completely bare down to her toes, in one of the last places she would ever chose to go.

Stopping just at the edge of the faerie ring where the redcaps had cornered her a few days before, Suzanne closed her eyes, controlled her breathing, and shoved the anxiety down, struggling not to give in to her despair. This place marked her greatest triumph and likewise cost her Lance's love. Clenching her teeth she locked down on the impulse to keen, instead shoving her heartache deep and wrapping the coolness of the night about her until all emotion drained away. Her body adjusted to the autumn air as her heart took on winter's chill.

The tremors of both sorts stilled. With each breath she found her balance, became more detached. She allowed her eyes to open. Took in every detail of her surroundings. Not much seemed to have changed. More leaves on the ground, more empty branches overhead, some scuffling in the dirt nearby that spoke of curious creatures nosing around. Something tugged at her gut once more, compelling, rather than repelling, this time. Kneeling down at the edge of the circle, Suzanne sampled the air among the deadfall, in a deep, slow draw. Decay...rich loam...a hint of frost...and a coppery scent all too familiar to her. On the exhale her breath quavered and her pulse sped up. She caught herself scanning the ground, as if she could sense where her blood had soaked into the soil. As if she must find it and reclaim the precious drops.

Her eyebrow twitched and her mouth moistened. Something akin to a craving kindled in her belly. Unsettled by the impulse, Suzanne scrambled back. Lost her cool. For the first time she noticed the red cap clutched in her hand. Conflicting nausea rose up to clash with the hunger. She pushed to her feet and stumbled back, shaking her hand as if to cast the cloth away. It would not go. If anything, her grip tightened. Her anguished cry silenced the night creatures. Spinning, she loped through the forest as only a fae could, weaving among the trees and leaping bushes, ducking branches and dodging rocks, in near total darkness, determined to distance herself from the circle, as she could not from the cap, before she found herself in the middle of it crawling among the leaves like a hound after blood spoor.

Crisp, cool air greeted the members of the Wild Hunt's mother chapter as they gathered in the lot in front of *Delilah's*. The sun hadn't yet cleared the surrounding trees, but light glowed in cheery brilliance through the branches and boles. Physically, Suzanne gloried in the fall day, her body comfortable, though she only wore a tank top, silkscreened with strategically placed mistletoe, under her jacket. Emotionally, she still struggled with the nightmare her life had become. For today she had to push that aside. It would be rough, given it was the first year she hadn't ridden at Lance's back for the annual run.

She scanned the gathering crowd, trying hard not to feel his absence. Around her, the humans stood out from the Fae; most of them wore sweaters or long-sleeved shirts over their lighter gear. The Fae, not so much. All of them had some nod to Christmas on or about them, from Santa hats to light-up earrings, sprigs of holly wreathing their headlights, or tinsel wrapped around the bitch bar. Every face held a smile. Today they made their Hunt for the Toys run, visiting various businesses to gather donations and presents for the kids at St. Frances's Orphanage and the long-term pediatric patients in the local hospitals.

Those there milled about chatting while everyone waited for the stragglers...and the special rides to be brought out of the storage shed out back. Not feeling social, Suzanne straddled her Shovelhead and tried not to fidget. The delicate hairs along her neck prickled the longer she sat there, and an all-too-familiar tension built in her shoulders. She had an overwhelming urge to scan the area to see who watched her. Part of her expected to see Lance; the other part expected the redcaps. Both should be impossible.

Because she didn't want to be proven wrong about either one, Suzanne sat still and stared intently at her gas cap. Idly she picked at the back of her wrist, which she'd torn on a shelf in the supply closet last night when she was retrieving napkins. She frowned and forced herself to stop.

"Hey, you," Tilly said, wandering over from where she'd been chatting with Kelly and Gavin's current lady...a human woman whose name Suzanne didn't know. Hardly worth asking; she hadn't been around long and she likely wouldn't be next week.

"Hey yourself," Suzanne answered with a lift of her chin. She smiled as she noticed her pendant once more circled Tilly's neck. "What's the holdup?"

"Mongo's staying here with his cousin this year to organize the wrapping party for after; The Winds are in the back trying to wedge Bubba into the suit."

The very image of that startled such a laugh from Suzanne that she nearly slid her off her seat. "Oh my..." she said. "You can't be serious."

Mirth sparkling in her gaze, Tilly nodded, her belled Santa hat jingling. That was when Suzanne noticed the rest of Tilly's outfit: white knee boots, sexy red hot pants, black-spangled suspenders, and a white V-neck tee under her usual leather jacket. Her cheeks were rosy but it did not seem to be from the morning chill.

"You're playing elf in the sled today, right?"

Tilly's gaze hardened briefly. "Of course. Like you'll ever catch me on a cycle without full protection."

Five years ago a hotshot SQUID tried to impress everyone by pulling an endo with Tilly on the pillion pad. Suzanne shuddered at the memory of the 600-pound bike crashing over on top of them both. Tilly'd cracked her head open, but fell clear of the bike itself; the SQUID ended up pinned beneath it and landed in the morgue with a broken neck. Ever since then Tilly, even impaired, had been obsessive about wearing protective gear.

Suzanne raised her hands in surrender. "Sorry...habit." She, along with everyone else, had gotten used to riding herd over Tilly because her judgment as to what constituted effective armor had at times been suspect.

"Yeah, I know. It's all going to take some getting used to..." Tilly said with an unsubtly pointed look. "Hard not to try and protect someone you care about, even when they don't need it."

Before Suzanne could react a loud rumble came from around the side of the building. Everyone turned toward the pop of hard rubber rolling over gravel, watching as an odd mechanical beasty rounded the corner. At first glance it looked like a conventional Santa's sleigh, all red and gold and green, with intricate scroll-work and jingle bells hooked to front and back and sides. But underneath all that hid an all-purpose, military grade ATV with six chunky wheels and a powerful engine. Behind it trailed a number of special trikes hauling small box trailers, all similarly festive in appearance. Bubba himself perched on the driver's seat of the sled with a big-ass grin on his face and a white beard hanging by its elastic around his neck. The fur-rimmed hat sat on his head a bit oddly, too tight to snug down around his ears as it should. He stopped beside them to let Tilly clamber atop the rumble seat in back for the "elf." She quickly strapped herself in then took up a red velvet sack of candy canes to pass out to any kids they encountered.

"What is this, Bubba? Can't have you looking all Shabby Santa," Suzanne said with a grin. Drawing a bit of magic from the surrounding air, she fashioned a glamour with the actual suit as a foundation, until Bubba put the best department store

St. Nick to shame. And if among the glamour rested a thread of protection, what the harm?

Bubba winked, then, as the Ride Captain for the run, he stood in his seat to scan the crowd. "What's the hold-up, anyway? Santa says: *get your ass in gear.*"

A wave of rebel yells split the air, along with a lot of cheering and laughing. Suzanne felt a chill of a different sort as she pulled on her helmet, started her cycle, and fell into formation as they headed to town. Locals honked and waved as the Hunt rode by, while those just passing through slowed and stared, perplexed at what they saw. By the time the Hunt was almost done the packages in the sleigh alone practically buried Tilly. In addition to those, they'd nearly filled the trailers and several sidecars full of Christmas joy to come. Some of it they paid for out of their own pockets or from funds they raised throughout the year at various rallies. The rest were accepted as donations from those businesses that partnered with the club to spread some cheer to the cheerless. One more stop and they were done their circuit.

Everyone else was revved, but Suzanne only felt weary. No matter how successful the run, she couldn't find the cheer in her own heart. Throughout the day, the sensation of being watched came and went, and each time it did, she felt Lance's absence even more. The irony of missing her self-appointed protector when ultimately that was why they split was not lost on her. Riding on the fringes of the loud and rowdy procession, Suzanne stayed alert, looking for problems, not to mention whoever might be spying on her. Neither one presented itself. When they came to an intersection she rode up the side of the pack and parked herself in front of the on-coming traffic so everyone could get through even if the light turned red. Gavin and his lady did the same in the opposite lane. Occasionally a cager honked, but a glare from the bikers, and even their fellow drivers, shut them up real quick.

At their final stop, McRory's Department Store, they milled a moment in the parking lot while Tilly and the other elves found safe spots for the last few toys so Suzanne took a moment to stretch her legs. Striding over to where Bubba lounged in his sleigh, she dug for a valid reason to excuse herself from the ride. The thought of going back to *Delilah's* to celebrate depressed her even more. Staring at the mounds of toys piled behind him, she didn't have to dig far.

"Hey, Nickie," she said, tongue firmly in her cheek. Very much in a good mood, Bubba chuckled and gave her his full attention. She squirmed, wishing he wasn't watching her so closely.

"I'm gonna head over to St. Frances's and grab the updated list of kids in residence," she continued. His eyes narrowed, but he nodded in acknowledgment.

"Stay vertical," he called after her as she turned and mounted her Shovelhead. She waved to him and the gang as she throttled out of the lot faster than she really should have.

The ride couldn't have been more uneventful. Yet when Suzanne pulled up in front of the orphanage every nerve she had stretched so taut it burned. She swung her leg over the bike to dismount and nearly toppled it. Moving with stiff strides, helmet still on her head, she peered around her like a wolf scenting a trespasser. The space between the lot and the building stretched before her much longer than she remembered. She quickened her step, instinct pushing her to get out of the open.

In the coolness of the main foyer Suzanne stopped and forced herself to breathe. In. Out. Slow and deep. Filling her lungs until her belly pushed against her jeans, then letting it all out until her gut nearly touched her spine. Her head pounded, but her muscles slowly released. Under control, she blew out a quick, heavy breath and turned to the main office.

"Morning, Mrs. Alberti, is Director Lane in?"

The woman behind the front desk looked up. A smile blossomed across her face.

"Suzanne! Hello, how are you, dear?" Mrs. Alberti then frowned, a bit confused. "You're not on the schedule today, are you?"

Suzanne shook her head. "If you could put me on for next week, though, I'm healed up and ready to come back," she answered. A look of relief rippled across the older woman's face; after the attack, Lance had contacted the places where Suzanne volunteered to let them know she'd had an accident. No one had complained, but she knew each of the places where she worked felt the blow of her absence. There were never enough volunteers, and Suzanne had always done her best to ease the burden at the local charities. Though physically healed, she'd been a mess emotionally. In the weeks after her rescue she hadn't been in any condition to face the world. Hell, she found it hard enough now, even without the PTSD!

With a shudder, she pushed those thoughts away. "Director Lane?" she prompted gently.

"I'm afraid she's in a meeting right now, but she should be done in about ten minutes. If you want to visit while you wait, the children are out in the play yard."

"Thanks. I'd like that." Suzanne turned and made her way down the main hallway to the back of the building, where simple, but generally well-maintained playground equipment bristled with energetic children. The sight hit her like a stiletto through the heart as the loss of her dream came home to her hard. As her eyes teared up she almost turned to leave; only she couldn't do that to the children. Instead she gave herself a moment to get it together, focusing on the equipment rather than the kids. Some of the swings looked the slightest bit frayed and a couple of spots of surface rust dotted the monkey bars.

Time to get some of the club over to clean things up, she thought, cataloging half a dozen other projects that needed doing until she had herself under control.

With so many of the Wild Hunt either without family or separated from them, they had unofficially adopted St. Frances's, helping with the upkeep and showering as much love as they could on the kids, short of actually taking them home. Like Suzanne, some of the club members even volunteered time as unpaid staff. Given their lifestyle and, for many of them, lack of status as citizens, official adoption was rarely an option. Besides, how could they decide who deserved to be loved, when, with a little more effort, the Hunt could love them all?

Suzanne stepped out of the shadow of the building and, as one, the children turned, smiles wide and joy lighting their faces. Their cries of greeting drowned out the sounds of the passing traffic and soothed her heartache. Grinning, Suzanne let herself inside the fenced-in play area, bracing herself for the stampede of children, ranging from as young as two, all the way up to seventeen. She made sure each of them received a hug, spending a few extra minutes on Sally, one of the special needs orphans. As she embraced the little girl she also ran her hands along the brace encasing much of Sally's little body, strengthening the mage protections she'd placed there when the little girl first arrived at St. Frances's. When the child placed a kiss on Suzanne's cheek and tugged herself away, Suzanne dropped her arms and straightened while Sally ran back to her friends, her gait slightly less awkward than before. Smiling, Suzanne waved at Helen, one of the teachers and sometimes helper, before the children again dominated her attention. Laughter and questions erupted around her. She soaked it all in, letting it soothe, if only for the moment, the dark places in her soul. A single tear tried to move past her lashes as the little ones clung to her knees, a bittersweet reminder that she had thrown away her chance at a family with Lance. The heartache nearly overwhelmed her once more before she shoved it down with both fists and gave the children the love they hungered for.

Once the hubbub died down she allowed herself to be led to the swings, where she proceeded to push as many little ones at once as she could manage, delighting equally in their squeals and the physical effort required, which left her little attention to spare for paranoia. Even so, the hairs on her neck still prickled.

Finally Suzanne looked up as a motion by the building caught her eye. Director Lane stood by the back door, a contented smile on her face. As Suzanne extracted herself from the benevolent horde, her nerves unexpectedly spiked. Gaze homing in on the far corner of the yard, Suzanne spied several sudden flashes of red; there, then gone. She held it together, but her control nearly slipped as she turned back and noticed one of the staff watching her. A new woman; short with deep, deep red hair and a bold stare. Suzanne didn't care for the vibe coming off of her. Locking down her instinctive snarl, she caught the woman's eye and stared a challenge.

Maybe Suzanne would have gotten in the woman's face; maybe not. Fortunately, her restraint remained untested as Director Lane motioned again with a little more urgency.

"Be good, everyone. I love you," Suzanne said to the children as she got herself under control and went to where Lane waited for her, following her inside for the list she'd come for.

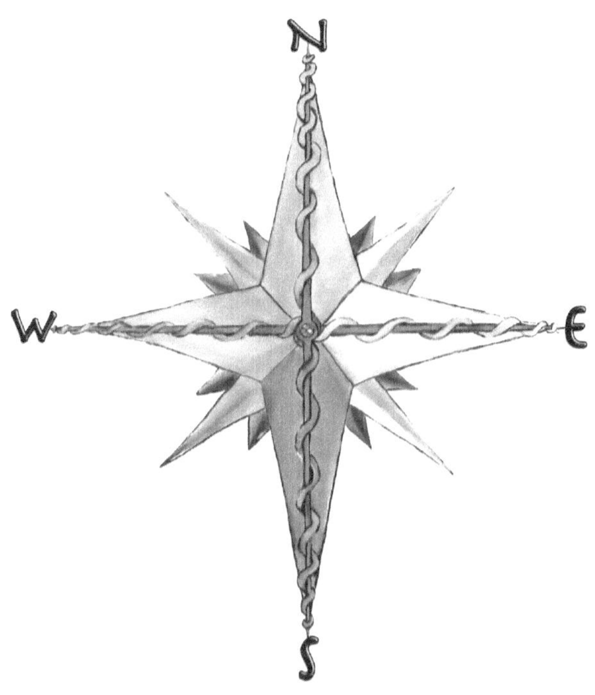

N
W
E
S

Molotov Cupcake

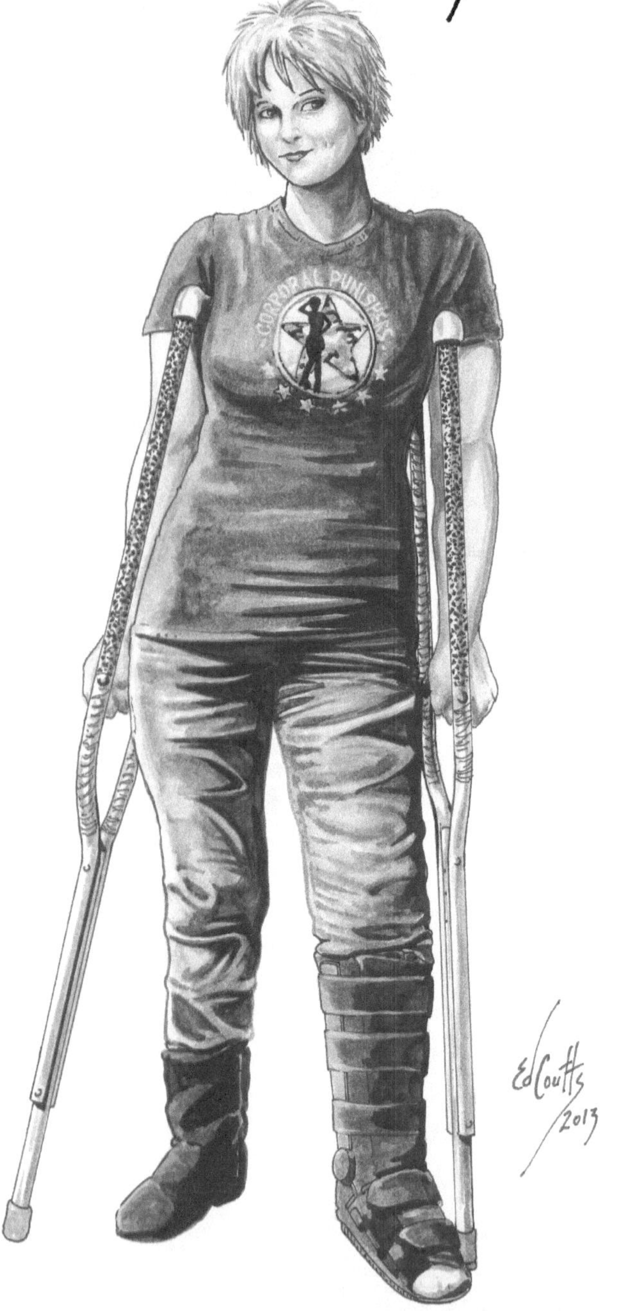

Chapter Five

Saia's bee buzzed. In the middle of a Guardians' Conclave, the blasted bee buzzed and kept on buzzing. Smothering a groan, she pressed her chatelaine and its burden between her calves in attempt to muffle the sound.

The Morrigan glared the length of the table. Someone else tittered. Saia...she blushed and lowered her head, vowing to avenge herself on Jonathan, Jason, and Coyote while she was at it, at her earliest opportunity. Normally, she made specific effort not to draw attention to herself, an effort the men of the Mead Hall gleefully foiled at every opportunity.

Finally, the day's business came to a close and Saia pushed to her feet, causing the sudden swell in the buzzing as her chatelaine swung free. It seemed to have increased in intensity apace with her mortification. Before she could escape, the Morrigan motioned for her to stay. As the seven other guardians left the chamber Saia worried her lip and resisted the urge to rub the area above her eye where tension tightened the muscles.

The Morrigan crossed her arms about her waist and watched Saia with a shuttered gaze. The set of her mouth gave the impression she either smelled something offensive, or tasted bitterness on her tongue. "You have a duty, spoke vows. Remember that in the days to come and do not allow incidentals to distract you," she said after a long pause, her gaze sweeping down to where the buzzing went on.

"My vow is my bond, I will serve as Avalon requires."

The Phantom Queen's lips twisted briefly, before a neutral expression veiled her features. "As do we all." She dropped her gaze, but not before Saia caught a glimmer of pain, deep and startling. The Morrigan looked up again, intent as she spoke. "I am to tell you that within you is the crux of many futures. Choose wisely, when you must, and do not hesitate, or more than one world will see darkness descend."

Before Saia could speak, the Morrigan moved past with hurried, yet dignified strides, leaving confusion in her wake. Not precisely the admonition Saia had expected. She found it difficult to process the relevance of the Morrigan's warning. Bemused, it took a sharp twinge in the finger Jonathan had bled for Saia to realize the buzzing began to fade.

Gathering up her robes she ran from the room and down the broad steps of Avalon's Hall, nearly stumbling as she gained the path to the orchards.

"No! No, please, no!" she gasped, desperate not to have missed her miracle. Jonathan had warned that this might not work, and if it did, nothing guaranteed it would succeed more than once. She could not miss this chance. Every instinct drove her to reckless speed. As she gained the center of the grove she spied the Mead Hall doors once more framed by the gnarled branches. Either her eyes lost their focus, or the doors had begun to fade. Not even slowing, she plowed through the pool at the center of the grove and threw her weight against the age-darkened wood. She stumbled forward and started to fall as the doors slammed shut at her heels, only to find herself caught by furred, well-muscled arms.

"I love it when pretty ladies fall into my lap!" Coyote said to his apprentice, Nuub, with a comical leer. "I love it even more when they're wearing white linen and sopping wet…"

Saia struggled out of his grip and smacked him hard upside the head. "A gentleman would pretend not to notice!" Quickly, she ran her hands over her near-transparent robes, transforming them in an instant to a supple—and completely dry—vest and matching pants in black leather.

"Oooh! Even better!" Coyote's furred ears perked up and his tongue actually lolled out the side of his muzzle. She suspected he played up the cartoon antics on purpose; the only thing missing was the telescoping eyes.

With a quelling look, she extracted herself, only to realize he'd assumed an outfit *nearly* identical to hers. He'd opted for chaps instead and foregone pants all together. A shameless smile completed the ensemble.

Not one to encourage him, Saia swiftly turned away to look for one of the Js. She felt a sudden pinch to her bottom, though she'd walked out of arm's reach. Eyes narrowed, she stalked back and smacked the Trickster again, not so much for his lewd behavior, but for the doggerel she'd unnecessarily chanted on the occasion of her last visit. "And mead is *not* wine!"

Howls of yipping laughter followed her as she hurried to the stairwell leading to the Js' loft. The spiral steps left her dizzy and short of breath after her previous mad dash and trans-dimensional shift. She found herself leaning against the jamb as she knocked politely, if impatiently, on the office door.

It opened straight away, taking her unaware. For the second time in as many minutes, Saia landed in the arms of a man, not quick enough to stand upright.

"Really! This is too much," she grumbled, this time extracting herself from a startled Jason's grip, careful not to meet his delighted and somewhat hopeful gaze. Across the room, Jonathan entered through the door marked FLIGHT DECK. He chuckled as he divested himself of aviator's goggles and a leather bomber jacket, hanging both on a hook by the tinker's bench in the far corner.

"We were afraid you wouldn't make it, m'dear," he said, walking over to place a light kiss on her cheek. She smacked him too.

"Buzzing? Really? And in the middle of a Conclave?!" She glared at him, equal parts frustrated and relieved. "Next time warn me! The Morrigan nearly incinerated me with a glare."

Jonathan gave a little frown and stroked his chin. "I can see where that would be problematic, but we could hardly have known."

Before she could smack him again, he held up his hand and slightly cocked his head in the direction of the hall. Saia turned toward the still-open door and heard the increase in the normal uproar. Above all a familiar voice captured her attention.

"Someone better explain what the hell is going on here before I start break heads."

Tears edged Saia's lashes and a smile overtook her face. Relief bubbled through her. With eager, yet hesitant steps, she hurried through the doorway and out onto the small landing. She caught the guardrail before she tumbled down the stairs as well. Below stood her brother, his expression fierce and his shoulder fins fully expanded until tendrils of rich forest green cracked and snapped the air about him, leaving him in a clear space surrounded by the Hall's normal patrons. She tried to call out to him but joy held her throat too tight. A sound like a sob entwined with a laugh escaped, but nothing more.

Her brother looked up, his thrust jaw like iron and eyes raging beneath his lowered brow. On seeing her, the aggression drained away like warm honey in the noonday sun. His jaw dropped and his eyes moistened. His wings, on the other hand, flared, sending golden sparks up into the high rafters and patrons scrambling back a few more steps. The instant transformation set Saia laughing. Even to her ears the sound held an edge of hysteria. From behind, a bracing hand gripped her shoulder, the fingers thin, but strong, and Saia felt a twinge of heartache for what could not be. Patting Jonathan's hand, she gathered herself and cleared her throat.

"Such manners, Jonraphal..." She smiled her delight. "Is that any way to greet guests?" And then her brother stood beside her, climbing the stairs so swiftly she would have thought he flew, had she not known better. His arms wrapped around her as he muffled his cries in her hair. Her own tears soaked his shirt, but both of them laughed. Neither of them let go as two sets of hands herded them away from the rail and into the office. Saia barely heard the door close as the Js left, giving the two of them a moment of privacy.

"How?" Jon murmured, his breath tickling her ear.

"They don't call this place the Miracle Mead Hall for nothing."

Jon drew back, his brow furrowed. "What?"

"This place…it's trans-dimensional. That means it moves in the between spaces, existing everywhere and nowhere, all at once," she explained the best she could, not knowing precisely how it all worked. "I asked a boon of the proprietors, that they would open a portal to *Delilah's* as they have to Avalon. Here I have not broken my vow…the doors are anchored in their respective places. The Hall itself is both no place and every place. That means I have not left Avalon, and you have not…"

With an impatient shake of his head, Jon cut her off. "I don't care. I don't care in the least." He hugged her tight enough the hasp of the chatelaine crushed against her belly. "I missed you, Tilsaia."

The one-time princess indelicately bawled, her heart bursting as the person she loved more than any other—whose death she had been forced to relive countless times in her visions—held her and spoke her name, which she had not heard in full from another's lips since ascending to Avalon. She allowed herself to savor the closeness only briefly before drawing back, her gaze intent. "We need to talk."

For days, Mongo's and Debbie's words taunted her. *Tough. Aggressive. Bloody.* It always came back to bloody, she realized in horrified fascination. Mostly, she was glad for the distraction. It kept her from dwelling on the mess with Lance. *Get a load of me,* she thought as a jag of pain sliced across her heart. *Mess, like all we need to do is clean things up nice and tidy…*

She sucked in a quavering breath and willfully turned her thoughts back to roller derby. She had only a vague notion of what the sport was about. Her mind kept replaying half-remembered images from Saturday afternoon TV of tough women battling it out on roller skates and pulling crazy-ass stunts more suited to a sideshow. She remembered purpling bruises. Rink rash. Crimson gashes in smooth flesh. Riding a cycle took strength and skill. Barreling around a slick track with eight wheels strapped to your feet, circling at insane speeds with five aggressive women trying to take you out, took more balls than sitting on a rocket recliner ever did. Not that Suzanne hadn't ever eaten asphalt on a bike, but never in the equivalent of a combat situation, and she wore a hell of a lot more armor.

Clearly derby girls had to be a touch crazy to do what they did.

Yet, unexpectedly, something about the prospect drew Suzanne. Whenever she helped out in the bar her attention kept gravitating toward the flyer Cupcake had tacked to the bulletin board. Drifting over to it now, she took a closer look.

Battle of the Babes!
Flat-Track Roller Derby Bout

Dame's Derby Death Squad
versus
The Jerzey Derby Brigade

Saturday Night, 7pm

Inline Dalton
17-40 Rte 43, Dalton

$10 in advance, $15 at the door

Proceeds to benefit St. Frances' Orphanage

Suzanne worried her lip. The more time that passed, the more she obsessed about going. Saturday was three days, away, though. Then she remembered what Mongo's cousin had said. Practices. Every night. A glance at the clock showed it just approached five-thirty. She had plenty of time to get to Dalton. Grabbing her helmet and her keys, Suzanne waved to Joan, who'd just come on shift, and took off, letting the door swing shut behind her hard enough to jangle the bells on the wall.

The scene before her played out like a circus on skates. A well-choreographed circus on skates. Suzanne leaned her arms on the rink wall and watched as the Jerzey Derby Brigade completed warm-up circuits around the practice track. The team wore a hodge-podge of straight up black and in-your-face color—quirky printed tights, fishnets, bold tees, and hot pants—with innuendo-laden skate references emblazoned across their boobs and asses. Suzanne did her best to ignore the abundance of red, the second most prevalent color after black. Otherwise she'd be even more wired than she already was. A bad idea, that. Instead, she focused on the skaters.

They were an odd mix of sexy and scary. Suzanne felt right at home.

"Yo, Suz!" a familiar voice called from her right.

Suzanne turned a stony look in that direction. Time for a talk with Mongo's cousin; only Lance got away with messing with her name. Then Suzanne caught a look at Cupcake hobbling toward her on a set of stripy aluminum crutches and she forgot her annoyance.

"Hey! What happened to you?"

Cupcake scowled in the direction of the track. "Rolled my ankle at practice last night, doc says I may have torn a tendon. No skating for me for at least two months." The look of utter dejection that she wore appeared almost comical, jumbled, as it was, with bald-faced defiance.

She sighed and turned back to Suzanne. "So, whatcha doing here?"

"Just hanging," Suzanne answered, schooling her expression to cool indifference, except her eyes kept drifting toward the rink and the thud and hiss of spinning wheels as the skaters powered around the track, moving counterclockwise. The woman in charge wore a black helmet with a skull and crossbones emblazoned across the front. She barked out an order and the rest gave a sudden hop/spin that landed them in the opposite direction standing on the toes of their skates in a dead stop. They immediately pushed off, now skating clockwise as crazy fast as before.

"Ah! Checking us out..." Cupcake said with a smirk. Before Suzanne could deny it, the woman nodded at her teammates. "Doom's trying to keep them balanced."

Suzanne's brow twisted and she tilted her head in the other woman's direction trying to puzzle out what she meant. Cupcake laughed and let go of the cross arms on her crutches to pat her thighs. "The captain,"—she pointed toward a muscular woman all in black with "Doom Hilda" printed across her back in big, bold letters—"is making the team skate in the opposite direction we normally do so they work both sets of thigh muscles to keep one leg from getting bigger than the other."

As the derby girl continued to explain random bits of detail, Suzanne's focus remained riveted on the practice taking place in front of her. Occasionally, Cupcake yelled out as someone took a particularly spectacular fall, or laughed when they hammed it up or showed off their already darkening bruises. Suzanne joined in, but always paid particular attention each time Doom demonstrated a move or corrected one of the skaters. When her fingers flexed as if she would pull herself over the wall, Cupcake laughed.

"Bet we could hook you up with some skates and gear, you know..." the woman offered.

Suzanne started to decline. "I just came to watch..."

"Oh, come on. You want to...I can tell, so why not?" Cupcake persuaded.

Suzanne did. She really did. That's kind of what scared her. Her gaze followed one skater who'd lost a bit of skin in an earlier fall. Beads of blood dotted the fresh scab where it'd cracked open as she continued to skate. Suzanne swallowed.

"I can't skate like that."

"How do you know, if you don't try?" Cupcake asked, a note of taunting in her voice as her chin tilted up in a dare. "Besides, who says you have to? It's just a bit of fun."

Suzanne chewed her lower lip and remained silent as the team passed in another round of hard skating, blocking, and the occasional stumble.

"Come on, I'll give you some pointers first," Cupcake offered. "The Brigade is short one"—she grimaced and gestured toward her foot—"so it's not like they'll scrimmage or anything. You'll just be trying out some drills, and only what you're up to."

Now if that wasn't a gauntlet tossed down...

Without waiting for an answer, Cupcake got Doom's attention and tilted her head toward Suzanne, mimicking the putting on of a helmet. The captain gave them a considering look, then nodded.

Surprised at her own lack of resistance, Suzanne let herself be herded into the locker room where she excused herself to the restroom. In the privacy of a stall she took the plastic baggy containing the redcap from her jeans pocket and slipped it into her bra. She'd learned the hard way early on not to leave it behind. When she was done, she met Cupcake by a plastic storage tote filled with a jumble of neoprene, Velcro, and molded plastic in various joint-specific configurations.

"We haul this stuff along with us in case someone forgets something or someone's gear falls victim to a mash-up," Cupcake explained as she sorted through the mess, taking out bits and pieces as she went until Suzanne had a pile of knee, elbow, and wrist guards, topped with a bright red practice helmet covered in sarcastic skate stickers. From another, smaller tote she took a plastic package and tossed that at Suzanne as well. Inside was a brand-new mouth guard. "Extras. We're always losing them.

"What size shoe do you wear? Looks like about the same as me..."

"About a seven."

"Perfect! Come on, follow me, and bring the safety gear." In the end Suzanne found herself outfitted in Cupcake's spare practice clothes and skates.

"Not like I'm gonna need them," Cupcake grumbled.

Except for the skates everything fit more than a little snug, but from what Suzanne had seen outside absolutely no one would notice.

When they returned to the rink the team had halted for a break. Cupcake hobbled over to the bench where the skaters sat as they downed bottles of Gatorade and Vitamin Water. Suzanne followed, but hung back once she got there, perching at the empty end of the bench to put on the skates. As she tied them off she paid attention to all the banter and back-and-forth between the women. She couldn't deny this was a tight-knit group, every bit as close as the members of the Wild Hunt. And dedicated... though sweat-dampened and breathing a bit fast, they all looked revved and ready for more. When Cupcake saw her just sitting there she motioned Suzanne over.

"Hey, this is Sandra...Doom Hilda's her derby name, but we usually just call her Doom," Cupcake said with a grin. "Sandra, this is Suzanne, a friend of my cousin's. She's local."

Suzanne nodded in greeting. "Thanks for letting me horn in on your practice."

"No problem, always glad to see more women get interested in Derby."

If she only knew... To Suzanne it felt like a swiftly growing obsession. She didn't know whether to thank Mongo, or punch him for introducing her to his cousin and the sport. Maybe derby would stop distracting her so much once she got a chance to skate. Falling on her ass a few dozen times might take the shine off it.

"So, come on over and meet the brigade," Doom said, clearly emanating 'leader' vibes as she skated off, not even waiting to see if Suzanne would follow. Her first impulse was to resist on principle, but truly she didn't want to start a pissing contest, despite the instinctive response. She gently rolled over to where the woman waited, surrounded by her team. "You already know Debbie, aka. Molotov Cupcake...and over here we have..."

The urge to laugh at the brutal humor nearly overwhelmed Suzanne as Doom started calling out the girls' derby names: *Criss Catastrophe, Assault Shaker, Maggy Kyllanfall, Little Mo Peep*—she tried to keep track of what tags went with which players, but the creativity of the names kept distracting her—*Inna Propriate, River Slam, Voldeloxx, Skank Tank, Raven Rage, CaliforniKate, Beast Witherspoon, Brass Muscles*... No one mentioned given names, which struck a chord with Suzanne, paralleling the club's use of 'legal' names.

When Doom finished Suzanne waved in greeting to all the players and said, "Suzanne...or Fresh Meat, I guess you'd say?" Everyone laughed.

For a few more minutes everyone chatted and retightened their gear, filled up on fluids and talked trash at the few guys there, refs helping out with the practice. It became a little uncomfortable for Suzanne. They all knew one another; things were relaxed and easy among them. They didn't go out of their way to make her feel the interloper, but what did they have to say to her? They picked up conversations interrupted by the introductions while Suzanne stood there and smiled as the comforting camaraderie wove around her.

"Okay, ladies! Break's over. All of you, hit the track!"

The team went into what Doom called suicide drills while Suzanne kept to the sidelines with Cupcake calling out instructions from the bench. The Tomahawk stop seemed tricky at first, but the knee drop left her groaning. Even a fae felt the shock and discomfort of a sharp impact, knee guards aside. As she worked on the moves, her awareness pinged the nerves across her shoulders and up her neck. Someone watched her. Someone other than Cupcake. Suzanne shook her limbs to release the tension, reminding herself there were likely plenty of others sneaking a peek at the newbie, if nothing else to catch her spectacular falls.

She made sure to include a few. Others ambushed her all on their own.

After about fifteen minutes of the basics she itched for something more challenging. The skating came to her easily, thanks to her Fae nature and elemental edge, and she found the rest pretty simple too, once she understood the moves. Frustrated with the baby steps, she kept glancing over her shoulder to where the team practiced blocks. She noted when they used a move she'd just learned and did her best to mimic their smooth execution. From there she attempted some of the things Cupcake couldn't explain through verbal instructions.

"Way to go!" Mongo's cousin actually started clapping so Suzanne couldn't have been doing that badly.

The ruckus caught Doom's attention.

"Hey...Meat!" she called out. "Stop wastin' time and get over here."

Something stirred in Suzanne's blood and she had to tamp it down. Great that they included her, but no way would she let that name stick. She lifted her hand in acknowledgment and skated over to Doom's side, showing off with a Tomahawk stop she stuck hard without even a hint of a wobble. The captain clapped twice slowly with a get-real look on her face, but her eyes glimmered with amusement and respect.

The derby bug bit Suzanne hard as she joined the drills. Doom let her try a little of each position, like it was a test drive or something. Suzanne had the speed and flexibility to be a decent jammer, but when they tried her out as a blocker the adrenaline kicked in and a fierce grin crept across her face. Strength, speed, power... All the things she craved in life in a single, bad-ass position. At one point she stumbled a bit as the sensation of being watched returned. Gradually, the feeling faded until by the end of the practice she relaxed. Feeling calmer than she had all week, Suzanne lost herself in the moves. Her pulse sped up with the thud and hiss of the wheels and she started to feel as confident on the track as she did on the road.

When Doom called an end to practice and motioned them over to the bench, Suzanne noticed a woman standing on the sidelines, arms braced on the wall and a calculating look on her face. Suzanne frowned. Her watcher? Maybe so, maybe no. Either way, something about her put Suzanne back on edge; a hint of the familiar that she couldn't place. Part of her really wanted to educate the woman on why it was a bad idea to stare. She tried to ignore the unexpectedly strong impulse, thinking it bad form to end such a good day by treating her new friends to front row seats at a catfight.

As she plow stopped in front the bench area, Suzanne loosened her borrowed helmet.

"Looks good on you," Doom told her, "why don't you keep it for now. And if you're ever in Jersey we'll see if we can't pencil you in to the roster."

A rough, gravelly voice cut in before Suzanne could respond.

"Stop poaching, 'Hilda...if she's local we need the new blood more than you do."

It was the woman who'd been watching throughout the practice. Suzanne hadn't noticed her come up. If she had she might have been ready for the surge of aggression that clawed its way up her back and tugged across her shoulders. Turning, she looked the intruder up and down. The woman had the build of a granite retaining wall. Solid, innately powerful, but short. Really short. Suzanne had to look down a good five inches to stare her in the eye. Unlike most of the derby girls, the woman wore a long-sleeved tee in stark black, no markings at all, and matching yoga pants, with red-red sneakers on her feet. What stood out the most, though, was her hair. Also red—a deep, violent shade that didn't look like it came from a bottle—it bore an uncomfortable resemblance to the cap tucked against Suzanne's boob.

Then it clicked. The orphanage. This was the worker she'd caught staring when she visited the children. Suzanne's paranoia came out to play as the woman's blunt gaze drilled its way under her skin even more than the assumptions did. Only an iron control kept Suzanne from drawing magic in preparation of defending herself. Instead, she let a sneer take her lips and challenge blaze in her eyes. "Funny, you'd think I'd have a say in where I played, or if I even chose to at all."

"You could always do worse than the Death Squad, but that's up to you," the woman answered in kind, her stance shifting to bring her center of gravity even lower than it already was. "Not like we're looking for prima donnas or anything."

"Hey, Dame...Suzanne, let's take it down a notch," Doom interjected, a nervous expression on her face. "It's all cool here."

Grimacing, Suzanne held up her hands. "Sorry...been a stressful week." Turning to the Brigade captain she smiled, letting warmth seep back into it. "Thanks, that was great. Can't wait to see you guys in action on Saturday." Despite her best efforts, the words came out gruff. She pivoted on her borrowed wheels and skated away without further acknowledging the one called Dame.

Once in the locker room it didn't take Suzanne long to shuck the gear and wipe everything down with antiseptic pads she found in the storage tote. Grateful for the effortless way the team drew her in this afternoon, and feeling the warmth of their acceptance, Suzanne took a moment to trace faint runes of protection on each piece of protective gear in the tote, not even bothering to resist the impulse to protect her new friends. As she turned to the locker where she'd stowed her clothes she came face to face with Dame. Suzanne lost a touch of the warmth softening her expression as the woman spoke.

"We need to talk."

"Excuse me?" It felt good to loom for once, though it pissed Suzanne off that she even needed to.

"Listen...you need to can the alpha-bitch tendencies a minute and hear what I have to say."

Suzanne had to laugh. The sound held a dark edge to it, but it wouldn't be denied. "You failed Persuasive Talking 101, didn't you?"

Dame grimaced, her brow lowering in a thunderous manner. She cursed and visibly reined herself in. "Can't help it any more than you can," she said, biting off each word as her hand darted out and tugged the plastic baggy from Suzanne's shirt. "We're territorial beasties."

Panic tightened Suzanne's chest as she remembered what had happened when she'd tried to set the cap aside. She shuddered and Dame snagged her hand, tucking Suzanne's fingers around the bag, but holding on to the resulting fist. "Let's try this again," she said, clearly making every effort to keep her tone reasonable. "We really do need to talk. Whatever you decide about derby, that's up to you, but this other problem...you need my help."

The edges of Suzanne's vision actually started to take on a reddish hue. That had never happened before. It shocked her to the point where her control slipped. Her shoulder fins started to unfurl, pressing taut against her borrowed shirt as instinct pulled mage energy from the air.

"Is that why you're following me? Because you didn't get a chance to ambush me at St. Frances's?" Suzanne jerked her hand out Dame's grip. "Fuck off and get out of my way, bitch, before I jack you up right here." The uncharacteristic words were out before Suzanne could think them through, and damn if she would take them back. Must have been those alpha-bitch tendencies Dame had mentioned.

The woman's eyes narrowed and her lips thinned. "Your call...but be warned, we're most likely to hurt those we love." With that cryptic comment she turned and left the locker room, her body rigid, as if she held herself tightly reined.

Suzanne stood there a long time with her pulse racing frantically. Instinct ordered her to go after Dame, but she wouldn't do it. Not even if hell came knocking on the door. She could take care of her own problems. She felt calmer already...really.

Forcibly releasing her hold on the magic, she just stood there, battling the aftermath of the sudden flood of aggression.

When the derby girls started drifting in, Suzanne shook herself out of her funk and finished changing, calling goodbye over her shoulder on her way out. As she left the locker room she encountered one of the refs, a tall guy wearing a black-and-white striped jersey with Stud Muffin silk-screened across the shoulders.

"Hey!" he greeted her, an easy, pleasant smile on his face. "Good skating out there, Meat."

"That's D'Eath Lily to you, zebra," she shot back with a touch of lingering heat, the newly coined derby name bubbling up seemingly out of nowhere. She must have looked startled, and rightly so as she hadn't realized it, but her subconscious had been kicking around names since Doom first called her Meat.

Stud Muffin laughed long and hard, slapping her shoulder as she passed. "Good on you!" he said, still chuckling. "See you around."

He looked hopeful and that should have felt good, but Suzanne found herself close to crying. She merely nodded as the heartache she'd temporarily set aside rekindled in her chest, swirling together with the lingering tension left over from her encounter with Dame.

She barely managed a casual wave as she headed out the door.

Lance peered through the doorway of the empty bedroom, a black look on his face and his gut roiling. He couldn't help himself. Though he'd called it quits between them days ago he couldn't stay away. A stubborn, masochistic part of him had to make sure *Suzanne* was okay.

When he'd come in last night she had been tucked in over on the far side of the bed, her rigid back to his pillow. Once he knew she was there, he'd gone to sleep in the spare room. When he woke she'd been gone and he saw no sign of her anywhere in the apartment. He knew she'd been pissed at the way he'd closed her out during the battle, but hadn't she done the same thing to him before that? Bitterness seeped into his soul at the double standard.

The worst of it...? He hadn't even realized what he'd done until she'd called it to his attention. Of course, he had to admit that if he *had* known that closing the link was possible he would have with conscious intent and without remorse to spare her sharing even part of the *Dubh Fae*'s hard, brutal death.

Anyway...as it was, his ignorance made no difference. She would not believe anything he could say in his defense and he'd reached the point where that barely mattered to him. He just couldn't take the bullshit anymore. She screamed distrust, yet she didn't show one bit of faith in him. That had always sat like a splinter in his heart. *Enough.* He couldn't keep giving her all he had and be happy with the scraps she returned.

Silently his soul raged at the lies he told himself.

Needing to focus, he pushed all of that aside. While he stood in the doorway, the early morning twilight slowly brightened the room, highlighting a dark patch on Suzanne's side of the bed. His breath caught sharp as he saw it across the room. Flicking on the light switch he reached the side of the bed in two long strides and snatched up the pillow. Blood. Dried blood, and not just a speck. Looking more closely, he noticed a few streaks on the bedding as well. The sight threw open the tap on his adrenaline. His hands fisted and his heart pumped faster. He searched the room, and then the apartment looking for any sign that this was anything more than a nose bleed or a tumble from the bike. He didn't find any more blood, and what there was on the sheets really didn't amount to a whole lot, but tell that to his *he-man impulses*.

Lance gritted his teeth and, out of habit, glanced down at his arm where the image of Suzanne usually hugged his skin. He flinched at the sight. The inked image remained, but the life had gone out of it. The colors had dulled and the woman depicted hunched in a despairing pose, her expression etched deep with grief. All he had left of his Suzanne was this stark reminder of the pain he'd caused in that final moment before he severed their link. Already, his regret ran deep, but done was done. He had too much respect for both of them to settle for crumbs. Besides, there was nothing left that he could say. Clearly, neither of them trusted the other and without that trust they had nothing to build on.

Lance's jaw tightened and his eyes narrowed. He told himself this was for the best and to let things alone.

He sucked at listening.

Snatching up his cell phone from where he'd forgotten it on the dresser, he flipped it open; no messages. From Suzanne or anyone else. The urge to hit the speed dial almost overwhelmed him. His ears buzzed. Blood continued to mock him from the smooth cotton pillow. Drawing a couple of deep breaths, he pulled on a long-sleeved shirt to hide the tattoo and headed downstairs. Maybe Suzanne had gone to hit Mongo up for breakfast or more likely a cup of coffee. Closing the door of the apartment behind him, Lance headed downstairs... only to find himself somewhere completely unexpected. Someone had planted a bar where the back room used to be. He stopped short a few steps from the bottom of the stairs. Already tense over Suzanne, every muscle bunched tighter at this further sign that *Delilah's* wasn't as secure as they'd thought it was. What he saw made no sense to him. Like the place had been taken over by Rennies or SCAdians. And it wasn't anything as simple as some drapery or false walls. The room he saw bore no resemblance to the one he'd passed through when he'd gone to bed last night. It looked like a movie set for a spoof of the Lord of the Rings overrun by the extras from whatever other movies were shooting on the lot that day.

Lance scanned the room for anyone he knew. There were a few patch holders in the corner tormenting the waitresses. Rock and Blow tossed knives and axes at the butt end of casks lined up along the wall and Dream had bellied up to the bar, but he saw no sign of Jon, Delilah, or Suzanne. As he finished scanning the place a table in the center of the room caught his attention. He blinked, shook his head, and blinked again, before bringing up a hand to rub his eyes. Either someone wanted to mess with him, or he'd somehow stepped through Alice's looking glass. Or maybe he had the wrong Alice...either way, there in the middle of friggin' Midgard sat Tilly and Gort apparently playing poker with two dogs. And a little dragon. In the middle of the table a pile of what looked like cookies stood in for poker chips. Garm sat beside the table, his head lowered to rest on it, soulful eyes never leaving the pile.

No one looked like they grasped that reality had turned on its ear.

Lance left the stairs and cut through the room. His expression must have been warning enough, because not one person among the chaos got in his way.

"What the *hell* is going on here?" he said, looking to Gort as the supposed rational adult there. Startled, the fae looked up, a slight, perplexed frown on his face, as did Tilly, though her frown leaned considerably more toward fierce.

The hound-headed guys also went still and pivoted in their seats to pin their gazes on him. The one shaped kind of like a coyote just grinned and tipped the green plastic visor he wore on his head. The other—looking like someone took a can of hot pink spray paint to a statue of Anubis—just narrowed his long-suffering gaze and ran his eyes up and down the length of Lance before looking away dismissively. The dragon ignored him all together, chortling at his cards and blowing smoke rings without the aid of a cigarette.

Lance bristled and leaned forward. His lips peeled away from his clenched teeth.

"Just a friendly game," Coyote said. "Hand's almost over if you want to be dealt in."

"Gort!" Lance's fist came down on the table, startling the dragon into fumbling his hand, the cards landing face-up. The entire table gave Lance disapproving looks.

"Way to ruin a perfectly good game of poker, he-man!" Tilly said as she tossed her cards on the table and pushed to her feet. Smacking him, she stormed off in the direction of the bar where a hefty man in a bowler attempted to console her.

Lance's frown deepened.

When he turned back to the table the others rose as well and walked away, waving casually at Gort and acting like Lance wasn't even there. Except the dragon. He first flicked a long, pointed tongue across the center of the table until only one cookie remained, and then—after shooting a thin jet of flame in Lance's general direction—scurried away. Garm pounced on the lone surviving cookie, darting under the table with it before Mongo could catch him with the illicit treat.

Gort remained where he sat. He did not give Lance grief as the others had. Instead, he gathered up the cards and put them away, then waved a hand around the table. "Have a seat…there seems to be plenty."

His calm demeanor brought Lance's temper down to a simmer. Worry for Suzanne took over. Clearly, whatever transformed the place wasn't a threat, or Dream—the West Wind and his fiercest warrior—at the very least would be busting heads.

"This doesn't feel like Underhill," Lance said, idly flicking at a crumb the dragon had missed.

"That's because it's not."

Lance grunted. "Mind telling me what it *is*, then?"

Gort just gave him a scathing look and brushed off his High-Court attitude. "Did you need something when you came barreling over here like a bear with a thorn in its paw?"

"What do you expect?" Lance said, leveling a glare of his own. "Don't even think of judging me with all the shit that's been going on."

"Point taken, *A Shoilse*." *Majesty.*

Lance let the sarcastic dig pass. "Have you seen Suzanne?"

"Not since this morning," Gort answered, concern beginning to darken his gaze. "What's wrong?"

"How about Jon?" Lance asked, ignoring the question.

Gort didn't pursue the matter. Turning in his seat, he pointed upward over the bar. "According to Tilly, Jon has been closeted up there since before I arrived."

Lance turned to leave, but Gort reached out and grasped his arm. Lance's gaze snapped down to the druid's hand, then looked up, his eyes rekindling with anger already primed. Slowly he snarled. Kudos to Gort that he didn't even blink.

"I wanted to warn you…there are those Underhill who consider you a rival."

"That's their hang-up. As long as they stay on their side of the Veil we won't have any issues."

"You don't understand," Gort said, tension drawing the muscles of his neck taut. "As long as you exist…*any* of you exist…no one else can truly assume power in the Fae realm."

"What do you mean 'any of us'?" Menace threaded Lance's response.

Despite the tremor that rippled his features, Gort stood firm. "Those of the *Rudha-an* blood: Jon, Tilly, yourself...the three of you are all that is left of the current royal line. As long as you live, the power over the realm can never be claimed." He paused and held Lance's gaze long and hard. "You've crushed Dair na Scath, but his hound is now unleashed. Callan has ever been the greater threat."

Lance drew in sharply, forcing himself to listen to the sense of what Gort said, no matter that the druid still wasn't his favorite person. "Thanks, consider me warned," he said with a slight nod. He wheeled away and headed for the spiral staircase leading up to the room Gort indicated earlier. Before he reached halfway there the door above opened and a woman in black leather walked out, resting a hand on the railing as she searched the crowd below.

Something about her sent a shiver through Lance's gut. Something almost familiar... Before he could figure out what, Gort gasped behind him. Lance twisted to see the druid push up out of his chair quick enough to send it tumbling. His face went pale and his eyes wide and shocky. "Tilsaia!" he cried and Lance had to fight off the swirling tempest of Gort's emotions.

Then the name registered. Tilsaia...Gort had mentioned it before, back when they argued over Tilly's name what seemed like forever ago. Pivoting back, Lance lifted his gaze and stared into the face that echoed Tilly's and Jon's and even his own. Stunned nearly as badly as Gort, Lance lifted his hand, as if he could touch her, despite the distance between them.

The motion drew the woman's...*Tilsaia's* gaze. She appeared a bit shocked herself, but then her eyes focused on him and she really did smile brighter than the sun.

"Oh, good...you're here." His aunt held out her hand to him and a fierce joy flooded his heart. Lance took the stairs three at a time.

The sound of high-speed rolling sang out like a siren song as Suzanne entered the rink. She glanced at her watch and cursed. Just past seven o'clock. The bout had already started. Dropping her cash at the window, she hurried inside, program book clutched in her hand. Before she made it past the foyer, anticipation lit a fire in her blood. From here it looked like the spectator seats were full. The rink area echoed with yells and cheers and Doom's voice cracking orders, punctuated by the occasional squeal of flesh sliding across the track. Suzanne winced, knowing firsthand how much that stung.

As she came around the guard wall looking for somewhere to sit, she caught sight of Cupcake and Skank Tank on the visiting team's bench in their jerseys and jeans, with sneakers on their feet. The rest of the team not skating sat beyond them in their gear. Beyond everyone, she spied River Slam clutching the wall as if ready to slingshot out of there the minute she got a signal. No one noticed Suzanne, all their attention on the rink.

She followed their gazes to where taped-down rope replaced the neoprene pads the Brigade had used to mark out the practice track. Ten ladies zoomed around—mostly—within the boundaries, crouched low, coasting around the corners and pounding hard through the straight-away. All of them either wore arm bands bearing their numbers or had written them on their arms with a Sharpie. Five of the skaters she recognized as members of the Brigade: Little Mo Peep wore the jammer's panty, a helmet cover marked with a big red star on either side, and Criss Catastrophe wore the pivot's white stripe. Voldeloxx, Beast Witherspoon, and Doom herself served as blockers. Suzanne didn't recognize the members of the rival team, Dame's Derby Death Squad. She'd only met Dame.

"Hey," Suzanne called out in greeting to those benched. They waved her in to sit beside them. She settled in on the end then leaned out to look toward Skank. "What are you doing in civvies?"

"I've been banned from the team." She sounded bummed and her expression ran a little long and wistful, but her face glowed. "The nine-month injury," she explained, her hand unconsciously drifting down to her belly.

Suzanne smiled and reached past Cupcake to bump Skank's fist. "Congrats!"

"Thanks." She smiled broadly. "I'm a kill 'im when I get home, but yeah, thanks."

That ended the conversation as everyone's attention riveted back on the bout.

Cupcake started to explain what took place but Suzanne waved her off. Tonight wasn't about figuring things out; it was about losing herself in the high-energy feel of roller derby. Watching and feeling the flow with every sense she had. The exhilarating anarchy you could only have by sticking ten women on skates, telling them to go really fast, and not to let anyone past them. While she gave the track her complete attention part of Suzanne's mind catalogued the bits and pieces she learned the other day, eagerly noting the proper use and execution.

At one point, when the pack of skaters bunched particularly tight and the Death Squad's jammer zipped up the inside of the track, the girls on the bench started chanting: "Doom! Doom! Doom!" until the frenzied crowd picked up the call. Then, with sudden and brutal force, just as the jammer dropped low to take advantage of a seeming hole in the pack, Doom slammed sideways, sending the derby girl stumbling out of bounds. The crowd roared and shouts of "BOOM!" echoed from the rafters.

The girls beside Suzanne shouted loudest of all, laughing and shoving each other in rough camaraderie. She grinned and received a few shoves herself. She tried to relax and go with it, but the day had been one of frustration and nerves. Hell that described the whole week. Even now her shoulders twitched and a shiver ran down her arms. She scanned the rink, the crowds on either side, everywhere, but nothing stood out. Well...except for way too much red. Hats, shirts...slashes of war paint across a hell of a lot of cheek bones. It made sense; both teams had red as one of their team colors. Good thing she was solid now, no longer phobic. That didn't mean she found being surrounded by red on all sides comfortable, but at least she didn't feel a freak-out coming on. Really. Just because about a hundred redcaps could infiltrate the place and not even stand out...

Suzanne shivered again and told herself to stop being paranoid.

She jumped as a whistle blew to signal the end of the jam.

With the action on the track halted she turned to those on the bench. This was the first time they'd really had a chance to talk. She'd checked out their website before coming tonight; they all had such diverse backgrounds. She had a hard time imagining what about derby appealed to all of them. Looking down the line, she asked, "What got you all into derby?"

There was a barrage of answers, some of them serious, others wiseass. Most of them along the lines of great exercise and an even better way to blow off steam.

River Slam quirked her lips in a sassy smirk, "It lets me use my experience as a figure skater but I get to hit people." She leaned over and mock whispered, "They frown at hitting people during figure skating."

Everyone broke out laughing just as Doom rolled over from the track, pulling out her mouth guard and tucking it in the top of her helmet as she reached the wall. "Yeah, well can the hitting for tonight before you spend the whole bout warming that bench."

River grinned unrepentantly.

Doom mock-growled and swung open the player's gate. "Go! Get out there, I need a break," she said, nodding toward the restrooms. "Try to stay out of trouble until after I get back."

The bench cleared out a bit as the rest got up to move around. Suzanne found herself sitting alone next to Skank. The woman wore a wistful expression as she watched the skaters roll by.

"What are you going to miss the most?" Suzanne asked her.

Skank got an endearingly evil look on her face. "The sound they make when they hit the floor," she answered, nodding toward the opposite team.

"But you can still go to the games."

She chuckled. "Yeah, but it's not the same unless you're the one that dropped 'em."

Suzanne laughed at the unabashed aggression glimmering in Skank's eyes. Here was another brawler who would be right at home in the Wild Hunt. They fell silent as the next jam began.

By the end of the bout Suzanne screamed and yelled right along with the crowd, rising to her feet and gripping the wall much in the way River had earlier, wishing she had skates on her feet. The past few hours were the most relaxed she had been since…since before she and Lance split. The match had been close, but the Death Squad pulled it out in the end by a single point. Suzanne watched alone from the bench as the Brigade lined up along the edge of the track and collectively went to one knee. They held out their hands, which the members of the Death Squad smacked as they skated by in a ritual that totally perplexed her.

"Respect," Skank said as she returned from the restroom. "It's kind of like shaking hands to say good game."

Suzanne nodded, a thoughtful look on her face.

"So, we leave in the morning to go home," Skank said after a minute as the Jerzey Derby Brigade cleared the rink and headed for the locker rooms. "But a bunch of us are going to the diner next door if you want to join us."

As the home team took a few more victory laps, waving wildly to their fans in the stands, Suzanne considered. The offer touched her. She couldn't remember the last time she did something as normal as go to have a meal with some girlfriends. Of course, she couldn't really say she *had* any girlfriends, but that was beside the point.

"Sure," she finally answered, "that would be great."

"Cool, I'm gonna go ahead and score us some tables. You wanna go with me, or wait here for the gang?"

"I'll come with," Suzanne answered, but before they had a chance to head out one of the Death Squad's team members skated over, lightly bumping the wall.

"Hey! I thought that was you!"

Suzanne frowned, turning to stare at the woman, not quite recognizing the voice.

The derby girl undid her helmet and pulled it from her head, revealing thick, glossy black hair, mussed up and sweat-soaked, but enough to trigger recognition. Between the hair, the war paint, and her bold features, she looked like an Indian warrior princess.

"Jamie! Oh my god!" Suzanne leaned over the wall to hug Gavin's old girlfriend, one of the rare ones she had really liked. She relaxed, happy to see the woman. It had been a few years since Jamie had been to *Delilah's* but she hadn't changed much, once the gear didn't obscure the view. "I didn't know you were into derby…"

Jamie laughed. "Well…you know…I had some time to fill. *Et voila!* Bod Hopper was born," she said and with a flourish, gave a surprising leap straight up in the air, tucking her knees up tight—easily clearing the height of a fallen skater or two. Suzanne found herself most impressed with the way Jamie stuck her balance when her wheels reconnected with the rink.

"What are you doing here?" Jamie asked.

"Mongo's cousin is a member of the Brigade. She got me curious."

"Cool…hey, why don't you come over and meet the Squad?"

Suzanne didn't particularly care to deal with Dame, but that was something she better get over fast because after the rush of tonight's bout she didn't think she could stay away from derby, and she didn't know another team in the area. Pursing her lips, she glanced at Skank, who still stood there quietly waiting.

"No problem. Catch up with us when you're done."

Smiling her thanks, Suzanne nodded then followed Jamie out onto the rink.

The whole team watched them approach, while around them the bleachers emptied and maintenance started dimming the lights. The effect made Suzanne feel like she stood in a spotlight. Her nerves bunched up, tingling and itching as if every eye in the world locked on her. But then, that was a familiar sensation lately, whether there were people around or not. Suzanne shook it off and wedged a smile on her face, trying not to give the impression she braced for a fight.

"Hey," Jamie called out to her team mates as they drew near, "this is my friend, Suzanne."

The easy way she said it brought out an instant, more relaxed grin on Suzanne's face as she nodded at the women being introduced—again, derby names only, something she had noted with the Jerzey Derby Brigade as well. As if what these women were here was their heart and soul, and what they showed the rest of the world was just a social mask. While the names rang out she noticed a decided theme, which shouldn't have surprised her given the team was the Derby Death Squad. Dame O'Destruction, whom she had already encountered, was the captain. The rest returned Suzanne's nod as their names were called: Bruishilda Bonebrake, Unda Taker, and Meecha Maker, had all played blocker that night, as had Halla on Wheels. Surprisingly, hers was another familiar face, one that had always come across as quiet and unassuming. Suzanne knew her from the orphanage, where they called her Helen. She taught the kids arts and crafts once a week and served as an aide. The rest of the team kind of blurred together: Valhal E. Girl, Luv Tap, Chicka Die and Chicka Boom—a set of rough-and-tumble, heavy metal book ends—Brit SchitHaus, Fluff n'Knuckler, and lastly, Bouncing Betty Bammer, looking like a pin-up girl with punch. The explosion on the side of her helmet confused Suzanne until she got the WWII reference. She laughed and gave the woman a thumb's up.

With the exception of Dame, Suzanne immediately felt comfortable with everyone, and even with her there seemed to be more of a stand-down than a showdown. Not wanting to let go of the camaraderie but needing to get next door, Suzanne exchanged her information with Jamie and gave a loose promise to check out their next practice.

"You better," Jamie said in a mock-fierce growl as she and the rest of the team skated toward their locker room. "Val's moving the end of the month. We have a slot to fill in the roster."

"I'll be there," Suzanne said, grinning as she turned and headed for the back exit, closest to the diner. Only five minutes had passed since Skank left, she might be able to catch up to her.

Suzanne moved beyond the rink area, to the dimly lit hallway. The shadows pressed in on her. So did the feeling of being watched. Suzanne slid her hand into the pocket where she kept her butterfly knife. She didn't draw it, but her fingers worried the casing as she braced herself for trouble. On the edges of her awareness she heard mutters and whispers that may or may not have been an auditory flashback. Not taking the chance, she lengthened her stride, strong-arming the bar on the door to the parking lot, where she would have more room to defend herself, if it came to that.

More likely she'd look like an idiot barreling into some poor fan just heading for their car. Her hindbrain had control, though, and it screamed 'defend!' As she powered out the door her hand instinctively drew the knife and flipped it open in a single, smooth arc. At the same time she drew just enough magic to set her shoulder fins tingling.

She stared out over a near-empty lot, glistening and damp with rain. To her left stood a series of dumpsters; to the right a bit of wall supporting an overhang that sheltered the entrance. Fifty feet away to the right glowed the diner lights, intensifying the darkness in her sheltered spot. From the front of the building she heard the faint rumble of traffic and laughter as the crowd left. She slowly pivoted, searching for the source of the menace that deepened the shadows and seemed to steal the oxygen from the air. By the dumpsters she spied a dark, wet streak against the rusted, white metal. She stepped closer despite instinct screaming at her to leave. To be safe and far from where she was. As she neared the bins the whispers at the back of her mind grew louder, more chaotic. Vicious and hungry. At a whiff of fresh blood her belly both rumbled and turned. Eyes watched her from the shadows. She could not see them, but for a faint red glimmer, yet the weight of their gaze challenged her.

The night went still. The sound of the cars faded. No more laughter drifted on the air. In the silence, Suzanne's ears picked up a low, desperate groan, harsh and edged with rage. She stalked forward and, with strength no mortal could bring to bear, shoved the dumpster away from the building, toward the lot.

A half-dozen redcaps watched her slyly from the sheltered corner. Gazes canny and considering, the fae also poised to strike; between them, backed into the corner, crouched Skank, with her body positioned to protect her belly and a broken two-by-four clutched in her hands like a bat. Blood ran down the side of her head and bruises marred her face. Across the ground her gear lay scattered in the muck such places bred. She'd clearly put up an impressive fight to hold off so many.

Madness darted around the edges of her expression as she turned glazing eyes toward Suzanne, whose presence didn't seem to register. Skank screamed at the redcaps around her, swinging wildly, though none of the evil fae moved closer. "Give it a try, fuckers! Give it another try…I will fucking kill you!"

The redcaps chuckled, a dry, ominous sound, and turned to the skater. They tensed and crouched, as if to leap at her.

Suzanne barked out a "No!" that would have made a marine snap to.

And the redcaps stopped. They grumbled and glared and clawed at one another in frustration...but they stopped, if only for a moment, then Suzanne trembled, her body suddenly battling impulses to both protect her friend and see her blood spilt. Something clattered to the pavement and only vaguely did she realize she now clutched an object both soft and moist in her other hand. The hunger spiked and Suzanne gritted her teeth, resisting. It took all of her focus, freeing up the redcaps, who crept forward once more, teasing and taunting their prey.

Suddenly, the door behind Suzanne crashed open spilling derby girls from both teams into the lot. Even Cupcake came to the rescue, hobbling on one crutch while raising the other like a club. In the forefront stood Dame, brandishing a crowbar, and beside her, Doom, armed with a length of pipe. The rest had grabbed whatever else came to hand that looked capable of dealing pain. They stalked forward, ferocious, lethal.

"Put that away before someone else gets hurt," Dame snarled as she came even with Suzanne, a free hand locking on her arm, snatching back the hand that clutched the cloth. Suzanne looked down, a fog licking at her thoughts, doing its best to obscure reason. Horror burned through Suzanne's fog as she realized she'd drawn out her trophy cap. Not just pulled the baggy from her pocket, but actually removed the cap from the plastic without even realizing it. The implications left her paralyzed long enough for Dame to growl menacingly and shake her.

Suzanne brought her head up with a jerk. Setting her jaw tight against the urge to snap at the woman helping her, she blinked away the last of her confusion and shoved the cap back in her pocket. Dame's eyes narrowed in assessment, then she nodded sharply and let go to stalk within striking distance of the 'caps. The derby girls moved with her in a well-spaced pack, each girl leaving no gaps for the attackers to escape, but plenty of room for her sisters to swing. Before they could rain retribution, the redcaps straightened and screeched, hissing at the derby girls and grinning suggestively at Suzanne. As one they seemed to fold the shadows around them and, with a sideways step, disappeared. In the split instant in between, Dame threw the crowbar like a hook, snagging the cap off one of the powrie. Both he and his cap disintegrated with a shriek as if she'd torched him. The sound deafened the derby girls; it sent Suzanne to her knees, one hand clutching her head, the other wrapped around her gut. Bile surged up her throat and she heaved, adding an acrid stench to the slime already coating the ground.

"We will have that talk," Dame snarled as she and the rest rushed to Skank's side.

Doom, however, stalked toward Suzanne, muscles standing out everywhere, her expression ominous. "What the *hell* was that? What just happened?"

How to explain? Suzanne couldn't, not without opening the derby girls to the threat of more danger from the fae. Instead, she drew subtle threads of magic from the air, wove them into a memory near identical to what transpired, if more mundane, then with a gentle breath blew it across the minds of everyone there. Most of them shook their heads sharply, as if clearing water from their ears, before they hurried over to help Skank, muttering about the thugs they'd run off. Not so for Dame...or Halla. There was something 'other' about each of them, but other *what* Suzanne couldn't say. Neither woman said a word. They just turned and joined the pack, Dame muscling in close while Halla bent and gathered Skank's gear.

Shaken, Suzanne watched a moment, not knowing what to do, her help seemingly not needed or wanted. She released a shuddering breath and went away before she brought more harm down on these women she found she really liked.

Suzanne wandered aimlessly a while, frightened and not a little shocky. She ended up on the other side of town, down by the lake, where a pseudo village of retro trendy shops stayed open late, looking cheerful draped in their twinkle lights, with old-fashioned gas lamps lending ambiance to the spaces in between. Parking her bike near the soda shop, she pocketed the key and started walking, keeping to the well-lit path along the picturesque lakefront, very glad of the many people out enjoying the crisp autumn night.

Suzanne definitely couldn't say she enjoyed it. She barely noticed. Doom's question kept swiping at her. It reached out from the depths of her mind, surrounded by the surreal horror of Skank's attack. The sequence of events was quite simple to explain, but what *happened*... infinitely harder. Her pulse kicked into a frantic pace while a chill sank deep into her bones. Bad enough to see Skank and her unborn child at risk, but infinitely worse to have the insidious cap stir such unnatural impulses in Suzanne, impulses that could have meant harm to one of her new friends, or other innocents. Her chest locked tight at the thought.

She stopped beside the path and exhaled hard, then forced herself to fill her lungs slowly, calming her heartbeat and stilling her frantic mind. When she opened her eyes she jumped and nearly screamed. Dame stood before her, one hand in her pocket, the other holding out Suzanne's closed butterfly knife.

They stood there, not quite face to face, the difference in their heights leaving Suzanne staring at that ridiculous, yet disturbing hat. A faint shudder traveled through her.

"Mine's just for show."

Suzanne blinked, then scowled. "What?"

"The hat...just for show," Dame repeated with a brief waggle of her head, though her eyes were dead serious. "Unlike the genuine article you keep hidden in your pocket. The plastic baggy was a nice idea, by the way, but as you saw, not all that effective."

After the stress of the night and the hours Suzanne had had to work herself up since then, Dame's attitude propelled her past her point of control. She thrust out her jaw and got down into the woman's face. "What the hell are you and where do you get off shoving in to my business?" Suzanne's intense aggression rattled her more than it did its intended target. Dame didn't even blink. Instead she reached out and ran the bare edge of her pinky across a fresh scab on the back of Suzanne's hand.

"This will stave it off a while, but not forever."

"What the hell are you talking about?" Suzanne snarled. "And while you're at it, keep your fucking hands off me." It took every bit of her self-control to not to get into it right there. Something about this woman really set her off.

"Not that I can't believe you already had that temper," Dame said, her tone at once both concerned and reproving, "but how long has it been getting worse?" She moved a little closer, staring intently into Suzanne's eyes as if the answer were hidden there.

Suzanne screamed in her face and threw a punch before she even realized she intended to. Just as quickly she found herself on her knees, her fist caught in Dame's hand. Around them, people gasped and hurried on, some of the men looking like they'd intervene, if it weren't for their women tugging on their arms. Suzanne barely noticed. Dame demanded her attention. The woman's expression didn't change, nor did her stance. She radiated calm until Suzanne realized she'd been shaking only by the fact that the tremors began to fade the longer she was in contact with Dame's skin. Suzanne stopped and breathed, focusing on nothing but the act of slowly inhaling and exhaling, her gaze locked on the multitude of wire-thin scars lacing the woman's skin.

When her blood no longer felt on fire and her muscles went as lax as soft-set pudding, Suzanne looked up and met understanding eyes the color of jet, reflecting a faint glimmer of red. Her teeth snapped shut at the sight and she tasted the tang of fresh blood before memory reared up and smacked her down again. Redcap…Dame had the eyes of a redcap.

Not possible. It wasn't just the vagaries of legend, redcaps were *all* male.

"How?" Suzanne asked in the barest of whispers.

The woman frowned and released Suzanne's fist only to grab her elbow and help her rise. Suzanne closed her eyes against a wave of dizziness or she would have jerked away. When she steadied, Dame motioned that they should keep walking.

A while passed before she spoke. "Murder's not the only means of spilling blood," Dame finally answered, not bothering to hide her frisson of pain. "Though likely that was how things were meant to come out in the end. Someone happened by before he got that far and the woman who bore me came out of it with a big belly instead of an early grave."

For the second time that night, bile surged from Suzanne's gut to burn the back of her throat. "Your mother…"

Dame shook her head sharply. "Not mother…incubator be more accurate." Her manner of speech shifted from neutral to some slight, old-world cadence Suzanne could not place. "Not her fault the trauma of rape at the hands of a monster twisted her brain, but I can hardly call the woman mother when she tossed me to the cobbles and me not ten minutes old. The hedge wife took me in, raised me up. The other washed up dead on the bank afore the dawn broke over Derry."

"How old are you?" Suzanne had to ask, though it was the height of rude, even for the Fae.

The halfcap laughed, if a bit caustically. "Older than I ought to be, and younger than you think. The first I fed was on my own blood, which sealed my fate. I imagine things might have rolled up different if I'd a taste of mother's milk instead. The mam what raised me really did have the patience of a saint, not to mention the strap of a Catholic nun."

"I didn't know such a thing was possible."

"No, you can get them anywhere, really…they don't just give them to nuns." Dame said, her gaze artfully innocent.

Suzanne wanted to punch her.

"You know what I mean."

Dame shrugged. "I've seen a man or two changed when they somehow came by a cap, but I can't say as I've run into another like me aside from you, and even that's not altogether the same."

Suzanne grimaced. "No, not hardly."

Silence reigned for a moment, heavy and uncomfortable. Turning, Suzanne stared out on the lake.

"What's happening to me?" she asked low enough she barely heard herself as she drew the cap from her pocket.

"Did you think the twisted man you took that from was the powrie?" Dame asked. "That bugger was as much victim as you were. The cap is the beasty, glomming on to whatever poor soul comes to hand and warping it until you have what everyone thinks is the creature of legend, instead of just a piece of it. You're the replacement. An you let it graft to you, that thing'll shape you until it feels right at home. That happens, and you'll be damned forever."

All warmth bled out of Suzanne and she swayed where she stood. "Me?"

Dame nodded, some of the red glow leaching from her eyes as sympathy darkened them. "It's already got a piece of you without you hardly realizing. You have to fight it if you intend to keep from tumbling all the way."

"How do I get rid of it?"

"You don't. Least not that I know how. You deal with it. You resist for every day of your life until you can't resist anymore."

"What happens then?"

"You fall...or you die."

Stunned, Suzanne barely noticed as Dame briefly gripped her shoulder, promised her help if she wanted it, then walked away.

Lance

Chapter Six

"I don't believe you."

"Lance…" started the woman…*Saia*. His aunt.

Lance cut her off, his jaw bunching as a snarl twisted his lips. His fists pounded the thick plank table as he pushed to his feet. "I said I don't believe you."

He paced the bizarre room above the equally strange bar, his fists clenching and unclenching. When he found himself in front of delicate glass and other potentially breakable materials he wheeled around before he ended up trashing someone else's toys. Breathing heavily, he pinned his newly discovered aunt with a furious look before flickering his gaze to Jon, who sat beside her, and addressing him.

"I know her, *know* her, as deep as here," he said, thumping his chest. "Suzanne could never do what *she* says she will."

Jon stood, his stance loose, but ready, as if he might need to defend his sister.

"Do you?" Jon asked, his own gaze plagued with doubt. "Lance, she's Callan's daughter. *Callan*, who has already tried to kill you."

"So…does that mean you think I'm going to go bat-shit crazy and try to take over the world because my grandfather went insane and usurped the throne Underhill?" Lance dared Jon to refute the comparison.

Saia rose beside her brother and laid a gentle hand on his tensing arm.

"Lance, Fleur is conditioned to obey her father."

At the sound of that name and all that the conversation implied Lance nearly lost it. He snapped the tension from his neck in lieu of anything more satisfying, the rapid-fire cracking causing Saia to flinch. He then spoke through clenched teeth, his eyes still on Jon. "And why is it we didn't know that before now?"

Jon twitched uncomfortably. "I left Court a long time before Saia ever did. I never knew Callan or his daughter."

"So...what you are asking me to believe is that the woman I love and have been devoted to for over twenty years is someone completely different and capable of homicidal butchery. And you want me to believe this because a woman I don't know saw it in a puddle of water?"

Before Jon or Saia could respond to Lance's hostile question, the sound of a clearing throat came from by the door. Gort stood there, his gaze flickering from Lance to Saia and back again.

"Saia speaks the truth of Callan and his daughter," he said in soft, hesitant words. His eyes lowered a moment, briefly hiding their regret. "As for Avalon's Oracle Pool it is legendary for revealing only true visions."

Lance had trouble getting his breath as what Gort said sank in. Gort, whom he'd come to respect, if not like. Gort who had lived and served at the High King's Court for God knew how long right up until mere weeks ago. Doubt clawed a foothold in Lance's soul. "And why didn't *you* tell me?"

Gort shrugged, an almost Gallic gesture. "I had no idea you were unaware."

Neither did Lance, and that hurt worse than anything he had ever experienced. Here he railed at his family in defense of a woman who had never really shared herself even as much as he'd thought she had. Not even her true name. And yet he still loved her. The beast tearing at his heart wanted to destroy more than a few glass beakers.

"What's the plan?" he asked in a dead voice.

"The visions are true visions," Saia said, "but they are not immutable. We've sent Coyote and Nuub to wait in your *Delilah's*. They will bring Fleur here to us so we can begin to divert the events that I have seen."

"The dogmen?" he asked, a bit incredulous, remembering the scene downstairs around the poker table.

"Bounty hunters," Saia answered.

Lance grunted with disgust and turned away, headed for the bar downstairs to see if this Miracle Mead could work the miracle of making him forget.

Suzanne couldn't help herself. Despite the state of things between her and Lance she gravitated toward *Delilah's*. It was home, and had been for a very long time. Without *Delilah's* she had nowhere to belong, in the mortal realm or Underhill. Besides, she needed Lance. What happened tonight...what she'd learned...terrified her and no one had her back like he did, whether she wanted it or not. She tried the door and found it locked, though closing time was twenty minutes off. Perplexed, she drew out her key—still worn on a lanyard around her neck—and let herself in.

Whoever worked closing had started putting the place up, but hadn't quite finished. They'd dropped the lights to after-hours low and turned the sconces along the walls off for the night, but the bar area remained lit up and only half the tables bristled with overturned chair legs pointed skyward.

Oddly enough, Kelly still manned her post at the counter and a stranger anchored the far end. Yet the door had been locked. When Suzanne tried to get a good look at the guy her vision blurred, then, with what she could only describe as a peculiar itch across her eyes, returned to normal. She frowned as she considered him. He sat upright and proper, elegant in a white silk shirt and matching pants just the perfect shade to complement his blue-black skin. Narrow, neat, cornrows hugged his head and draped down to just past his shoulders, giving the impression of a cowl. She expected to find an Armani blazer and a fedora lying somewhere nearby.

In other words, he looked distinctly out of place.

Suzanne frowned, her gaze never leaving him, as she walked up to the bar and got Kelly's attention.

"Where is everyone?"

"We seem to have sprouted another bar..."

The odd fellow at the end of the counter curled his lip and lifted his chin with an air of offended sensibilities even more out of place at *Delilah's* than he was.

"And they brought their own wenchresses," Kelly said with a wry twist to her lips, ignoring the jackass's reaction. "Everyone decided to barhop for a change."

What could only be described as a sound between a bark and a guffaw jarred across the unnatural quiet. Suzanne jumped. Her head snapped around to find another man peering at them from beyond the stiff-necked fellow. Again, that peculiar itch. Suzanne blinked, trying to dispel it so she could get a better look at what she instinctively thought of as Trouble. He wore a grin just this side of crude, with a touch of mischief threaded through.

How the hell hadn't she noticed him until now? Again, a stranger, but one in faded jeans and a well-worn leather jacket over a Harley tee. He looked altogether more at home where he sat.

"Ooh...say that in front of the Maidens...please!" He said in a voice that was a strange blending of gruff, gravelly, and melodious all at once. For some reason that and his narrow face and broad, toothy grin put Suzanne in mind of a ride she'd been on out in Arizona years back, roaring across the desert on a moonlit night to a serenade of coyotes.

His friend smirked and turned cold, bottomless eye on them. "Yes...please do. And it's a Mead Hall, not a bar." Again, his lip curled.

Suzanne treated the Citizen to a scathing glance of her own, learned at Father's knee. Cold, hooded eyes slowly took him in as the barest edge of her lip lifted infinitesimally on one side. She let it linger a moment before unhurriedly bringing her attention back to Kelly.

"What's going on here?" she demanded, unconsciously still channeling her father.

Kelly returned her look and raised a warning brow at her tone but merely shrugged and answered. "Don't know, but Jon said everything was cool."

Not much of an explanation, but what could Suzanne expect after pissing the woman off? She gave Kelly an apologetic smile. "Where can I find him?"

Without a further word, the bartender nodded toward the back room.

"Lance in there to?"

Again, Kelly just nodded, then went back to her closing routine of wiping down the counter and drawing the riot gate down over the liquor shelves. "Bar's closed, gentlemen. I'm going home." Her tone bore no argument.

Suzanne waited for them to rise, anxious to have them leave so she could go find Lance, only they did not head for the front door. The two of them unfolded lean, muscular bodies from their respective stools and turned toward the back room. As they reached the door, the one without a stick up his butt paused and looked back at her. For an instant Suzanne's vision again blurred and the itch crawled across her eyes briefly before things cleared. She cursed and shook her head, more than fed up with her body doing things she couldn't explain. From that moment an impression floated in her mind of a muzzled face too fine to be called wolfish wearing a grin for which that description was most definitely apt. A pair of upright pointed ears crowned the effect, and all of it topped a lean, cut body decidedly naked but for some well-placed fur that absolutely served no one's modesty.

Gasping, Suzanne shook her head more vigorously to try and clear the image. Her eyes flew open to the sight of the guy still paused by the door, his grin definitely wolfish, but everything else at odds with the image yet tormenting her brain. She would swear that in the brief instant it took her eyelids to rise she had seen the plume of a feathery tail wag from the ass of his jeans.

He cleared his throat, the grin growing impossibly wider. Suzanne jumped for the second time that night. She jerked her eyes upward and gritted her teeth as she felt her cheeks go uncharacteristically flush. Nothing about this night in any way resembled sense and it pissed her off.

"Might we escort you to the next fine establishment? You won't find anything like it anywhere…I promise." he asked. His tone and half bow were distinctly at odds with the rest of the impression he gave as he swept his arm forward to the door. Somehow, despite his pleasantness, his question did not come across as a request.

Suzanne didn't know what 'we' he was talking about. His friend hadn't bothered to wait. Her gaze trailed past the guy still patiently standing there.

Her jaw dropped so quickly it popped.

The back room no longer held the back room. Unable to speak, she stepped toward the inexplicable sight before her, walking as if in a dream. As she passed the stranger he chuckled deep from his belly, the sound abruptly changing to a high yip that again reminded her of the desert. She turned on him, glaring, her heart racing more than she wanted to admit.

The guy wore innocence as well as he wore nothing at all. "Welcome to J&J's Miracle Mead Hall," he said. "*Our* home base of choice."

Another smile graced his lips and his teeth gleamed white.

"Nice to finally meet you, Suzanne," he said as he slipped her arm through his and drew her into what she could only suppose was the Mead Hall. She found herself too stunned to react or respond, though mental alarms jangled at his use of her name. "I'm Coyote, and my friend there, he's called Nuub. Let's go, you can ogle me more in there."

In shock, Suzanne didn't even resist. Or snatch him bald for the comment. As she passed the threshold, the one called Nuub pivoted and actually seemed to sniff her, the look on his face giving her the impression the assessment had not been favorable.

"I am a jack*al*, not a jack*ass*," he informed her, drawing back in distaste, "and you smell of spilt blood and dark deeds. I should have liked you, but for that."

It was like being slapped by a stranger. Suzanne paled, then showed him her teeth, snapping them a fraction of an inch from his long, pointed nose. Where did he get off judging her?

"You should see him at parties."

Confused, she looked to Coyote.

She shook her head at the completely irreverent comment and walked deeper into the room, leaving the wiseass behind. Her shoulders tensed as the two of them fell in behind. Glancing around, she searched for Jon, finding him at a small, round table off to the side of the room. He sat there with a woman decked out in black leather. Suzanne felt she should recognize her. Something about the eyes…the slight smile, but her mind refused to make the connection.

Someone made a noise. Maybe her, or maybe someone else, but in either case those at the table turned their gazes in her direction. Jon twisted in his seat, something in his expression both wary and pained. The woman pushed to her feet and stepped out into the open. The smile faded and her eyes hardened.

"Fleur…I hardly recognized you."

Suzanne couldn't breathe.

"Yeah, *Fleur*…me either."

Suzanne spun around and the room kept on spinning. Anguish tore at her heart on seeing the look Lance gave her. Darkness closed in, sending her to the floor.

Suzanne woke up in an unfamiliar bed, soft and deep, with an ornate headboard that looked like something out of a movie. From the other room she heard the muted sound of talking and someone moving about. Slowly, she opened her eyes. She could not see her surroundings for the shadows. The only light in the room streamed in from the half-open door. Lance sat in one of the chairs from the mead hall, his booted foot braced on the edge of the mattress. The light slashed across only a portion of his face. Suzanne wished she hadn't seen even that much. Sullen and brooding worked hard to describe his expression and still failed miserably. Defeated came closer. She lay there in the shadow, unmoving as she watched him, sorrow clawing at her. Likely that was what gave her away.

"You should have told me," Lance said in a low rumble.

Before she could agree, someone moved into the doorway, blocking the light.

"What, so you could judge her based on her kin too?" Gavin asked, anger threaded through his words. "I would think you were the last person justified to do that."

Suzanne had missed something. Something important. She saw a glimmer of it in the raw rage twisting Lance's features. An acid wash of negative emotions swirled around the room, pushing all of them closer to the edge. He dropped his foot and stood, menace in every line of his body.

"*You* should have told me, too. We can have that conversation if you want, but right now I'm talking to *Fleur*."

"No! Don't you dare use that name," Suzanne cut in. "If you ever cared anything about me you'll forget you ever heard it." Maybe not the best thing to say, given the circumstances.

She took a breath and tried to filter the aggression out of her voice.

"I didn't tell you because it shouldn't have mattered who my father was. It had nothing to do with this life, and I thought it never would. *Callan* has no claim on me, nor any interest, even. I left anything to do with that life behind for good, save one." She looked at Gavin before going on. "Neither one of us had any intention of deceit. We didn't even know he was involved before he walked through the blasted gate."

"And after?"

She glared at Lance, royally pissed off with the distrust in his voice. No longer caring to keep things civil she vented her frustration. "Hmm... let me see, when would I tell you? When you shut me out after the battle and stormed off?" She cocked her head as if considering it. "No...maybe not. After you came back, when you were fucking me? I can't imagine why it didn't occur to me. Of course, I could have waited until after, but I was a little busy being dumped!"

By the time her tirade ended the sound of her yelling echoed from the walls. Slowly she realized she knelt on the bed with both hands fisted so tight that blood trickled from beneath her fingers. Lance and Gavin stood in stunned silence.

A sob slipped free and Suzanne pounded her fists on her thighs in frustration.

"I came to you for help," she cried, her voice cracking. "I came because I need you and I want to make things right."

Disgusted with both them and herself, she scrambled from the bed. As she stormed out of the room Lance finally spoke.

"Would you have told me?"

Suzanne stopped and looked over her shoulder. "If I didn't have to? No."

In the room beyond she stopped abruptly. The woman from earlier sat there on some kind of fancy couch, and beside her sat Jon. Behind them—between Suzanne and the door—stood the guys who'd shown up at the bar. She flinched as her eyes itched much more intensely than before until suddenly she saw the men as the avatars they were: truly Coyote, and what...*looked* like Anubis. Though the latter caused her to frown and squint, confused not only by the neon pink of his fur, but what she suspected was a tiny satin bow perched atop his head.

Then he growled and bared a multitude of sharp, pointed teeth.

"*Coyote...*"

The next instant the jackal was resplendent in elegant black from his fur to his tux and right down to his burnished claws.

Suzanne stumbled backward for the first time wondering if she was in fact going mad.

"What is this?" she asked. The words came out stilted. Distant.

"An intervention," the wiseass hound answered.

"Coyote!" Saia chided him, a glimmer of anger in her gaze as she looked over her shoulder. "And yet, aptly put. Are you familiar with Avalon's Oracle Pool, Fleur?"

Suzanne straightened, her expression hardening. "If you insist on using that name, this conversation is over."

"Suzanne," Gavin said from behind her. "Knock it off and listen so we can clear this up."

She turned to glare at him over her shoulder. "Clear what up? I've done nothing but try and claim my life for myself. What else is there precisely to clear up?"

Her answer came from the woman on the couch. "I am Tilsaia, sister to Jonraphal and one of the guardians of the Blessed Isle of Avalon. I am here because the Oracle Pool gave me a vision of you."

Suzanne frowned. "But the guardians never leave the shores of Avalon."

"My superior instructed me to choose wisely and not to hesitate," Tilsaia answered, her voice soft and a touch grim. "I believe that I have done as instructed. By remaining in the Mead Hall, which is not seated in time nor space, I am confident

I have kept true to my vows, but should I be wrong, I will face the consequences gladly if it means that I may intervene to prevent the horror of that vision."

"It doesn't work that way..." Suzanne murmured half to herself, before Tilsaia's implications diverted her thoughts. The blood drained from her face at the vehemence of the woman's words, paired with the flicker of what could become cold hatred in her gaze. How dire was this future deed of which she was accused? She swallowed hard and squared her shoulders. "And what will my crime be?" she asked.

"Murder," the guardian answered.

Behind her, Gavin gasped and Lance swore, followed by the sound of flesh pounding into the wall.

Suzanne didn't take note of anything else as images that surpassed her worst imaginings played through her mind, followed by a thought-whisper in Tilsaia's voice. *I will not let you do this to those I love.*

Screaming, Suzanne shoved against the presence until she expelled both the voice and the horrors from her thoughts. She stalked forward, her hands clenched and her throat raw. "I have done *nothing* and you have no right to judge me. I reject your claims, and I reject you and your threats, *oath breaker*, because this thing you have shown me is not and will not *be* me, upon my very life." Suzanne spat at the woman's feet, then turned and headed for the door.

The hounds moved to block her way.

"Let her go," Lance ordered from across the room, his voice laden with menace.

They stopped closing in on her, but did not step back. Suzanne growled and shouldered her way past them. Inside, her heart shattered and she knew what she must do. Whatever those in the room behind her thought, her oath was sound.

She stood before the faerie circle, raised arms stained red with her own blood, which had streamed from now-healed cuts along the length of both veins. The cursed cap restored her flesh even as she sliced it, repeatedly and without fail. And thus she had come here, only to find herself foiled once more. Her chest heaved like she'd run a marathon and her jaw clenched tight enough to fuse. She fought to step forward into the circle. Fought to end this horror where it had begun. Just a few more steps would carry her into the faerie ring. From there she'd open a portal to the furnace. She visualized stepping through, knowing it would kill the monster she was becoming. Her muscles stood out in taut ropes and she strained forward until it seemed her skin would split and fall away. No matter how she tried, she remained in place, physically unable to move past the row of mushrooms guarding fae ground.

Not one for the futile, Suzanne eased back. She considered the obstacle with her other senses. A grimace twisted her lips. A shield. *Her* shield. Set weeks ago to ensure the redcaps did not escape from inside the faerie ring. The irony tasted bitter on her tongue.

Well, what magic raised, magic could bring down. With none of her usual restraint, she drew upon the pools of magic surrounding her as Lance had back when this all began. A tempest lashed the trees around her. The forest screamed. Magic flew to her grasp in an endless stream until her shoulder fins unfurled with a whip-crack.

Suzanne nearly lost control at the sight of her "wings." Once all lavenders and blues, accented by threads of pale green, red, and gold, the energy tendrils that now crackled around her snapped like blood-red flame. Had she truly changed so drastically? If such darkness had crept into her magic, what had entered her soul? She renewed her efforts, panting shallow breaths in desperation. The air sizzled as the tendrils lashed around her, until Suzanne's stomach turned at the stench of burning ozone. And still she could not shatter the barrier. Something more held her back.

"No!" she screamed. "I do not choose this!"

She reached in to her pocket and yanked out the hated red cap, her stomach roiling with more violence at the sickening sensation of it hungrily absorbing the drying runnels of blood that trailed over her hand. Snarling, she threw the cap toward the ground only to keen a tormented wail as her hand clung tight to the cloth.

Why had she thought she could handle this? Even with Lance beside her, how could she hope to overcome the curse? When she thought of those visions that Tilsaia had fed into her mind Suzanne's soul crumpled beneath the horror, the dreadful certainty that, left unchecked, they might well come true.

For the first time ever, Suzanne began to believe the poison her father had told her for so many years. For the first time ever, she truly felt weak. Tears burned down her cheeks. Wails assaulted her ears, shrill and broken. Her chest quaked with them. The energy drained from her and the glow of her wings faded. She swayed and would have slid to the ground, but for two massive hands that came from behind to grasp her shoulders. Their touch burned her skin.

"Shhh...that's enough screeching, girl," Bubba said, his voice low and soothing, deep and unshakable. He lifted her from the ground and scooped her into his arms in one effortless motion. "Time to stop this nonsense, too...what the hell were you thinking?" As his gaze swept over her blood-coated arms his tone did not invite an answer.

Suzanne released a shaky breath and let her head fall back until she saw his face. He looked fierce. Worried. Creepy. The rough patch on his forehead—just over the spot mystics would call the third eye—glowed like banked coals, slowly dimming and flaring as she watched. She shuddered as she thought again of her wings and their startling, fiery transformation.

"How did you know to come here?" she asked.

"There's more fire in you than there used to be," he answered, concern pulling at his features. "It called to me. It's not the first time."

"Help me..." Suzanne's expression tensed as she pleaded with him. Her eyes drifted back to the circle, the quickest way she knew to dump herself back into the furnace.

Bubba scowled, his forehead drawing down so low she could barely see his eyes. "I am."

"No! I need to go through," she argued. "I have to do this...It's the only way." *Before I lose myself,* she thought. *Before I become a danger to those around me.*

He didn't raise his voice. "No."

"I don't want to be like this anymore," she said in a bare whisper, burying her head against his chest, too tired to actually fight him.

"Then stop whining and fix it."

"But how? How do I stop what I'm becoming? I don't hardly recognize myself anymore. Even my magic is changing. You have no idea what they said I will do."

The Fire Elemental stopped in the middle of the woods and dropped her legs to the ground. Turning her toward him he gripped her shoulders once more and gave a shake that rattled her teeth.

"Doesn't matter. Nothing's happened until it's happened. You don't like where you're at right now? You change it! You find your balance, girl." Impatience threaded his words like steel bands. "How else do you keep from falling?"

"I tried that!"

"NO! You walked away from that!" Bubba snapped in a rare show of temper as he gave her a little shove that nearly sent her on her ass.

Suzanne compensated without thinking, only to have him shove her again and again, finding each push harder to adjust for until finally she grabbed for his arm to keep her feet. When she had her balance she hissed at him and shoved back. He barely even rocked back on his heels.

"*Sometimes* finding your balance means knowing when to hold on to something...or someone," he said, his tone low and reasonable enough to make her want to shove him again. Suzanne's cheeks burned as she glared up at him, her jaw set and every muscle projecting resistance.

Bubba's face twisted, his lip curling as his scowl deepened. "Don't you get it? Haven't you ever wondered why we formed the Wild Hunt? Why the Four Winds even exist the way we do? This isn't exactly the natural order of things."

She didn't want to hear what he said, let alone accept it. Every insecurity within her reared up in protest. Suzanne bit her lip. Hard. Tasting the blood on her tongue, she spat it out, growling in frustration as the demon inside reared up and demanded more. She had to fight herself not to bring the redcap, still clutched in her hand, to her lips.

Bubba got down in her face, his expression as hard and unyielding as the mountain he resembled. "Why? Come on...say it."

Rebelliously she remained silent, continuing to glare up at him. The ember at Bubba's forehead flared into a flame. Suzanne had never seen him so pissed.

"Lance," she murmured grudgingly.

Bubba nodded and stepped back, banking his flame. "He centers us. He's our balance. Keeps us in check. Just being around him makes us stronger, more stable...There's a reason we call him Dušan."

Dušan...*Spirit.* Aristotle's fifth element. Yeah, she had an affinity for that one too. Still Suzanne remained silent. Doubt divided her. One part desperate to run back to Lance, the other certain she would lose everything of herself if she did.

Bubba glanced over her shoulder in the direction of the faerie circle, then back at her, eyes hooded. "Aren't you doing that already?" he said, as if she'd spoken her fears aloud. "Never figured you for a weak-ass quitter... You do what you want. I'm going back to bed."

With that he shook his head and turning, walked away in the direction of *Delilah's.*

Suzanne had never seen herself that way, either. Setting her jaw at a determined angle, she swiped her tear-stained face with the edge of her shirt and started to follow Bubba. She had taken but a few steps when the forest sounds went silent and the air chilled as something sucked the magic away. With a snap as sharp as cracking marble a portal opened before her. She had a glimpse of her father's sneering face before he reached out and snatched her to him, his muscular arms binding her to his chest before she could even react.

"I told you long ago, child, you can never be free of me," he breathed against her ear. "There is nowhere you can go that I cannot follow if I chose to."

Suzanne screamed, more in rage than fear, but it went unheard.

The gate closed, leaving the wold dark and desolate, drained of its essence, still echoing with Suzanne's cry.

Tilly. Mongo. Bubba. The three of them ambushed him.

Lance had gone to his father's place to work on the Knuckle-head and to bounce some of this off Cam. He had to try and get his head on straight before everything went completely to hell and stayed there. Suzanne had taken off. His aunt, the lovely woman who started all this, disappeared with the Mead Hall, and Gavin wasn't talking to him, leaving him without the support and confidante he'd had grown to depend on for longer than he and Suzanne had been a couple. His father helped, but mostly he just listened, letting Lance ramble and rage and find his own way to the truth. Despite hours of talking, there hadn't been much success yet.

As the three of them walked up, Lance looked away from the carburetor he was rebuilding with parts from several junked units. Beside him, Cam kept working on the tranny. When Lance saw their faces he set the part down and got to his feet.

"And I thought I'd had as much shit as I could take," he said, his tone more weary than warning.

"No one should have to save themselves all alone," Bubba answered cryptically.

Lance shook his head. "Plain and simple, folks, so we can wrap this up."

"You want simple," Tilly snapped. "Simple is Suzanne is up to here in hot water, and you're screwing around rebuilding parts."

His expression tightened, and Lance had to rein back hard on his temper.

"I don't know if you missed it, but she doesn't want my help."

"Wanting and needing are two very different things," Mongo added quietly. "Something real bad is going down."

Bubba nodded. "She was ready to come back last night. She was ready to listen and talk. Clearly things didn't get that far. I don't know what happened, but she's gone. Just gone."

A frown deepened the strained lines of Lance's face. "And this is peculiar why?"

Tilly stalked up and got into his face, smacking his shoulder hard as she said, "Her bike's still here!"

"Excuse me?"

"Poof! Thin air, no waiting!"

Lance's knuckles popped as his fists clenched. "When?"

"Sometime between last night and now," Bubba answered, a thread of guilt in his tone. "That's the last anyone saw her, but we didn't realize until now. I had a little chat with her in the woods behind *Delilah's*. We already combed them, she's not there." Though he sounded done, Bubba's voice went on, speaking directly to Lance's mind, as all the Winds could, though they seldom did. *She tried to end it, Dušan. She's so afraid of whatever went down, that she tried to take her life to prevent it. How about we find some more constructive way to help her put it all behind her?*

That sent Lance reeling. His heart screamed and his vision hazed, and suddenly he wasn't so sure he couldn't be happy with whatever she gave him, as long as she was there and well and not dead because of something that *might* happen. Seeing her around the place brought peace to his soul, even while it tore out his heart fresh each day. Just imagining life without her somewhere in it left him dead inside.

Why? Lance thought at Bubba, knowing the Elemental would pick the question up from his thoughts.

She's changing and that scared her shitless already; whatever the guardian showed her made that worse.

The guilt went straight to Lance's gut. "What about Gavin?" he asked, remembering how Suzanne's brother had followed their blood line to find her the last time she went missing.

"He's freaking out. Can't sense anything, can't find her," Mongo said. "Doesn't even know where to start. Right now he's riding around physically searching anywhere she might be because he just doesn't know what else to do."

It grew harder and harder for Lance to keep his temper in check. Behind him he heard Cam set down his tools and slide off his stool. Then his hand came down on Lance's shoulder.

"Son, what are you still doing here? You know what's important and what isn't. Go. Find her."

Lance reached up to grip his father's hand before setting it aside. "Thanks, Cam. You got things here?" Cam gave him a look and slowly shook his head.

"Get out of here."

Grabbing his jacket, Lance shrugged it on as he walked, then slid his hand into the pocket where he'd left his cell phone. "You guys coming, or what?" he called over his shoulder as he punched the speed dial on his phone.

"Yo, Gavin. Cut the bullshit and get your ass to *Delilah's*. We'll meet you there."

The stink of decay surrounded her, must and mildew and rotting things. Suzanne's nose pinched against the assault as she groaned and shifted, straining to become conscious. Slowly her lids half-rose, fighting whatever spell her father had dropped on her. She lay in the gloom of a large, open space she resisted calling the Great Hall, but only for the state of it. Though she had never been happy in this place, she mourned the devastation that assaulted her gaze. She struggled upright, noticing her own clothes were gone, replaced by a shabby mockery of Court garb. She grimaced and wiped at her head as something tickled her skin. Her fingers encountered a cold, moist softness. When she lowered them the tips were marked with blood.

Her shriek echoed through the hall.

"No! I will never choose this," she yelled out, snatching the cloth from her head, shuddering at the clammy feel of the air on her blood-dampened hair. "And you will never choose for me!"

"Pathetic posturing," her father said, his voice coming at her from behind.

Not one to be caught at a disadvantage, Suzanne pushed to her feet and with a cold, challenging look, reached down and tore the hem from her gown, lifting it to wipe the blood from her head. And then, because she knew she could not cast it from her, she balled up the redcap and tied it in the scrap, tucking it in the kerchief pocket she knew had been worked into the seam of her skirts, as was the fashion.

This confrontation echoed so many others in their joint life, but only faintly. Gone was the hunched and submissive little wisp who had once trailed behind him like a kicked dog. For the first time ever Suzanne faced her father square on, eyes raised and shoulders back. Despite the situation her heart was at peace and her confidence firmly rooted.

"Get bent, *Daddy*," she sneered.

Now that she stood she spied the source of the rotting smell. Arrayed around her, crouching in anticipation, were the redcaps. She growled and stomped until the nearest scrambled back, only to hiss and bob in defiance, and yet she sensed no malice or danger from her unlikely guardians.

"Talk the rebel all you want, Fleur," Callan said, his tone mocking and his high brow lifted in distain. "You will do as I wish, whether you will it or not."

She crossed her arms, not caring that her right sleeve shredded at the seam. In fact, she reached up and gripped the restrictive garment, first one shoulder, then the other, tearing the sleeves off. "You keep telling yourself that, *Pop*," she said as she looked him up and down, her lip curling. None of this was new to her. The manipulation, the crushing comments, the lack of regard. Old hat. She'd shrugged it off once, before she knew her strength. It meant nothing to her now. She'd grown stronger in the mortal realm, confident and unhesitant. It had taken her a long time, but she knew who she was and not even someone she respected had been able to change that, let alone someone she didn't.

Giving him her back, though instinct screamed at her not to be foolish, Suzanne started to stalk away. One of the redcaps crouched in her path. Rather than go around she snarled. "Out of my way!" Her eyes began to widen as the powrie ducked his head and scurried back. The revelation set a cold, little smile dancing over her lips, short lived.

Before her next step touched the ground a cruel yank arched her back as tendrils of magic constricted around her chest. Her father's hated laughter mocked her from behind. With slow, brutal tugs, he drew her back. When he had her pressed against his chest Callan leaned down and whispered in her ear, insidious and hateful.

"I chain all my dogs, little bitch, not just those with fur. You've worn your harness since birth. The only reason I never came for you before is you were hardly worth the effort."

She fought the urge to growl and scratch and otherwise prove him right. If there was any creature in existence she would gladly kill and bathe in its blood it was him. Her breath heaved and her muscles twitched to make it so. At the edges of her mind the murmurs that so recently plagued her came a little clearer. *Yes. Do it. Slick and sweet, so very good. Powerful. Yes...*

"NO!" Suzanne yelled, rejecting the muttering and her father both.

Callan chuckled at her. "You will do as I wish, by one manner of persuasion or another," he said as he grabbed her arm and twisted until the shoulder popped and shoved her away. "As you can see, there is no more need to maintain appearances."

Suzanne refused to cry out in pain, not even once he'd left and she forced the joint back into place. She prowled the Hall only to discover her "tether" kept her within the confines of the "nest" where she awoke. If she stretched even an inch beyond her range agony shot though her limbs as the bonds her father set constricted.

The entire time she paced her open-air prison, violent bloodlust shoved against her will one moment, then whispered to her soul the next. For a moment Suzanne had trouble remembering why she must resist. Then the cap made its first error. It dredged up a memory of the visions, tormenting her with glimpses of Lance and his loved ones, egging on her rage and trying to convince her through persistence that the impulses were right and good. Suzanne recoiled and came back a bit more to herself, realizing two things: one, her agitation aided the enemy, sapping her strength and weakening her defenses; and two, acting like the caged animal Callan thought her did nothing to free her from his control.

For lack of a better place to rest, Suzanne lowered herself back down to the moldering bedding. Once again, the redcaps settled around her, close, but not too near. By their expressions—alternating from hateful to hopeful—they were as conflicted as she.

Putting them from her mind, she turned her thoughts inward, searching for any weakness in the link binding her. As she examined her soul she gasped aloud. One stout cord came round her from her father, but hundreds of threads trailed away.

The lot at *Delilah's* overflowed. Cycles, cars, trucks...all jammed in until it looked like there was hardly room to squeeze between them. Lance drove right up the front walk and parked next to the door, leaving the others to find spots where they could. Kicking down the stand and yanking his helmet off, he didn't even take the time to set it on his bike. He stalked into the bar with it tucked beneath his arm.

Gavin and a hell of a lot of others waited inside. The din hurt Lance's ears, but not for long. As soon as he walked in the heated debate cut off. Gavin came forward and invaded Lance's personal space.

"We have to do something," he said, his mouth rigid and his eyes wild.

Lance just gave him a stare until he backed up, then said, "Keep it together, bro." He reached out and clasped his friend's shoulder as he walked past him deeper into the room. When they were side by side he murmured, "I'm sorry, Wingman."

Gavin jerked a nod and fell in behind him.

Lance took a deep breath and glanced around the crowded room. "Report," he said sharply. And for fifteen minutes everyone took turns sharing what they knew. For those fifteen minutes Lance fought down his increasing anger. As the last person finished, Lance trailed his gaze from face to face.

"Has anyone called her?"

Silence a moment, then someone spoke up. "We found her phone upstairs."

"What else have we tried?"

"I've combed the area as far as Dalton," Gavin answered. "Not one whisper of Suzanne anywhere, and I couldn't home in on her—blood, body, or magic."

"The boys and I took out a bunch of others to canvas the woods," Sammy added next. "Someone was out there at some point, by one of the faerie rings, but we didn't see any sign of Suzanne or a tussle."

And so it went on, a whole lot of nothing, until suddenly Gort staggered through the door from the back room. He'd gone so pale Lance could barely see the ivy markings normally scrolling his skin. The High King's former advisor swayed before bracing an arm on the jamb.

"Callan has her. I sensed his magic in the woods. I have tried ever since to cross to Underhill but he has somehow closed the ways." Lance cursed and thumped his helmet, letting his hand rest there as Gort went on. "With a strong enough link to her, we might break through in spite of his efforts to bar us."

Gavin's gaze snapped to Lance, homing in on his arm.

"Godammit!" The oath tore from Lance's throat, leaving it shredded. Clenching his teeth and unclenching his hands, he fought to throttle down his rage. Losing control would not help Suzanne. With a grim look Lance shook his head and bared his arm to Gavin, the static tattoo screaming loudly of how thoroughly Lance had screwed up.

Gavin's expression hardened. The light in his eyes dimmed and took on a bleak cast as his head fell forward. The hopeless need to act radiated from him like a toxic cloud.

"Lock it down or get out," Lance growled, then turned to the rest of the room, his gaze singling out the fae and mages in the room. "Give me options, people. Anything and everything, I don't care how far-fetched."

The answers flew and, while Lance noted each one, none of them triggering a spark of hope.

When the voices fell silent and strain wired the room a woman stood and came forward, someone Lance didn't recognize, and certainly not one of his. He frowned, about to ask her what she was doing there, when she spoke, her gentle words radiating calm.

"You're all thinking as if it will take just one single thing to break this hold." She looked around the room, her grace steady and unyielding.

"I don't know this Callan or most of what is going on, but I know Suzanne. Her love. Her compassion. The way she's incapable of moving through life without touching everyone that crosses her path. That woman has left more bits of herself with each one of us that I'm surprised she has anything left for herself. That's what you want. You gather up the bits of strength she's selflessly doled out on us and there's your link. There's your way to reach her no matter what the bastard does to block you."

Forget spark, her words jolted Lance like a live wire.

His hand, now idly rubbing his helmet, stilled. His other hand came up to press against his chest where the bike armor Suzanne had gifted him wrapped him in protections beyond the physical.

"Who are you?" he asked.

"Helen. I work at the orphanage." With that, the woman plucked magic from the air and wove a simple spell. Behind her ear, a small wheel-like symbol began to glow as she lowered the spell over her head like a hoop. When it dropped past her shoulders and slid toward the floor, the woman vanished back to wherever she came from.

Murmurs went through the crowd as no one knew what to make of what just happened. The woman wasn't fae, and she wasn't mage, but she'd spun that spell in the middle of protected ground. Lance didn't really care at this point. His knuckles lightly tapped his helmet as what Helen said penetrated his worries. He couldn't believe he hadn't realized it himself. As determined as Suzanne was to not depend on anyone to take care of her, she herself tried to take care of the world. Not just him, though he knew he got special attention. Scooping up his helmet he moved to the pool table across the room, shoving past whoever didn't have the good sense to get out of the way. He smacked the helmet down and turned to stare everyone in the eye.

"Every single thing Suzanne has given any one of you, I don't care if it's as small as a toothpick, you get it and you get it now. Right here on this table," and he brought his fist down, bouncing the helmet.

Tilly came forward first, drawing the crystal pendant she'd worn for over five years and placing it beside Lance's helmet. "She would never let me take this off... before... now I guess I understand why."

Part of Lance wanted to shove the necklace back in her hand, dreading the thought of his cousin coming to anymore harm. He resisted the urge. This might be their only way to reach Suzanne. Instead he drew Tilly into his arms and hugged her.

Someone cleared their throat. Lance looked up to see Lyman approach. He stepped back so the man could reach the pool table. Lyman lay down an odd little bundle of dried flowers.

"Don't have a clue if this is anything, but Suzanne gave it to me yesterday to give to my sister when she heard she was sick."

Lance nodded his thanks, then, as the quiet man retreated into the background, he turned toward the crowd gathered in the bar.

"Come on, people. Everything Suzanne gave you. You have ten minutes. Make it happen." Before he was done speaking, a steady stream of charms and trinkets and bits of clothing, each of them bearing a tiny portion of Suzanne, passed from hand to hand until the pile half covered the pool table. He made no exception for himself. Besides the helmet he laid the leathers she'd given him for his birthday on the table. That one hurt, but nowhere near as much as losing Suzanne would.

Lance looked up at a commotion from the door. The first time Suzanne went missing one of the Wild Hunt's probates had told Lance what was going down. Now that same SQUID came struggling through the front door pushing a sweet Harley Softtail.

"You have got to be kidding me..." Lance said, slowly shaking his head as the kid came closer.

The guy blushed. "She said my ride wasn't even safe to sit on. Swapped mine for this when I wasn't lookin'." Squirming beneath Lance's stern look, he added, "I been payin' her for it...honest."

Lance had no doubt, and he couldn't be mad at the kid for taking advantage of her because Lance knew full well she would have done it somehow whether the kid accepted it or not. Running his gaze over the sweet ride he saw her mark all over it: runes of protection, mage-reinforced struts, even a glimmer of something around the gas cap that probably made sure he didn't forget to fill up. Lance stepped back so the kid could move the bike into place. The look on his face screamed dejection.

"What's your name?" Lance asked soft and low.

"Kyle."

Lance winced. "How about I call you Trooper..."

Now Kyle winced. "How about Troop?" He countered, slouching and trying to cock his head tough.

"Done." Not laughing—though he really wanted to—Lance held out his hand and they shook. "So, Troop, don't sweat the ride. When this is done I'll help you trick out something fine to take its place."

Troop ruined his bad-boy act by grinning like a kid on Christmas. "Oh, *man!* Yeah!"

Okay, so Lance laughed. Not that it lasted long.

He stood back, stance wide and arms crossed, waiting for wisps of Suzanne to come back so he could go after the rest of her.

It took quite a bit longer than ten minutes, but Lance could hardly complain. The mound piled on and around the pool table boggled his mind. For the first time he truly grasped what Helen had said when she wondered how Suzanne had anything left for herself…though he had to wonder how Helen had known to begin with. The items before him were likely only a portion of those out there, rather than everything, but Lance had to hope it was enough of her essence to make a difference. As he stood trying to figure out how to do this the Four Winds gathered at his back, occasionally circling the pile, their gazes intent.

"This is going to be tricky," Blow muttered.

Dream nodded, then tilted her head slightly, as if trying to get a better perspective. "It'll take all of us, but we have to use caution." She brought her gaze up and met Lance's eye. "I cannot say what effect releasing the essence will have."

"Well," Bubba cut in, "We know what doing nothing will accomplish, so unless you have a better idea stop talking it to death and let's do something."

Lance shook his head at the Elemental bickering and looked toward Rock, who had yet to speak. He just shook his head back and crossed his arms over his barrel chest, his expression screaming get on with it. They were the only ones left in the bar. No sense taking risks with the club members' lives when none of them knew what was about to happen.

Rooting through the pile until he uncovered his helmet, Lance pulled it free. "Best to start small," he said as the Winds gathered around him.

"So, like we did before?" Bubba asked.

Dream gave him a scathing look. "Preferably without the 'Someone dying horribly' part."

Lance shot her a quelling glance. It had about as much effect as yelling at the rain.

No one spoke again as Lance gripped the helmet firmly in his hands, then the Winds placed their hands on his arms, shoulders, and chest, each of them at their proper cardinal point. Slowly they breathed, in and out, their muscles relaxing and their focus turning inward. One by one their breathing synched and the edges blurred. The five elements linked, melded, each one's strengths compounding the others.

I can see it, Blow said into their joint mind. *Look...* and he shared his vision, which the others had not yet grasped, their sight not as sharp as the far-seeing wind. Lance gasped and his grip tightened on the helmet. A scintillating thread of lavender/blue laced the runes of protection, steady and strong, for all the light touch. It trailed from the helmet out into the ether. He ran a mental finger along the close end of the strand. The magic tingled at first then gave him a jolt as the strand stretched taut. It took effort not to flinch.

Do we follow it? Dream asked.

I doubt it's enough, but let's try. He didn't wait to see if they agreed.

Like walking a mental tight rope, Lance sent his awareness along the line, trusting the link to keep him anchored to himself. At first his balance wavered but as his spirit found familiar paths, he steadied. Emboldened by this small success, he sped his thoughts down the length of the thread, willing his body to follow it, certain his link with Suzanne ran deeper than even her brother's, which had proved too weak to guide him.

The thread went taut. A tremor ran the length. Lance stilled but acted too late. As the connection snapped, his spirit fell away.

She woke once more with the cap atop her head and her teeth gnawing her lip. Suzanne sobbed and tore the cloth away. Desperately, she tried to throw it from her, but only succeeded in flapping her hand, droplets of blood spattering the nearest redcap.

Those in the room stilled.

In a slow turn, the powrie brought his gaze to hers. The hunger overwhelmed her. The savage, desperate hunger. His. Hers. She couldn't say, but Suzanne sobbed harder, too weary to care at the weakness she showed.

In her dreams Lance had been near. He touched her, caressed her, then something snapped and her soul remained alone again, stinging as a sudden spark jolted her like a 9-volt to the tongue. For a brief instant, she felt stronger, then the weight of her situation bore down. With the crushing sensation her brief peace faded and the horrors crept back through her thoughts on the redcaps' muttering.

Awake and alert served her no better than nightmare-drenched sleep.

Suzanne lay herself down again and reached the hand holding the cap as far from her as she could get it, then slowly released her hold, finger by trembling finger, until her only contact with the hateful beast was the barest pad of her pinkie. She then turned her head into the crook of her other arm and quietly cried herself to sleep once more, her thoughts desperately locking on Lance and the succor even her most painful memory offered.

Likely it was wistful thinking, but eventually Suzanne calmed as what felt like her lover's thoughts brushed hers once more in an echo of the sundered link between them.

Lance gasped as he fell back into his body, the impact shattering the five-way link. He groaned, then swore as he came to on his knees, hand clutching the nearest table edge.

"Son of a..."

Dream cut off his curse with a well-placed smack to the back of his head. When he glared back at her, her expression met his, stern and laden with warning.

"Don't do that!" Rock growled, his tousled head held gingerly in his hands. "No more going rogue when all of us are linked or I'll bust *your* head!"

Lance jerked at the vehemence in the normally mellow Earth Elemental's words. Hell, just the sheer number of words alone shocked him, as Rock usually doled them out sparingly.

Rubbing the back of his neck, Lance groaned and silently agreed with Rock's sentiment. Recklessness got people killed, on a bike or anywhere else. If some dumb kid had pulled something like that on a ride, Lance would have jacked him up.

"Sorry, everyone…won't happen again."

"Just so we're clear, what did happen?" Blow asked.

Lance gave him a grim smile. "I tried to rush the fort, but the pass couldn't take the weight."

"Huh?"

"The link snapped under Dušan's massive ego."

Elbowing Bubba hard in the thigh, Lance climbed to his feet and staggered to the pool table. "Hey! Mongo!" he called out, certain the cook had ignored his order to vacate the building.

He waited a moment and yelled once more.

"What!?"

"Break out a bottle of that mead the maniac men gave us. The good one."

"Gave nothing!" Mongo bellowed. "Cost me three batches of my best brownies…*each*!"

"Just do it!"

Still grumbling, Mongo stomped out with a bottle of J&J Miracle Mead – Avalon's Kiss cradled in his arms.

"Say good bye, papa," Lance said as he lifted the bottle and pulled the cork, swigging straight from the bottle in the absence of a handy glass. Energy instantly flowed through his body, not from the mead itself, but through every mage channel; healed, cleansed, and soothed by the potent drink. A shudder traveled through him at the sudden wealth of power. Wiping the neck of the bottle, Lance handed it off to Dream. It continued around the circle until all of them had been restored, leaving Mongo to stare mournfully at the nearly empty bottle. With a resigned shrug, he upended the container over his mouth and kept it there until every sweet drop of nectar slid past his lips.

"Now get out of here! All the way out," Lance ordered, crossing his arms over his chest.

Mongo got a sullen look on his face, but complied.

Once he was gone the Winds turned their attention back to Lance. He led them back to the pile of items. "Okay, here's where I think it went wrong—we need a rope, not a thread. We link back up and carefully snip each of the threads connected to these items, but not letting them go. When we have them all, we weave them together into one cord, and that will take us to Suzanne."

The looks on their faces grew thoughtful. Dream picked up a small stuffed bear in leather biker gear and a studded collar and turned it over in her hands, as if normal sight would show her Suzanne's thread. She pursed her lips, then nodded. "Okay...I've got nothing else. Any of you?" she asked, glancing at the other three Winds. They shook their heads.

"Okay then!" She tossed the bear at Lance and they began the long process of liberating Suzanne's essence. As they divested each item of its link the object crumbled to dust. Lance flinched to see it, knowing how much care his lady had put into those gifts. It had to be done, though. It took effort to resist the urge to rush again. The longer they took, the more chance Suzanne would come to harm. But what if going too fast doomed them to fail?

Slow and steady beat needing a mulligan or three.

Lance kept telling himself that, but his gut twisted tighter with every passing second. His thoughts and his spirit reached for Suzanne without even thinking about it. And suddenly, he was there, half-bundle of spirit threads clutched in his mental hand, and the Winds howling in the distance as they fought to keep his fool-ass soul anchored to his body.

Eternal twilight wreathed the Great Hall as Callan strode forward, stopping to stand over his sleeping daughter. The redcaps rose and crept near to him, just beyond his reach.

"Is she ready?"

They shook their heads and flinched back before he even raised his hand.

"You aren't trying hard enough. The cap's been taken, the soul must be claimed. I want her weak and fallen. I want her spirit shredded beneath the senseless hunger. You will make this happen," Callan ordered. "By whatever means, you push her to that edge and I will see she falls."

They bobbed and hissed, and cast longing glances toward the brat. Callan narrowed his gaze at them, not altogether certain their goals aligned with his.

Swatting at the nearest powrie, he turned and stalked from the chamber. Beyond the satisfaction of pressing his darling daughter beneath his heel for all time, Callan was determined she would prove the key to his ascension to true and total power. The blasted halfling and his cohorts would never doubt her loyalty; Callan had seen that much. With her acceptance assured it would be no effort at all to send her 'escaping' home, there to end the line of *Rudha-an* forever.

Pain. Intense pain. Suzanne cried out and rolled to her side, clutching her arm. Callan laughed and sent another mage bolt crashing down on her. She tried to dodge but he yanked her tether tight. Scrambling to deflect the blow, she could not draw energy quickly enough. This one lanced her thigh. Gasping, her body arched as the attack cascaded through her, tripping nerves and burning mage ways. She fought not to sob with the agony.

Time had little meaning Underhill and Suzanne had lost track of how long she'd been there. Ten minutes? Ten thousand years? It had ceased to matter. She did not have the energy to break free, and her ability to repel the hunger and resist her father waned.

Callan must have sensed this. He kept pushing and attacking, yelling hate and poison and violence, threatening worse if she did not comply with his wishes. So far Suzanne fought but he wore her down the more hope bled away.

Suzanne.

She gasped and managed to roll away from Callan's next blow before shoving herself to her feet. He screamed and tried to yank her back down to her knees. Her stubbornness revived and she resisted. Whipping around, she searched the length and breadth of the Hall for the impossible.

"Lance?" she cried, the sound barely above a whisper.

Her father heard her. His face twisted with fury and he renewed his efforts, slamming her full to the ground, following with a sharp kick to her ribs, the whole while screaming about the Abomination. She had never in all her life seen him this unhinged, this out of control. Father was all about control, not even himself exempt. But oh…had she truly heard Lance? She wanted to cry, thinking she had imagined it, but she could not give her father the satisfaction of believing he had caused her tears.

Shh…no…don't. I'm in here, Lance said, and she felt the caress of his thoughts along hers.

Her hands went over her mouth as she held back her outcry. The fierce smile on her father's face grew.

Oh, baby, I will never give you grief for henning me again! she thought back at Lance.

His chuckle danced around her head until Suzanne felt giddy with the sensation.

You can rescue me now.

Lance went silent and still. For a moment she feared he'd gone.

I can't. I've already tried. We all have, we just can't get through. Something's keeping us out of all Underhill.

The last of her hope dried into dust. She was too weak…they were too weak.

No! You cut that out! Cut it out now, Suzanne. Fight! Dammit!

She barely heard him. Somewhere deep inside she had been certain all she need to do was wait, that Lance would once again defy her claims of not needing him and swoop in to the rescue. She had been wrong and with that realization the fight went out of her. Years of false pride had kept them apart and now always would because Suzanne had been wrong. She couldn't take on the world all alone. Well. She could, but her current state was proof she couldn't win.

Her doubts and demons toppled the walls she'd built around them. In through the gaps they left behind in her defenses the murmurs returned unrelenting…persuasive. Between their wearing her away on the inside and her father's bombardment on the outside, Suzanne found herself overwhelmed. She deserved her fate for what she'd put Lance through. She cried out and her spirit curled in on itself, not embracing the hunger, but unable to resist any further. She felt herself fading as the cap exerted its influence, only to be jolted out of her apathy by what amounted to a swift kick to her spirit.

Suzanne! Move! Shove that crap down their throats.

She wanted to listen. To do as he said, but she just wasn't sure she could.

I can't do it for you, angel. I want to, but I can't. I'm just not strong enough to break through. You have to try... You been telling me all along you can take care of yourself...now's your chance to show me!

Drawing a quavering breath, she let her head fall back, too weary to hold it up as tears streamed down to mat her blood-caked hair.

"Yes, child," Callan said tightening his grip on the magic binding them, jerking her lower. She found herself prostrate before him and saw little point in struggling up again.

No! Don't give up on me, Suzanne. You can do this. You don't need me to get free. All that strength, it's yours. You are so much stronger than you realize.

Suzanne smiled faintly at his claims, hardly finding it possible to believe him, but heartened at his efforts to shore her up. She'd always came across as strong, fiercely defended that position, but deep in her heart she had never believed it herself.

Please! his spirit begged and behind it she felt his plea echoed faintly by the Four Winds. The touch of all five souls seemed to push back the darkness taking over her heart.

They made her want to believe, but dare she?

Her father's foot came down on the back of her neck as he reveled in her subjugation. He pressed her to the ground, and the hateful voices grew louder, flooding their toxic urgings into her thoughts to block out Lance's persuasion. But the voices, they were on the surface of her mind, constantly clawing her defenses, attempting to burrow deeper.

Lance? He was a part of her, though what a time to realize.

Come on, don't quit on me. She had never heard him speak with such desperation as she felt pounding against her soul. *I'm here for you...whatever you need...everything I am, you take. We'll do it together.*

Suzanne heard him. Echoes of her conversation with Bubba came back to her, from just before she'd been taken. Balance. For her, that meant all the elements: Earth. Air. Fire. Water...*Spirit*.

*Dušan...*she thought. And she felt Lance still as if waiting for her to act. His heart and soul stood wide open to her. No corner of his spirit remained hidden. She saw the truth of his words and his trust in her restored. But his love...the width and breadth of it set her trembling as he reached out down the threads of her spirit and bound his soul tight to hers in a link much closer than the one severed between them. At the same time he loosed his hold on the strands still trailing from her.

The mass of energy snapped back into her body with the force of a freight train barreling out of control. Her chest expanded and her pulse kicked up like someone hit fast-forward. Energy glowed from beneath her skin and the unmatted ends of her hair crackled and floated free. Callan cried out and stumbled back as her shoulder fins unfurled in one rolling snap, the tendrils lashing the air as they lengthened.

You blow me away, angel... come home and let me show you how to fly.

She heard him and she wanted nothing more to grant his wish. But it would be the wrong thing to do. "No," she answered aloud, her voice ringing out bold and strong. "Not yet."

She heard him protest but there was no choice. If she ran from Callan now she would never be free of him. He would never believe her strong enough to leave alone. Their lives would become one attack after another until someday she lost something more precious to her than her soul. She flinched as her demons snagged the memory of Tilsaia's vision and threw it into stark relief, bold and glaring and ugly. But she was not weak and a fear should be nothing more than a warning, something to guide her, not rule her. She did not stand alone. Lance's love and faith poured into her, for now and ever, undeniable. She wanted that back. She wanted the future he held out to her. Finally, she was ready to let loose her stranglehold on her own love; time to let it flow instead of doling it out in sorry little samplings. Suzanne pushed the darkness inside away and climbed to her feet. Drawing herself up with a regal grace Callan could only emulate, she turned to face her father.

She could kill him, the voices whispered, bathe in his blood as she'd considered before. She could even send the redcaps against him. They would listen, she had seen that, in the way they bowed and scraped as if she were royalty. But to do that would kill a part of her she valued and darling Daddy had already left more than enough scars. For a brief moment she closed her eyes and thought back to the Brigade, and the Death Squad, grateful for the outlet the derby girls had shown her for the aggression she fought and would continue to fight until she shucked off the curse of that damn cap. But first, time to rid herself of her other demons...

"You need to back off, old man," she told him. "My name is Suzanne and I am no longer your daughter. You have no claim over me. I have no allegiance to you. And if you ever come near me and mine again and we will not hesitate to protect our own. You will not come out on the winning side."

Callan snarled and snatched power from the air, a hint of panic flitting across his expression as he realized how little energy around them remained unbound. Suzanne flared her wings and, before he could lash out, once more stole the power from his grip, slamming it back down on him like a hammer blow.

He went to his knees, face pale and teeth gritted. With a surge he gained his feet again, only to be forced down once more as she channeled power in a way she never had before, without fear or hesitation, without the doubts he'd fostered. The barest edge of her father's lip trembled as she showed him how strong he had made her in his efforts to keep her weak. Suzanne actually laughed with the rush of mage energy tingling through ever cell in her body. If not for Lance—and through him the Winds—keeping her grounded she might have found herself again overwhelmed.

Hatred burned in Callan's gaze, but beneath it he swam in swiftly growing fear. She stalked forward prowling like a leopardess until she stood right before him. Her wing tendrils—the lavender and blue tones predominant now—crackled and snapped until Callan broke and flinched back. She leaned down and got into his face trapping his gaze and crowding him. The tableau held for no longer than a heartbeat for her, but she felt his panic surge and knew his torment would go on forever, his weakness revealed.

She smiled one of his unpleasant smiles, visualized the last of her demons purged from her body, and said, "Boo!"

The sound of his cry soothed her soul with guilty pleasure as she drew up her shields and turned her back on him. Not even the most optimistic part of her believed this would be the last of it, but sure as hell she knew it was the last they'd meet on his terms, or his footing. Whatever might unfold in time, Suzanne vowed that no one and nothing—not even her fears—would ever control her again.

I am so proud of you, babe, Lance said in her mind. *How about coming home now?*

Suzanne laughed unleashing her joy on the sick and twisted land of Underhill, driving back the edges of the darkness, healing the thinnest sliver of the decay.

Reaching down the link to her lover, she wrapped him close with her elation and pictured herself in his arms until they squeezed her tight and she felt Lance's laughter tickle her ear.

"Show-off."

She grinned. "You're one to talk."

At her words he went serious. "Speaking of talking, I think we need to."

Concern vibrated down the link, though Lance kept his tone calm. Suzanne nodded, knowing after everything she could not deal with this on her own. Nervous, she looked around them, noticing the place was packed. She felt raw and not certain she wanted to air her problems in front of the whole club. Lance smiled a slight, understanding smile. He squeezed her hand, telling her without words that it was okay, that everything was okay, even the things that weren't.

Suzanne inhaled deeply, her breath trembling, then tugged her hand out of his so she could take the cap from her pocket. She then turned and faced her friends and loved ones.

"I have a problem," she told them. "I made a bad call because I thought I had to do everything on my own to be strong." She dipped her head and swallowed hard. "A while back I went into the woods to conquer my fear of red and I came out with more trouble than I went in with."

A tremor went through her shoulders and Lance lightly laid his hand there, giving her his strength, his support. She reached back to grip his hand and continued on.

"I was cornered by some redcaps…the same ones who attacked me before, and I dealt with them." The memory tightened her jaw until it was hard to speak. "They died, all of them, but in taking them out, I snagged one of their caps. I've had it awhile now and it's been trying to change me…it *has* been changing me. I'm told there's no getting rid of it—" She paused to meet everyone's eye. "—but here's your chance to tell me I'm wrong and not piss me off. I would *love* to hear I'm wrong right now…"

Though everyone laughed, it did nothing to lighten the mood in the bar.

"Anyway, I can fight it, I know that much, and I figure…with all of you helping I might just keep it together without turning into the evil she-devil I could be." She caught some ribbing on that one, a couple muttered comments about it being too late, but Suzanne didn't mind; thanks to Lance she could feel the love and concern and support surrounding her, and mingled with that she sensed her own shame. These people. Her real family. They offered this all along, with no cost, no demands, and for years Suzanne held herself away, willfully weakened herself in the name of standing strong. What an idiot she'd been. The realization nearly sent her to the ground, but Lance caught her. His arms wrapped around her waist as he held her tight. He laid his chin on her shoulder and said to those around them, "Excuse us. We're going to go talk weddings."

Good thing Lance held her up. And held her down. Her spirit soared as his words alone showed her how to fly.

"Bubba" Nick
Ed Coutts
2013

Epilogue

In the family room of St. Frances's Orphanage, the children entertained guests. It was the day of their holiday party and the room was joyous and festive with decorations the kids had made to represent all of the winter holidays. The meal was over and, along with the children, staff, and friends, the Wild Hunt lounged on battered sofas and mounds of pillows on the floor, most of them tugged and tumbled by the boys and girls, who found it difficult to sit still, waiting as they were for Santa.

Suzanne sat in the vee of Lance's lap in a clear spot on the floor, near the tree, ready to help corral the eventual avalanche of paper. Santa had already brought her gift; on the ring finger of her left hand a perfect circle of faerie moonstone glowed softly against her skin. The mate to it rested on her knee, gracing Lance's hand. As was the custom of the Fae, they'd exchanged private vows, promising themselves they would plan something more formal soon for everyone to celebrate. In the meantime, they would work on the rest of her dream later...in private. Now was for the children of St. Frances's. Or it would be if the guest of honor would show.

"Where is he?" she murmured. Lance shrugged behind her, the motion brushing his chest against her back, distracting her until she didn't care when Bubba "Nick" came through the door.

There was a brief commotion across the room. Helen and Dame spoke in hushed tones before Helen ducked out in the direction of her classroom. And then the waited-for guest arrived. In the distance sounded jingles and thumps, followed by a familiar sound that had Suzanne clutching Lance's arm. She must have broken the skin because a faint whiff of blood's sweet, copper-penny scent woke the hunger until Suzanne gritted her teeth and fought it back. Lance just chuckled and unlatched her fingers, wrapping them in his where they could do no harm. She marveled at the love that man had for her, that after everything he held her so close. For a brief time, she'd forgotten the waxed silk bag tucked in her pocket—a gift from Helen, spelled with a form of witchy binding magic completely unfamiliar to Suzanne— and even the cap it contained. All because of this man. The one she didn't deserve.

And then her dark thoughts faded into the background as a very jolly incarnation of St. Nick rode in on a toy trike pulled by a whole slew of roller derby reindeer. Suzanne laughed and waved as her new friends played up the act to the delight of the children. Behind trailed a wagon piled with wrapped gifts.

The reindeer doubled as elves, apparently. Packages circled the room until every child had several. Their giggles and squeals were complemented by the enthusiastic shredding of wrapping paper. Suzanne was about to wiggle out of Lance's grip to see to her assigned duty, when Helen plucked the waiting garbage bag from Suzanne's hand and plopped a rather large and heavy package in its place.

"You will take this," Helen ordered sternly, definitely channeling her persona, Halla on Wheels. "The children helped pick them out off the internet and I will not have you disappoint them."

Suzanne swallowed her protests, smiling at the way the kids clapped and cheered as she tore at the wrapping, revealing a bright red derby helmet emblazoned with a skull and crossbones on the front and a pair of glossy black Antiks strung with red laces. Tears came to her eyes and she looked up and around at all the varied elements of her true family. She hoped her gaze spoke the thanks she could not voice for the tight grip happiness had on her throat.

"Yeah, well don't get too choked up..." Dame told her. "*D'Eath Lily* has practice at six p.m. sharp on Sunday, and I won't be going easy on you the way Doom did."

It was tricky to both groan and laugh, but Suzanne managed.

Glossary

A Shoilse – Irish Gaelic for "majesty."

Anatu – The name chose by the West Wind of the Wild Hunt; also called Ana. Variant spelling of Semitic (Ugaritic) Anat, meaning "water spring." In mythology, this is the name of a goddess of war, the sister and lover of the great storm god Ba'al. She is said to have been a consumer of blood and flesh.

Avalon – The legendary resting place of King Arthur where he went to heal after his battle with Mordred. Though tied to the British myth, Avalon is said to be in many places around the world and connected with several different myth cycles.

Bean Sidhe – Irish Gaelic for "woman of the hills," in Celtic tradition such women announced when someone was about to die. Sometimes only their wailing was heard, and other times they were seen washing bloody garments in the river. When the death was of a great leader, several *bean sidhe* would pronounce the death. The term has been Anglicized to banshee.

Bike Lane – The center line in the road, between lanes where there is enough room between the opposing traffic for a bike to zip through.

Bitch Bar – the vertical fender strut, passenger handhold combo on some custom choppers and other motorcycles, called so because most passengers tend to be female. Also called the sissy bar.

Bitch Pad – Another name for the pillion pad, again because most passengers tend to be female. Also called the bush pad.

Blocker – Roller derby term for the members of the team that run interference for the jammer. They form the pack. There are five on the team, which includes the pivot.

'Blood Band – A magical ring of the author's creation, worn by those of Rudha-an royal blood to protect them from magical attack. The ring bonds to the flesh and cannot be removed.

Bout – Roller derby term for a game. They are generally two thirty-minute periods broken up into jams that are up to two minutes long. There is a thirty-second break between jams.

BUG – Big Ugly Guy, a big hostile person.

Cage – A car or other four-wheeled vehicle where the drivers and passengers are closed in.

Cager – Someone that drives a car or similar vehicle.

Callan – The champion of the Faerie Court and aspirer to the throne.

Cherry-top – A police car.

Church – Club meetings.

Citizen – Anyone who is not a member of a Biker Organization.

Colors – The patch signifying the motor club or organization a biker is affiliated with.

Coupons – Speeding tickets.

Dair na Scath – Irish Gaelic for "Shadow Oak" or "Oak of Shadow" – The king of the High Court, Lance's grandfather.

Deifiúr – Irish Gaelic for "sister".

Derby Bride – Roller derby term for the player on the team you are the most comfortable with and who keeps you in line. She has your back on and off the track.

Donor Card – Put someone into a state where their donor card can be collected.

Dragon's Tears – A fictional corrosive fluid devised by the author for the purpose of the story, it is unclear if it is or is not the actual tears of dragons, but undiluted it will eat through anything but diamond.

Dubh Fae **(The)** – *See Kerwin.*

Dunter – another name for a redcap.

Dušan – The name the Four Winds gave to Lance. Czech name derived from the Slavic element *dusha*, meaning "soul, spirit."

Enki – The name chosen by the North Wind of the Wild Hunt. Sumerian meaning either "lord of the earth" or "lord of the underworld." In Babylonian mythology, this is the name of a god of creation, wisdom, keeper of divine laws, and half-brother to Enlil.

Endo – Stopping a motorcycle and having the rear wheel lift off the ground, a reverse of the catwalk. 2. Going back over front. 3. Pitching the rear of the motorcycle over its front, end over end.

Enlil – The name chosen by the East Wind of the Wild Hunt; also called Blow. Sumerian name meaning "Lord Wind," or more literally "Lord of the Command." In Babylonian mythology, this is the name of the chief deity and half-brother to Enki.

Fat Boy – First introduced in 1990, this cycle instantly became one of Harley-Davidson's most popular models. Originally available in only grey, later models came in any color except grey, including two-tone. The most distinguishing feature of this bike is the 16-inch solid wheels used both front and rear; it remains the only model so equipped. They ride the Softail frame, which hides the shocks beneath the engine. Power by an 80-cubic-inch Evolution V-twin introduced six years earlier, the Fat Boy uses belt drive.

Fluid Exchange – Biker term for a pit stop where the gas tank is filled and the bladder drained.

Fresh Meat – Roller derby term for a new, inexperienced team member.

Front Door – The lead position on a motorcycle run.

Gavin – Full fae, brother to Suzanne, Lance's lieutenant and best friend, member the mother chapter of the Wild Hunt.

Gremlin – Mischievous, mechanical-oriented fae often associated with the air force and blamed for plane malfunctions (Also see Road Gremlin).

Guardian Bell/Ride Bell/Gremlin Bell – Stems from actual biker folklore, a pewter or brass bell hung from a bike as protection from road gremlins. If the gremlin is already on the bike, the ringing of the bell traps it within the bell until it becomes senseless and falls off. If the gremlin is trying to get on the bike, the ringing scares it away. The magic of the bell is said to double if it is presented as a gift by a loved one.

Hecate's wheel – an ancient Greek symbol. An emblem of the Moon Goddess Hecate (Diana Lucifera), and her triple aspect. Used by practitioners of Hellenic Recon or Dianic Traditions of Wicca.

Henning – an author-created term for the act of being a mother hen toward someone.

Hose Your Ride – To wear out or damage a bike.

Jam – Roller derby term for a two-minute round in a bout.

Jammer – Roller derby term for the player on the team who actually scores points by passing all the other players on the other team. Generally the fastest skater on the team.

Keep the dirty side down – drive safe and keep the bike in the proper, upright position. The rest of the phrase is "keep the shiny side up."

Kerwin – The Little Black One – Also known at the *Dubh Fae*, the Black Faerie, another halfling, only one whose fae nature was dominant over his mortal half.

Knucklehead – A type of Harley-Davidson engine manufactured prior to 1948, which was characterized by large nuts on the right side of engine above the cylinders. Appearance is somewhat similar to knuckles. 2. Slang of Harley-Davidson Knucklehead engine (V-Twin, produced from 1936 - 1947). Name comes from the valve covers that look like the knuckles of a clinched fist. 3. Harley-Davidson's first overhead valve Big Twin.

Kobold – a Germanic sprite, usually invisible, it can manifest as an animal, fire, a human being or a candle. Generally house spirits, they can at times be helpful, though they are malicious if insulted or neglected.

Lance – Leader of the Wild Hunt, Suzanne's mate, best friend to Gavin, founding member of the Wild Hunt, also called Dušan by the Four Winds.

Leathers – The protective gear worn by bikers, could mean jacket, vest, gauntlets, chaps.

Mage bolt – a magical attack consisting of a bolt of pure energy cast at a target.

Lone Wolf Biker – Someone who lives the Bike Lifestyle but chooses not to ride with a club.

Love Nudges – Also known as swapping paint. Two riders bump in to each other while racing.

Mama – A woman that is available to all members of the club for sexual favors.

Mamó – Irish Gaelic for grandmother.

Mattress Cover – A young, pretty woman.

MC – Motor Club, biker gang.

Megatron – Speeds in excess of 150mph.

Meth – Methamphetamine, often abused drug that rapidly releases dopamine in reward regions of the brain producing the intense euphoria, or "rush," that many users feel after snorting, smoking, or injecting the drug.

Midgard – one of the Nine Worlds in Norse mythology.

Mulligan – A do-over.

Nur – The name chosen by the South Wind of the Wild Hunt; also called Bubba. Aramaic name meaning "fire."

Old Lady – A biker's wife or steady girlfriend.

1%er – Outlaw bikers, those one percent of the biker population that give the rest a bad name.

Open the Throttle/Throttle Down – Control the intake of air and fuel entering the engine to go faster or slower.

Organ Donor – Reckless biker, likely to get themselves and/or others killed, bikers that ride without a helmet.

Originals – A member's first set of colors which are never to be cleaned.

Panhead – A Harley-Davidson motorcycle engine, so nicknamed because of the distinct shape of the valve-rocker covers. The engine is a two-cylinder, two-valve-per-cylinder, pushrod V-twin. The engine replaced the Knucklehead engine in 1948 and was manufactured until 1965 when it was replaced by the shovelhead.

Panties – Roller derby term for the cloth covers worn over the helmets of the jammers (scorer) and pivots (pacer) on each team.

Patch Holder – Member of a motorcycle club.

Pillion pad – The passenger seat. Also called bitch pad or bush pad.

Pivot – Roller derby term for the player who paces the pack. Speeds up or slows down based on the jammer's speed. Wears a helmet cover with a stripe down the middle. A pivot can become a jammer if she is passed the jammer's panty (helmet cover).

Pooka – A shape-shifting fae that can take many forms but is most well known for appearing as a horse. If a human should mount one, it has been known to give them a wild ride, but do no real harm.

Powrie – Another name for a redcap.

Q-tip – An old, white or blue-haired driver, considered unpredictable and dangerous to others on the road.

Rat Bike – An older bike that hasn't been taken care of.

Redcap – Malevolent, murderous fae that dye their signature red caps in the blood of their victims. If the cap dries out they die. They carry an iron pike and wear hobnailed boots. Legend says that they inhabit the ruins of castles and murder unsuspecting travelers. Generally a solitary fae, for the purpose of this story they are under a compulsion to work together for the Fae Court.

Rennie – People that dress up in medieval garb and go to renaissance festivals.

Ride – Slang term for a motorcycle.

Ride Captain – The person in charge of a ride or road trip.

Road Agent – Another term for Highway Patrol Officer or State Trooper.

Road Gremlin/Gremlin – The evil spirits of the road that cause accidents and mechanical problems. Akin to the gremlins said to plague the air force pilots, who formed the first motor clubs. Gremlins like to ride. By hanging a bell on the bike a rider can either keep the gremlins from getting on, or trap them if they are already there, preventing them from causing mischief and damage to the bike or rider.

Rudha-an – Gaelic for rowan tree, also called mountain ash, Whispering tree, or Witch wood tree, among many other things. Many of these can be easily linked to the mythology and folklore surrounding the tree. The small, creamy white flowers are borne in dense corymbs. The fruit is a small pome, usually bright orange or red, but occasionally pink, yellow or white in some Asian species. It was thought to be a magical tree and protection against malevolent beings. This is also for the purpose of this story the ruling family line of the Fae High Court, of which Lance, Tilly, and Tilsaia are the last remaining members.

SCAdians – people who not only dress up in medieval garb and go to renaissance faires, but they often hold private events replicating aspects of medieval life and have created an alternative existence around those events with personas created specifically for those events. The precursor to the modern LARPer (Live Action Role Player).

Scoot – Slang term for a motorcycle.

Shoulder Fin – Author's creation for the purpose of the story. The anatomical feature that expands as the fae draw on magic. Something like a heat sink, it channels the magical energy into harmless tendrils that expand and resemble wings. This protects the fae from magical overload or burnout until the energy is used.

Shovelhead – Slang for Harley-Davidson engines produced between 1966 and 1984, so named because of the shape of the head resembles a coal shovel. The Shovelhead engine (V-Twin, produced from 1966- 1984). Harley-Davidson's third generation overhead valve Big Twin engine.

Sidhe na Daire – Irish Gaelic for Elf or hill of the oak. For the purpose of the story, Dair na Scath's fortress Underhill.

Softtail – Harley frame with hidden suspension; resembles a hard tail.

Spriggan – a Cornish faerie known for being ugly. They are portrayed as faerie bodyguards and often thieves. Though small they can swell to large proportions. They caused mischief to those who offended them.

SQUID – SQuirrely kID – An inexperienced young biker trying to ride beyond their skill level, often with no respect for the posted speed limit or safety, their own or others. Possibly a Southern term.

Statey – State troopers or police.

Static – A run in with the police.

Stay Vertical – Stay upright, don't crash.

Steel Horse Stampede – Where hundreds of bikers ride *en masse* down to Lynchburg, TN for a biker rally.

Surf the Asphalt – laying the bike down in a skid.

Suzanne – Lance's woman, full fae, sister to Gavin, member of the mother chapter of the Wild Hunt.

Sweep – The last position in a ride formation, generally assigned to the best and most trusted rider.

Tar Snake – Thick lines of uneven tar used to repair cracks in the road, a hazard to bikers.

Tat/Skin Art/Ink – Tattoo.

Team – A subgroup of four motorcycles within a larger group ride.

Thunderbolt – An expanding metal baton.

Tomahawk Stop – a roller derby move where you flip around and come down hard on your toe stops and then flip back around and keep skating. This is a way to intimidate and block the opposite team's skaters.

T-stop – a roller derby move where the skater drags their back skate behind them to stop, forming a T of both skates.

Tri-Armor – A brand of extremely strong protective biker gear.

Two Up – A term for carrying a passenger on the back of the bike.

Underhill – The land of the Faeries. Not always literally under a hill, but called so because of the time long ago when the Fae were force to live underground, away from mortals.

War Wagon – A vehicle used to haul a biker club's arsenal when trouble is expected from another club.

Whip – Roller derby term for a move where a pivot will link up and accelerate the jammer forward past the pack using their momentum.

Wind Walker – A respected biker that looks out for others on the road.

Wrench – A bike mechanic.

Zebra – Roller derby term for the referee in a bout, for the black and white striped shirts they wear.

There Ain't Nothing Like Us Dames

lyrics by Danielle Ackley-McPhail

(To the tune of There is Nothing Like a Dame)

We got derby on the brain,
We got spotlights on the rink,
We got quad skates and bandannas
Some are black and some are pink

We got scrimmages and suicides
And lots of dandy bouts!
What ain't we got?
We ain't got doubts!

We get bandaged up at home,
We got merch and we take blows,
We get speeches from our captains
And advice from all the pro's,
We got gear that's doused with sweat
'Till we get dizzy from the smell!
What don't we got?
You know darn well!

We have nothin' but fame to shoot for
What we got, there ain't no substitute for...

(Chorus—All)
There is nothin' like us dames,
Nothin' in the world,
There is nothin' you can name
That is anythin' like us dames!

We feel reckless, we feel bruised,
We feel rowdy, indiscreet,
We feel ev'ry kind of feelin',
But the feelin' of defeat
We feel ready as the champ felt
When he rumbled in the 'hood
What don't we feel?

(All) Misunderstood!

Lots of things in life are beautiful, but brother,
There is one particular thing that is nothin' whatsoever
in any way, shape or form like any other.

(Chorus—All)
There is nothin' like us dames,
Nothin' in the world,
There is nothin' you can name
That is anythin' like us dames!

Nothin' else is built the same,
Nothin' in the world
As the rough and tumble frames
Of the silhouettes of us dames!

There is absolutely nothin' in the game like us dames.

But suppose a dame ain't light
Or completely free of claws,
We're as fearless as a kitten,
And as tough as those with balls,
It's a waste of time to think about
the things that we have not,
We'll derby with the things we've got!

There is nothin' you can name
That is anything like us dames!
There ain't no one books like us dames,
And no one looks like us dames.
You can bet no one drinks like us dames,
No one jams like us dames,
Or even blocks like us dames.
There ain't a thing that's wrong with any man here
That can't be cured by a little bit of fear
Of us bad-ass, hard-case, tough and sexy dames!!

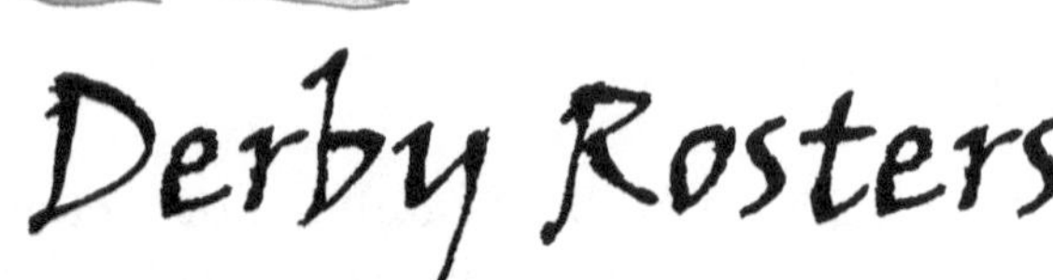

Derby Rosters

Dame's Derby Death Squad
(Fictitious – Dalton, Anywhere USA)

Dame O'Destruction – Plays all positions
Your day has come.

Bruishilda Bonebrake – Blocker
The name says it all.

Meecha Maker – Blocker
Let's get to the introductions.

Unda Taker – Blocker
Next customer, please…

Halla on Wheels – Jammer
Cus you're on the fast track outa here.

Valhal E. Girl – Blocker
That's where I'm a send ya.

Luv Tap – Jammer
Because I'll zero you out.

Chicka Die – Blocker
Don't let the cute and fluffy fool you.

Chicka Boom – Blocker, Pivot
It's all you hear before cute and fluffy gets ya.

D'Eath Lily – Blocker
Don't bother to smell the roses.

Brit SchitHaus – Blocker, Pivot
Try and deny it.

Fluff n'Knuckler – Blocker
She ain't no marshmallow and don't ever call her nuts.

Bod Hopper – Jammer
Aww…did somebunny fall down?

Bouncing Betty Bammer – Blocker, Pivot
Mine! Mine! Mine!

The Jerzey Derby Brigade*
(Actual – Morristown, NJ)

Doom Hilda – Plays all positions
Criss Catastrophe – Blocker, Pivot
Assault Shaker – Plays all positions
Maggy Kyllanfall – Mostly Jammer, blocker
Little Mo Peep – Jammer, Blocker
Inna Propriate – Blocker
River Slam – Blocker
Voldeloxx – Jammer, Blocker
Skank Tank – Blocker
Raven Rage – Blocker
CaliforniKate – Blocker, Jammer
Beast Witherspoon – Blocker, Jammer
Brass Muscles – Jammer, Blocker

To learn more about the Jerzey Derby Brigade and to see an up-to-date roster, visit:

http://www.jerzeyderby.com/

---

*This information was current at the time of the original printing but may have since changed.

The Jerzey Derby Brigade
Corporal Punishers

Photo © 2013 Tom Gaylord

front row:
Danielle Ackley-McPhail, Criss Catastrophe,
CaliforniaKate, Doom Hilda, (Skank Tank),
Heinz Catchup

back row:
Lawless Lizzie, Inna Propriate, Beast Witherspoon,
Molotov Cupcake, Maggy Kyllanfall, River Slam,
Raven Rage, Lil' Mo Peep, Voldeloxx, Easthell Getty,
Assault Shaker

About the Author

Award-winning author and editor Danielle Ackley-McPhail has worked both sides of the publishing industry for longer than she cares to admit. In 2014 she joined forces with husband Mike McPhail and friend Greg Schauer to form her own publishing house, eSpec Books (www.especbooks.com).

Her published works include six novels, *Yesterday's Dreams*, *Tomorrow's Memories*, *Today's Promise*, *The Halfling's Court*, *The Redcaps' Queen*, and *Baba Ali and the Clockwork Djinn*, written with Day Al-Mohamed. She is also the author of the solo collections *A Legacy of Stars*, *Consigned to the Sea*, *Flash in the Can*, and *Transcendence*, the non-fiction writers' guide, *The Literary Handyman*, and is the senior editor of the *Bad-Ass Faeries* anthology series, *Gaslight & Grimm*, *Dragon's Lure*, and *In an Iron Cage*. Her short stories are included in numerous other anthologies and collections.

She is a member of Broad Universe, a writer's organization focusing on promoting the works of women authors in the speculative genres.

Danielle lives in New Jersey with husband and fellow writer, Mike McPhail and three extremely spoiled cats. To learn more about her work, visit www.sidhenadaire.com, www.especbooks.com.

References

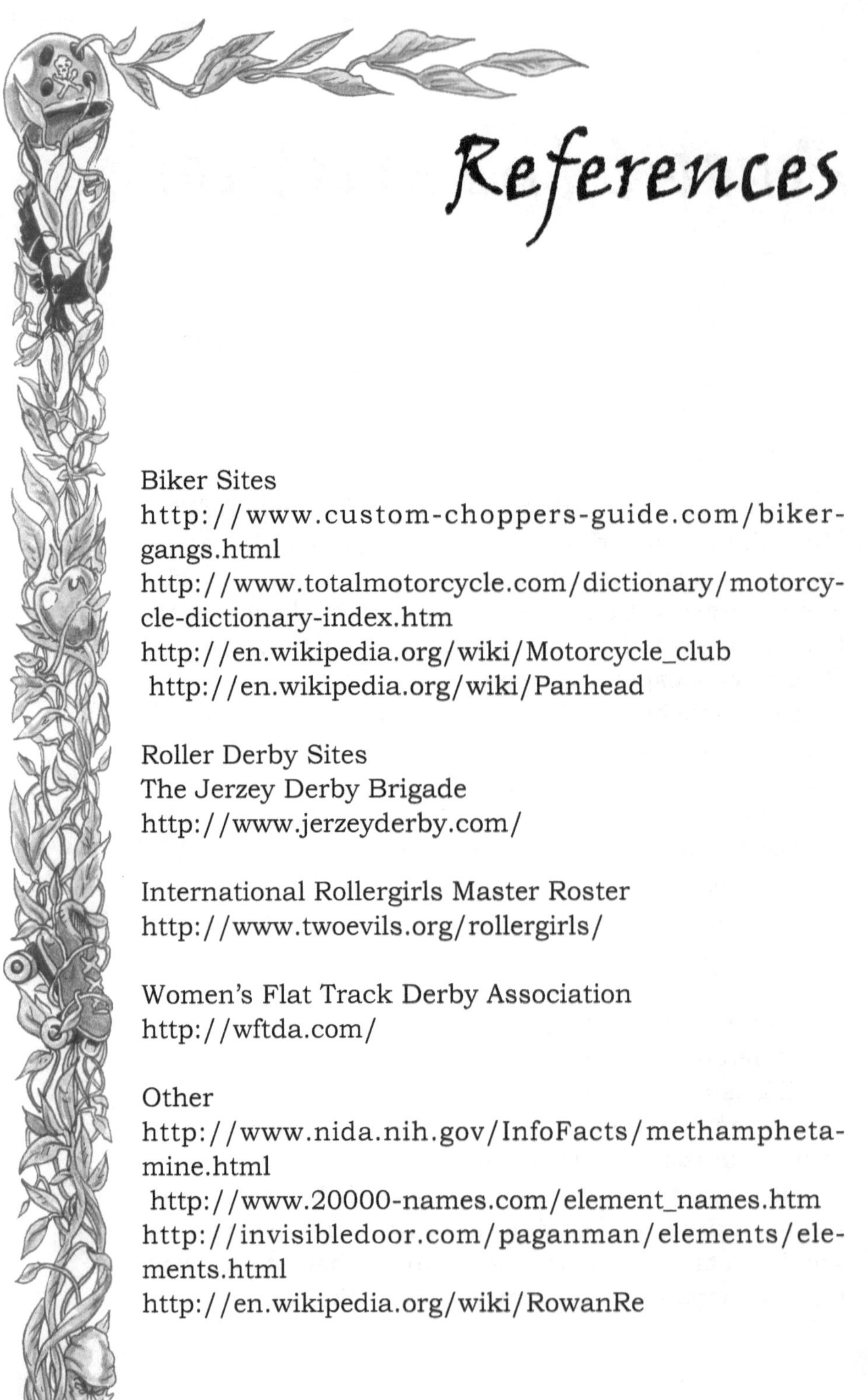

Biker Sites
http://www.custom-choppers-guide.com/biker-gangs.html
http://www.totalmotorcycle.com/dictionary/motorcycle-dictionary-index.htm
http://en.wikipedia.org/wiki/Motorcycle_club
http://en.wikipedia.org/wiki/Panhead

Roller Derby Sites
The Jerzey Derby Brigade
http://www.jerzeyderby.com/

International Rollergirls Master Roster
http://www.twoevils.org/rollergirls/

Women's Flat Track Derby Association
http://wftda.com/

Other
http://www.nida.nih.gov/InfoFacts/methamphetamine.html
http://www.20000-names.com/element_names.htm
http://invisibledoor.com/paganman/elements/elements.html
http://en.wikipedia.org/wiki/RowanRe